# Sandwich, with a Side of Romance

# Sandwich, with a Side of Romance

## Krista Phillips

**Abingdon Press** fiction
a novel approach to faith

Nashville, Tennessee

*Sandwich, with a Side of Romance*

Copyright © 2012 by Krista Phillips

ISBN-13: 978-1-4267-4592-8

Published by Abingdon Press, P.O. Box 801, Nashville, TN 37202

www.abingdonpress.com

All rights reserved.

The persons and events portrayed in this work of fiction
are the creations of the author, and any resemblance
to persons living or dead is purely coincidental.

Library of Congress Cataloging-in-Publication Data

Phillips, Krista.
 Sandwich, with a side of romance / Krista Phillips.
  p. cm.
 ISBN 978-1-4267-4592-8
 1. Christian women—Fiction.  I. Title.
 PS3616.H459S26  2012
 813'.6—dc23

2012017527

Printed in the United States of America

1 2 3 4 5 6 7 8 9 10 / 17 16 15 14 13 12

In honor and memory of Art and Lavina Johnson

All my memories of Sandwich revolve around these two sweet people: sneaking cookies from grandma's cookie jar, smelling (and tasting!) yummy homemade cinnamon rolls, learning to play a mean game of Rook, and reading my very first Christian romance novel from Grandma's stash.

Good times, every one of them, that I'll remember forever. Grandma and Grandpa, you are always in my heart.

# Acknowledgments

They say no man is an island . . . well, authors aren't islands either!

This book would not have been if not for:

My husband and kids, for enduring a crazy messy house during my "just let me finish this chapter" moments and during my manic editing mode, and for supporting me and cheering me on.

*Special thanks to my eldest daughter, Karalynn, for helping me brainstorm the first scene of this book in the parking lot of a grocery store while Daddy ran in to get milk. You done good, Sweetie!*

My mom, my cheerleader, and the one who thinks I'm the best writer ever. You're my own personal cheer section and I needed that *many* times throughout this process.

My dad, for all the "So, are you published yet?" questions that made me persevere until I could say *yes*.

My sisters, for telling me like it is at all points and times, for fun lunch dates, and for making me feel cool when you brag about your sister who is a writer. For a girl who has always looked up to her bigger sisters, that was a pretty neat and empowering feeling.

My super cool editor, Ramona, for taking a chance on this fledgling author and giving me hope at a moment when life seemed to be spiraling downward at a super fast and scary speed. God knew I needed that email, my friend.

My super cool agent, Rachelle, for seeing through my many rough edges and for keeping me away from those scary ledges that are so tempting to jump off of.

Jamie Chavez, for taking a scalpel to my book and exposing its flaws in all their messy glory. Any errors made in correcting and sewing it back up are completely mine.

Sarah, for knocking it out of the park in December, even while on vacation. I could not have done it without you.

To the many groups I'm in that inspire me daily, including but not limited to ACFW and MTCW, and Kaye, for allowing me to be a minion.

Aunt Marlyis, for helping with my odd Sandwich questions.

Sharon Shepard, for helping me with my Lake Holiday questions and not ignoring the strange lady who e-mailed her out of the blue.

And to all those who have prayed for our family these last few years. Without your prayer support, I would have surely crumbled into a heap and would not be where I am today.

# 1

*God, is it against the rules to want to strangle one's boss?*

Even though she was still very new to the whole Christian thing, six months yesterday to be exact, Maddie Buckner was fairly sure that thoughts of murder, even in jest, wouldn't be condoned by the Almighty.

Maddie bit the side of her cheek to keep from saying something not-quite-Christian as she swept the broom across the salon floor for the fifteen-billionth time. She hadn't driven an hour from Chicago with nothing but her clothes and a few hundred bucks to end up as a janitor.

But it seemed on her first day at the Sandwich Cut 'N' Style, that was all her new boss would let her do, considering it was already afternoon and she'd yet to cut a single strand of hair. She was supposed to be given walk-ins, but her boss refused her the few they'd even had, saying they were too "important" to risk on a newbie.

"You still missed some, Madison." Judy, her Nazi-of-a-boss, crossed thick arms over her ample chest and nodded toward two short brown specks in the corner. "And when you're done, the waiting area needs straightening up. I'm running to Art's, and I expect it done by the time I get back. Got it?"

The front of the salon was indeed a mess due to the five-year-old terror who'd just left. He'd thrown every magazine out of the rack and banged on each toy from the basket while his mother got a perm. Oh, the joys. And since Art's Supermarket was just down the block, she'd have to book it to get done before Her Majesty returned.

Maddie swept up the two errant hairs, then headed for the front. While she stuffed a *Good Housekeeping* magazine back into the rack, the bell over the door jingled and a fine specimen of a man walked in.

*Hello, Mr. Gorgeous.* Shaggy-blond hair, tan arms, a slight stubble on his chin. The old Maddie would have thrown herself at him to get a date. The new Maddie wanted to run away.

The guy leaned against the oak reception desk and ran a hand through his shoulder-length hair, then looked at his watch. "Cyndi gonna be much longer?"

Miss Agnes, their gray-haired receptionist/manicurist, nodded. "Sorry, Reuben. Cyndi's three o'clock is taking longer than she expected. It'll be another ten minutes or so. You okay to wait?"

The man eyed his watch again. "I need to get back before the dinner rush. Is there anyone else who can do it?"

"Only Judy, and she stepped out for a few minutes. If you really don't want to wait, we've got a new stylist who just started today."

Hunky-guy glanced at Maddie with a frown. "She looks a little young. Is she any good?"

Did the guy think she was deaf? Plus, Mr. *GQ* didn't look to be much over twenty-five himself.

Miss Agnes tisked. "Now Reuben, be nice. Maddie came highly recommended."

Only the prospect of her first client and a subsequent tip persuaded her to ignore the man's rudeness. Plastering on her best fake customer-service smile, Maddie straightened up from where she'd been putting blocks back in the bin. "My name's Maddie. I'd be happy to do your cut if you'd like."

Cyndi waved from the sink where she was removing perm rods from Mrs. Emerson's hair. "Maddie'll do a great job, Reuben."

Reuben crossed his arms, looked at Maddie for a moment, then nodded. "That's fine."

As she showed him back to her station, nerves did the hula in her stomach. Her first real, paying haircut. She'd been a natural at school and had cut her little brother's hair for years. But having her livelihood depend on it was an entirely new experience.

*Jesus, please don't let me mess this up!*

Grabbing a cape and towel from the rack, she forced another sugar-sweet smile and twirled the chair around. "Have a seat."

He nodded and sat down. She spun the chair toward the mirror and tucked the small towel around his neckline. "So what did you have in mind? Just a trim?"

"No, I want a perm." He rolled his eyes. "Of course a trim. Same style. No need for a shampoo."

Maddie bit the side of her cheek to keep from retorting with a rude comment of her own. "Not a problem, sir. I'm guessing to take off maybe a half inch?"

He shifted in his seat, his brow creased in a worried line. "Listen, if you have to guess, then maybe I need to just wait for Cyndi. I don't really care to be a practice mannequin today."

Maddie turned around and grabbed her comb so he wouldn't see the darts she hurled at him with her eyes. Her first customer had to be not only a male but also a demanding pig of one too. But still, she needed a good tip. "No sir, I was just making sure that was what you wanted."

When he didn't reply, she turned and saw him sitting, eyes closed, his fingers rubbing his temples. Maybe Reuben-the-jerk had a headache. She should *not* be gleeful at the thought. *Lord, forgive me.*

She walked behind him and ran her fingers through his hair as she assessed his current style. An ultramodern, long shaggy cut parted an inch to the right and layered to chin length with a chic "messy" look to it. The back curled out, giving evidence of a little natural wave. It was an attractive haircut, especially for his boyish, square face, but seemed a bit longer than it should be. He was cute now, but when she was done with him, he'd be positively swoon-worthy.

Minus, of course, his snakelike personality. Nothing she could do about that.

"What are you doing?" The man stared at her in the mirror.

Maddie withdrew her fingers from his hair and bent down, pretending to look at the back of his head. "Trying to make sure I get the cut right. Should be good to go now."

*Note to Maddie: Don't fall in love with a client's hair and spend several minutes running your fingers through it. Awkward moment will surely follow.*

Ignoring his brooding stare, she grabbed her scissors and began to work. The slivers of dusty blond hair floated to the ground as she snipped with a steady hand. She was doing it. Her first haircut at her first job. Her father's words echoed in her brain. *"You'll never amount to anything, girl. Just like your mom."*

She was proving him wrong, along with every other man who thought she was nothing but an object to be manipulated and manhandled. If only they could see her now. But, then, Maddie would be thrilled if she never laid eyes on any of them again. Especially her father.

As his hair began to take the proper shape, her confidence boosted. She was a success, and soon she'd have enough money to rent a little house and bring her brother home where he belonged.

While she trimmed the back, she glanced in the mirror. Was Reuben-the-jerk asleep? His head drooped, and his eyes were closed. At least he couldn't act like a spoiled brat while he slept.

She moved to the right and began to trim the front. The layers in his bangs started at the base of his ear and ended below his chin. Maddie combed the first swatch of hair and positioned her scissors to make the cut, but Reuben's head jerked farther down then up as she began her cut, causing her hands to slip.

Maddie gasped. Dread curled itself around her stomach and squeezed. In her trembling hand she'd caught four full inches of his hair. On the side of Reuben's forehead was a one-and-a-half-inch dusty-blond stub.

❧

The image in the mirror was just an illusion. It had to be. Reuben Callahan blinked twice.

No such luck. His hair was still in shambles, and a shell-shocked brunette stood next to him holding the evidence of her crime. He fought the urge to let a few words rip that rarely graced his lips. But with Miss Agnes over there gasping, word would no doubt get back to his mother since the two had been friends for years. And his mom wouldn't hesitate to take a bar of soap to his mouth, even if he was twenty-seven years old.

After what seemed like an eternity of eerie silence, the bell clanged against the front door, and Judy Meadows, the owner, walked in. "What in the world—"

Assessing the scene faster than a CSI agent, Judy dropped her bags and marched over. Snatching the scissors from Maddie's hand, she pulled her to the side. Reuben only caught pieces of the whispered conversation between boss and employee, but given the petite stylist's rushed escape to the back room, it hadn't been pleasant.

Judy grabbed a spray bottle and began wetting down his hair and combing it at a feverish speed. "Reuben, I am so sorry. Madison is new and came highly recommended. I had no idea this would happen. I'll fix it. I promise."

"How are you going to fix it? There's no disguising a missing chunk of hair." He was being rude; he knew it. He'd feel guilty later. But right now, on top of being up all night crunching numbers that just wouldn't add up and a pounding headache, he had a botched haircut too.

Okay, so it was just hair and no one had died. But his appearance contributed to the persona he tried to keep. He was the cool entrepreneur, the suave business guy on the verge of huge success. Now he looked like some dude with an over-grown mullet.

"We'll just find you a new style. One that'll look nice until it grows back out." Judy grabbed a hairstyle book out of the magazine rack and flipped through the pages. "Here, this is what I had in mind."

She shoved the book onto his lap. The page displayed a much shorter hairstyle featuring a rugged spiked look. With some hair gel, it wouldn't be too bad. "That'll do."

The portly woman took the book from him and laid it on the booth counter. "Good, good. I knew you'd like it. You just sit back and let ol' Judy take care of you. And, of course, it's on the house."

Judy made quick work of the haircut and took extra time to style it for him. The spiky look was different, but maybe a hair change was what he needed. Livy had been after him to cut it for ages.

As he set a few dollars tip on the counter, Reuben noticed a wallet-sized picture taped to the mirror. The new stylist, her brunette hair a little longer than her current short bob, had her arm around a boy who looked to be ten, maybe eleven years old.

Son, maybe? Doubtful, since by the looks of her ripped jeans and crazy hairdo, she couldn't be much out of high school. One never knew these days though.

Beside the photo was a slip of paper with a Bible verse, Jeremiah 29:11, typed on it.

Guilt tiptoed on his conscience making God-sized imprints. He'd been a bear to the poor woman. When he was in the zone, it was easy to forget that most people were more than just employees. They were mothers, sisters, or friends. Not to mention children of God.

As bad as his day had been, there was no excuse for how he'd acted.

Stifling another yawn, he waved to Miss Agnes, who frowned at him, and Judy, who had a too-bright smile plastered on her face.

He walked down the block to where his BMW was parked on Main Street and clicked the button to unlock the car. He opened the door and sat in the driver's seat, then flipped the sun visor down to look one more time at his new haircut, then turned his head from side to side. Yes, it would do.

He ran his fingers through the short hair, but stilled when the car rocked and a soft thud sounded on the hood. He flipped up the visor and stifled a yell. Someone lay plastered against the windshield of his car.

# 2

"What are you doing on my car?"

Maddie crossed her arms over her chest and smiled at the angry man staring at her. His new haircut actually made him look hotter. Too bad. "I'm sitting, what does it look like I'm doing?"

Reuben's hands were clutched so tight, Maddie wouldn't be surprised if there were nail marks on his palms. "I can see that. What I want to know is why. This is a brand new Beamer."

Crossing her legs at the ankle, Maddie pretended to relax, when in reality, her stomach threatened to heave. This was for Kyle. She had to stay strong. "I don't want to scratch your precious expensive toy, but you cost me my job, buddy."

His cheek twitched, and he pulled at his dress-shirt collar. "I didn't know she fired you."

"Bull. You were there when she told me to pack up my things."

A look of indecision flashed over his face. Was that remorse? "I didn't hear what she said, but I'll admit, I guessed as much. Listen, I'm sorry you got fired. But I don't know how sitting on my car is going to help."

Maddie pulled her legs up to sit crisscross on the hood, her tennis shoes resting on the shiny black paint. A good move given the stricken look on Reuben's face. "I want you to go back in there and tell them the truth, that you fell asleep and the whole thing was your fault, and then demand they give me my job back."

His clenched jaw shifted to the side. "First, I did not fall asleep. I was just resting my eyes. Second, it won't help anyway. When Judy makes her mind up, she rarely changes it."

Maddie hated to admit it, but he was probably right. Judy had been a strict dictator since she'd started that morning. She'd even highlighted in yellow the section of her handwritten, stapled-together employee handbook that stated the zero-tolerance policy for haircut errors the first month. But still, she had to try. "You did too fall asleep. And I'm not getting up until you fix this."

The man was eerily quiet, staring at her with those determined, hazel eyes. Panic flooded Maddie's resolve. What if he called the cops or something? Could she get arrested for sitting on someone's car? A jail record would not help her case in getting custody of Kyle.

Her stomach twisted when he walked to the passenger-side of the car and opened the door.

"Get in."

She blinked. "Excuse me?"

"I said get in."

The man must think she'd been born a hundred years ago. "I don't even know you. I am not getting into a car with a strange man. You could be a rapist, an ax murderer, a—"

"I'm going to call the cops in about five seconds and report you for vandalism if you don't get yourself in this car. I have an idea that may help both of us."

Maddie weighed her choices. Getting in the car could be the equivalent of suicide. Staying on the hood of the car would get her arrested. And giving up . . . that was just not an option.

She hopped off, stepped around him, and climbed in the car. He slammed the door and examined the hood slowly, his palm rubbing the spot where she'd sat, before plopping into the driver's seat.

"Buckle up." He spat out the terse command, making her wonder if he was a policeman in disguise. Just in case, she obeyed.

When he peeled out of the parking spot, she breathed a sigh of relief. He was definitely not a cop. A few minutes later he pulled into a restaurant parking lot. The sign read, "The Sandwich Emporium."

Not the most original name given its location in Sandwich, Illinois, but the front looked quaint and inviting, its gabled roof and stone façade giving a whisper of welcome.

Maddie ventured a look at Reuben. His hands still gripped the steering wheel, and he stared straight ahead. Should she interrupt him?

After a minute of silence, she couldn't take it anymore. "So, was your idea to buy me dinner as restitution?"

He sat back in the seat and glanced at her. "Would that work for you?"

"No."

"I didn't think so, and no, that wasn't my idea. I own the Emporium."

Maddie raised her eyebrows. "Really? You're awfully young to have your own restaurant."

His jaw clenched again, and Maddie could almost hear his teeth grinding. If he kept it up he'd need dentures by the time he was thirty.

"My dad left it to me when he died two years ago. And I'm not some young college kid. I'm twenty-seven and have been running this business for the last two years."

He was older than she'd guessed. "I'm sorry to hear about your dad."

"Thank you." His voice was softer, less harsh. "Now do you want a job or not?"

"Is that what you're doing? Offering me a job?"

He shrugged. "It's not glamorous, but I'd been thinking about adding another waitress anyway. If you want it, the job's yours."

❧

Reuben closed the door to his office and headed straight to his desk. He jerked open the top drawer and rummaged around until he found the bottle of ibuprofen, then tossed two pills into his mouth and washed them down with the bottle of water he kept in the mini fridge beside his desk.

For the millionth time in the last two hours, he questioned his sanity. He hadn't planned to hire another waitress anytime soon, although another one would be nice during the busier summer months coming up. Maybe he should have told Judy that he'd been partially to blame for the haircut mishap. He didn't remember falling asleep. But it was entirely possible.

He picked up the phone and started to dial the salon's phone number, but set the handset back on the hook a moment later. Better to see how Madison worked out first, then give her an option. Yes, that would work. Then maybe he could salvage his pride and his conscience.

He could almost hear his mother's lecture on pride going before a fall, but brushed the nagging voice away.

Sinking into his black leather office chair, he leaned back and closed his eyes. Five minutes. That was all he needed. Five minutes of quiet and no interruptions. The voice message light on his phone beckoned him, but it could wait until tomorrow. Probably his lawyer with more red tape to cut through or, worse yet, his accountant.

Sleep crowded in and he willingly gave in to it, but the opening and slamming of his office door jolted him awake.

"Who is she?" Livy stood inside the door, hands on her hips.

Reuben had no desire for this conversation today. He'd hoped she wouldn't stop by on her day off. "A new waitress I hired."

"Reub, you realize as manager that it's my job to do the hiring?"

That was the one thing she could say that would entice him to fight today. He'd promoted her a month ago to general manager, as the duties of overseeing all three restaurants as well as the planned new ones were getting too much for him. Since then, she'd gone from being a compliant employee to thinking she owned the place.

Considering they'd dated on and off, currently on, since high school, he let her get away with it most of the time. "Livy, you may be a manager, but I'm still the owner. I can hire a waitress if I want to."

"Did you do a background check? Call her references?"

No way did he want to explain the circumstances now. Livy would be furious. "She checked out just fine." A partial truth. If Judy had hired her, she had to be safe. That was enough check for him.

"Fine. What restaurant did she work at last?"

Maybe he could have asked a few more questions. . . . . "Livy, can we talk about this later? I have a splitting headache and I need to get back to the dining room."

Her face relaxed, and she walked behind him and began to massage his shoulders. *Much* better.

"I'm sorry. We can talk about it later. By the way, I like your haircut."

"Thanks. I, uh, wanted something different." Not a huge lie. The new style was growing on him.

Livy dug her thumbs into the nape of his neck. Sweet relief. "Well, I'm glad you finally listened to me. You look so much more handsome and clean cut. I'm not sure I would have gone that short, though."

Not like he'd had a choice. He patted her hand on his shoulder. "I'll just let you come with me next time then."

"I'll come with you if you go somewhere a little more classy."

"What, is Judy's place not good enough for you?"

She huffed but continued to knead his upper back with her thumbs. "She charges a whole twenty bucks for a cut. Your hair is part of your businessman image. You need to see it as an investment. I was thinking a few highlights too."

"I'm not spending that kind of money on my hair, Livs." She'd already gotten him to fork out way too much on that stupid BMW, which was looking more and more like a really dumb decision these days. Although he did admit it was fun to drive.

Livy flipped her fake blonde hair to the side, ignoring his comment. "Have you thought any more about what we talked about last week?"

Reuben searched his brain to try to remember that conversation. The only thing he could come up with was her suggestion to try a new vendor for the linen tablecloths and napkins. "Yes, I have. I think it has merit, but I'm waiting on some more price quotes first."

The hands on his shoulders stilled. "Price quotes? What are you talking about?"

"Uh, linens?"

She walked around and leaned a curvy hip against the side of his desk, her mouth turned down. "What do linens have to do with our future?"

Oh, *that* conversation. The one he wasn't ready to have yet. "I'm sorry, Livs. I'm just completely in over my head with these new restaurants. Opening two at the same time might have been the stupidest decision of my life. My brain is fried past that."

Livy's lips tipped to a half smile that didn't extend to her eyes. "I understand. You're stressed. We'll talk about it later."

Reuben nodded to her. "What are you doing here anyway? It's your day off."

"Just wanted to see if you could do dinner and a movie tonight. We're both always working; figured it'd be fun to get out for a while. The restaurant can survive a night without you."

Fun? He couldn't remember what that word meant anymore. "Sorry, but I've got a ton to do here. And I wouldn't be good company, trust me."

She leaned forward, pressed a kiss against his lips then turned to leave. "No biggy. Just thought I'd check."

When she reached the door, she looked back at him and smiled. "Don't work too hard. And keep an eye out on that new girl. I talked to her for a minute before I came in, and she seems a little rough."

"She'll be fine, but thanks for letting me know."

The door shut, much quieter this time, and Reuben sat back and surveyed his desk, or what he remembered to be a desk underneath all the paper. He had to get a handle on this, and fast.

If he couldn't manage things with three restaurants, what was he going to do with five?

A knock at the door interrupted his thoughts. "Come in."

Tilly, the head waitress, peeked around the door. "Boss, we have a little problem out here."

"What's wrong?"

"The new girl. She dumped a plate of food on Mayor Ryan's lap."

# 3

$S$ir, I am so sorry. Let me help you with that." Maddie moved her hands to pick up the sandwich, then realized doing so would put her hands in a rather, uh, personal position.

"No, no, don't worry. I've got it." The gracious gentleman picked up the bread and set it on the tray she held, then peeled the slice of rare beef off his black-dress-pant-clad thigh. The tea had done the worst damage, splattering all over his lap, making the poor man look as if he had bladder-control issues.

Out of the corner of her eye, she saw a frowning Reuben approach. He jerked his thumb toward his office, but Maddie wouldn't cower, even though she hated being a waitress and berated herself for not mentioning it to Reuben earlier. She'd tried it once after high school, but had been fired two days later. Her hands might be steady with a pair of scissors, but they were useless carrying a tray of food.

Dummy-her had thought maybe, given that two years had passed, her food handling skills had improved. Given the prime rib and iced tea she'd just deposited in the customer's lap, she'd assumed wrong.

Someone shoved a pile of cloth napkins into her free hand, and she looked up to see Reuben, his eyes as hard as stale bread. Fighting her reflex to defend herself, she turned away from him and handed a few of the white linens to the customer. "Sir, here are some napkins. I am so sorry."

"No problem, young lady. Accidents happen. Don't you worry."

*God, bless that man, will you?* Maddie blotted up the tea on the floor until a hand brushed against her shoulder.

She looked up and saw Reuben nodding toward the kitchen. "I'll finish this. Why don't you go get another drink and sandwich?" The command was forced through a clamped jaw with only a semblance of civility, for the sake of the customer, no doubt.

Maddie pushed herself up from the floor and handed him the rag, even though the floor was almost clean. Just like a man to offer to help after the dirty work was done. "I'll get right on that."

She rushed into the kitchen and yelled out the order to be remade pronto. While she waited, she refilled a glass with unsweetened tea and set it on a tray.

Minutes later, the cook handed her a plate with the new sandwich. Maddie picked up the tray and turned toward the door, only to have it taken from her grasp by her boss, his square jaw as hard as stone.

"I'll take it. Get in my office. Now." His voice came out in a low grumble.

Maddie took a breath, ready to argue, but decided against it. Sitting in the office alone would give her time to think up a good reason why he shouldn't fire her. If not, then she contemplated calling the *Guinness Book of World Records*. She was sure she topped the charts of how many jobs could be lost in the shortest amount of time.

She hung her head low, hoping to avoid stares, as she walked past the drink station to the other side of the restaurant and into his office, shutting the door behind her. She smoothed her apron, a black number with THE SANDWICH EMPORIUM written in bold, white letters.

Leaning against the door, she squeezed her eyes closed and prayed.

"Please God, don't let him fire me. I know I messed this up royally and should have been honest at the get-go, but I really thought I could do it if I tried hard enough. Apparently I'm just a big screw-up like everyone thinks."

She opened her eyes, knowing God was probably standing up in heaven, hands on his hips, just shaking his head at her too. Well, he could join the club.

Reuben's office was nowhere near as fancy as she'd pictured it. Given his expensive wheels, she imagined a pricy executive desk, cappuccino machine in the corner, and money all but dripping from the walls. Instead, the desk screamed 1950s with its thick, vanilla–ice-cream colored metal and a matching five-foot high filing cabinet against the back wall. Corny motivational posters lined one wall shouting "EXCELLENCE," "FOCUS," and "TEAMWORK."

The only new looking piece of furniture was a black leather office chair.

Her new boss was a puzzle. One she had no intention of solving.

Behind his desk were various awards for The Emporium hanging on the wall as well as diplomas sporting the name *Reuben E. Callahan* in bold letters. An MBA from some uppity school in Chicago. Figured that Reuben would be all hip on college.

Maddie had been lucky to get her GED and finish cosmetology school.

She moved to his desk and picked up a picture of Reuben cozying up with a tall blonde, the same one who'd been here not five minutes earlier. She'd walked into the restaurant like she owned the place and immediately asked Tilly what was going on.

The door behind her opened, and Maddie shrieked, almost dropping the frame.

"Careful, Miss Accident-Prone." Reuben shut the door and rescued the picture from her trembling hands. "Would hate to add to your list of disasters for the day."

She bristled. "Watch where you walk. I might accidentally step on your foot with my heel."

He set the picture down, leaned against the desk, and glanced at her feet. "You're wearing tennis shoes, Madison. I think I could handle it."

She glanced down at the scuffed Nikes she'd gotten from Goodwill and grimaced. Where were some spiked heels when she needed them? "What, you don't think I could still inflict damage?"

Reuben shook his head. "Oh, no doubt you could."

Despite her good senses, Maddie became aware of Reuben's close proximity. His cologne smelled spicy, but not overwhelming like her father's used to be when he all but bathed in Old Spice.

In an effort to create distance, she took a step back and moved to sit down in the chair, only to have Reuben grasp her arms and pull her back up.

Indignation coursed through her as she pulled away from him. "What? I can't sit down either?"

He shook his head. "Not unless you want to fall on your backside."

Maddie glanced behind her to see the chair a good foot farther back than she'd guessed. She stepped back again, felt for the chair, and sat down without incident. A good shower would help rid her of the grimy feeling of having a man's hands on her again, even if it was just her arms. A mouth full of chocolate would numb the embarrassment.

Reuben walked around the desk and sat in the swanky office chair. "Livy asked me if I checked your references."

"Obviously you didn't. And who's Livy?"

"Sorry. Olivia Sanderson is my, uh, girlfriend, and also General Manager at this location."

An "aha" light bulb popped on in Maddie's head. The dirty look that had been thrown her way as the woman left made sense now. "So that's why she wasn't happy to see me here. You were encroaching on her turf."

Reuben's jaw twitched, a now familiar sign that he was irritated. "No, I'm owner of The Emporium and have every right to hire you. But, she's right. I was a little hasty. Have you ever worked in a restaurant?"

"Once." An honest answer.

"And what'd you do there?"

"I was a waitress." Maddie bit her lip. She was on shaky ground between truth and, well, nontruth.

"For how long?"

There was the question she hoped to avoid. "Does it matter? Obviously waitressing isn't my forte. But I could be hostess, bus tables. You name it." Her speech reeked of desperation, but considering she was living out of her car, a job was a must. She'd do anything—well, almost anything—to secure one.

"I don't need a hostess or a busser. What I need is a waitress." The jingle of the office phone interrupted. He glanced at her for only a moment before picking up the handset. "Reuben speaking."

There was a pause, then he began shuffling through papers on his desk. "Yes, I have the quote right here. Livy and I were just talking about the linens earlier, in fact. Just a minute."

Reuben stood up and opened a file drawer behind him and flipped through the most unorganized stacks of paper she'd ever seen. From her viewpoint, it looked like the papers had been stuffed into hanging file folders at random, some standing straight up and others crinkled from being squashed in the drawer.

When Reuben pulled out a wad of papers and dropped them on the desk, she muffled a laugh. Given the dark eyes that glanced her way, the giggle hadn't helped her case.

While he rummaged through paperwork, Maddie's eyes swept over the chaos and landed on a piece of paper on the corner of his desk.

She picked it up and dangled it between her thumb and index finger until Reuben's eye caught the gesture.

He plucked the quote from her fingers, frowned at her, then turned his attention back to the caller. "Sorry about the wait. Found it. Let me see," his eyes scanned the sheet. "Looks competitive enough, but I do have two more quotes I'm waiting for. I'll let you know for sure by end of week. Will that work?"

He ended the call and hung up the phone. "Where were we?"

Maddie sat back and crossed her arms over her chest. "You were telling me how much you needed an administrative assistant, and that I'd be perfect for the job."

"When did I say that?"

Leaning forward, she tapped a finger on the disarray of papers covering his desk. "You didn't have to."

He crossed his arms over his chest and raised his eyebrows. "So you're telling me you're qualified to be an office assistant?"

*Qualified* and *capable* were two different, but related, words. "What I'm qualified to be is a hairdresser, but since you got me fired, yes, I think I could find my way around an office. I helped out as the school receptionist while I got my cosme-tology license." The job had only been part-time. But she'd enjoyed it, got compliments from her boss, and could prob-ably even call and wrangle out a reference if needed.

"Okay, let's say I agree to this. What exactly would you do?"

Maddie thought for a moment. She needed to make it so appealing he couldn't resist. "I would screen your phone calls for you, organize your filing, run your errands, keep on top of appointments and meetings, help with paperwork."

The wary look in his eyes slowly morphed into interest. He tapped a finger on the desk as he stared at her, then slapped down his hand, causing her to jump. "You're right. I do need an assistant. We actually have three restaurants, one down in Kankakee and another up in Rockford. I'm in the middle of finalizing the financing and building contracts for two more restaurants, too. My dream is to become national."

Butterflies performed a waltz in Maddie's belly. Not only did she have a job, but if she did well, she could ride this venture out. Maybe someday be the executive assistant to the CEO of a major restaurant conglomerate. There was no way the state of Illinois could say no to her custody request if she had that kind of future ahead of her.

"Then you definitely are going to need an assistant, and I'm perfect for the job. I may not be the greatest at carrying trays of food, but I'm a hard worker and could organize the sand on the shores of Lake Michigan if I had to."

He cocked an eyebrow. "The sand?"

Maddie shrugged. "Okay, a little exaggeration. My point is, you won't be disappointed this time. I promise."

They spoke for a few minutes about salary and hours; and since it was after five, they agreed she would officially start on Tuesday. When she stepped out of his office, Maddie couldn't wipe the smile off her lips if she tried. It took all her power not to skip out to the parking lot.

Instead, she held off until she was on the sidewalk, then did a little happy jig and squeal, complete with clapping hands and everything.

A throat cleared behind her.

Her cheeks burned as she turned to see Reuben standing there, a smirk on his face. "Nice dance."

Smoothing her hands over her shirt front, she stood up straight to gather what little dignity she had left. "I, uh, saw a spider."

"Clapping for a spider—very environmentally friendly of you."

Maddie bit down the comeback that sat on the tip of her tongue. No use making her boss too mad. She propped a hand on her hip. "Did you need something?"

"No."

"Well, I'll just be going then. See you in the morning."

"Eight sharp."

"I remember the time. We just discussed it a minute ago."

"Well, bye then." But the man didn't budge.

Maddie turned and took a step onto the parking lot, then paused.

Her car was still at the salon.

She swiveled back to see Reuben dangling his keys. "Need a ride?"

# 4

Reuben glanced at the woman in the passenger seat with her back turned to him, staring out the window.

He should have made the stubborn woman walk. The restaurant was only five or six blocks from downtown. She'd have made it fine.

What had he been thinking to hire her?

The thought had sounded good at the time. Someone to get all that cursed paperwork off his desk and into a place he could actually find it.

But his quick decision left him with a moody assistant who, by the looks of it, didn't even have decent clothes. Her jeans sported a hole in the knee and her button-up purple top had seen too many washes.

Image aside, he could barely afford the added expense. With the pending business loan for the new restaurants, he was going to be counting his pennies for the next year or so until they opened and started making a profit.

He should have sent her packing back to Judy's when he had the chance.

In fact, he could still probably pull a few strings and get her back on at the salon.

Reuben cleared his throat, and Maddie twisted her head toward him. "Yes?"

"I was thinking—"

An obnoxious drum beat filled the air, and Maddie dug a phone out of her pocket, flipped it open, and turned back toward the window. "Hello?"

Reuben stopped at a red light and pretended not to eavesdrop.

"Kyle? Hey, what's up?"

Kyle. Interesting.

Maddie laughed. Different from her usual snark. Nicer.

"I, uh, I've had an okay day. Not exactly what I planned but I've got a job, and that's what matters. It's actually better than the one I expected to have."

Great. Scratch plan B. The light turned green, and Reuben pushed on the gas a little too hard. The tires squealed.

Maddie glared at him, then turned her attention back to the phone. "Sorry, I'm riding with Mr. Speed Demon here." She paused. "No, it's just my boss giving me a ride back to where I parked. Stop being a worry-wart, the Tracker's fine. Now, how are you doing? Staying out of trouble?"

There was that laugh again. At least it wasn't annoying like Livy's. He loved the woman, but the snort-laugh combination was her least pleasing attribute.

Reuben pulled into a parking space on Main Street a half a block down from the salon and shifted the car into park.

Maddie didn't seemed to notice as her previous smile turned back into the frown he knew too well. "Yeah, you can put her on."

Whoever "her" was, he felt sorry for the woman.

"Mrs. Blakely, how are things?" A pause, then Maddie sat up straight, glanced at him, then turned away as if to create a shield of privacy. "Excuse me? Since when? You have no right."

Feeling like an ogre for listening in, Reuben got out of the car and shut the door.

A minute passed until Maddie got out and slammed the door. "That woman, I could . . . I could strangle her."

Reuben had no doubt the petite brunette, her eyes blazing fire, could accomplish just that. "Something wrong?"

She paced beside the car, back and forth, mumbling to herself. "If she thinks she can just, just barge in and take over, she has another think coming."

Pieces slid together. Mother-in-law trouble, or at least, future mother-in-law, given her ringless left hand.

No way was he getting in the middle of someone else's issues though. "Well, if you're good, I'll see you in the morning."

Maddie blinked as if realizing where she was. "Yes, in the morning. Fine. Eight o'clock."

Reuben got back in his BMW and shifted into reverse to head back to the restaurant, leaving his basket case of a new employee behind.

⥥

Maddie jumped into the driver's seat of her fifteen-year-old GEO Tracker and slammed the door.

She pounded on the steering wheel until her hands throbbed.

How dare that woman! Kyle was *not* hers. He was Maddie's brother, and blood trumped social status and bank account, right?

It did in her book, at least.

Once she got settled into a house and could show a stable income, she'd be eligible to petition the courts to obtain guardianship.

But if Kyle's foster parents petitioned first, as they were considering, she had no clue what would happen.

She should have told Kyle her plans. Gotten him on her side. But she didn't want to disappoint him if it fell through. She'd wanted it to be a surprise.

Well, the surprise was now on her.

Tomorrow, she'd call his social worker. Surely there was something she could do.

Maddie took a deep breath and blew it out.

God knew this was all coming. It didn't surprise him. Everything would get straightened out tomorrow.

As Rachel, the only decent girlfriend her dad ever had, used to say, "Don't worry, be happy, friend. God's got this."

Tonight, she needed a plan.

After digging out her steno pad, she flipped past all her feeble budget attempts, scribbled notes, and daily checklists until she found a blank page.

*Things To Do - Monday:*

- Figure out how to get to the Emporium
- Eat Dinner
- Find Laundromat
- Find cheap place to sleep

As she pulled out of her parking spot, item number three on her list appeared almost directly across the street. No clue how she'd missed it that morning.

She'd visit after work tomorrow, as she only had a total of four outfits with her, and between travel and work, she was almost out of clothes.

She added "used clothing store" on her list of places to find later. Her new job was going to need her to spiff up her wardrobe a bit. No hiding behind an apron anymore. But the two-hundred dollars in her wallet and an even skimpier bank account wouldn't allow for much.

Retracing the route Reuben had taken, she found the Emporium easily enough. She wrote down the East Center Street address, vaguely recalling passing it on her way in that morning.

If memory served her correctly, she could just keep on going down that road to get to both dinner and a place to sleep.

McDonald's . . . and the Walmart parking lot.

# 5

*M*addie officially had the most stubborn boss on the planet. "You expect us to share? Really?"

Reuben scooted a wooden, cushionless chair toward the front of the metal monstrosity of a desk and patted the seat. "I'm gone part of the time anyway visiting the other restaurants. You can sit in my big chair when I'm gone."

She put her hands to her cheeks and opened her mouth wide in mock surprise. "Thank you so much. I've always wanted to sit in a big-girl chair, Dad."

He scowled and sat down in his big-boy leather twirly chair. "Would you rather sit on the floor?"

Her hips still ached from sleeping in her car the night before, so she clamped her mouth shut and parked her tush. "Where should I begin, Master?"

"If we're going to be working together, you might tone down the attitude, Madison."

The man was right. No sense in losing a third job this week. The snark was second nature, though, and would be a hard habit to break. "First, the name's Maddie. Second, how about I start with filing?"

He nodded and went back to the computer in front of him. "Sounds grand."

Maddie surveyed the mess that was Reuben's desk. It looked like an F5 tornado had come swooping through.

One thing life had taught her was how to handle messy situations: Purge and start fresh.

With a sweep of her arms, she gathered most of the papers on the desk and dropped them on the floor behind her.

Reuben's eyes were so wide they could have popped out and rolled onto the floor too. "What do you think you're doing?"

She wiggled her eyebrows at him. "Filing. The cabinet over there is next."

He stood up quicker than a mouse devoured cheese. "You are not throwing everything in my file cabinet on the floor."

Maddie jutted her chin out an inch and straightened her back. "Am too. How do you expect me to organize that mess unless I take everything out first? If I had my own desk, I could use that. But since I don't, the floor will do just fine. You're the one who suggested it, Boss-man."

His steely glare burned into her for a good five seconds, but she stood straight and stared right back.

"Fine. I'll get you a desk to put in the corner as soon as I have time. I have an old computer at home we can set up to make Your Highness happy."

She folded her arms. "Do I get a fancy leather chair like you have?"

"Don't press your luck. This one was a gift from my mother. My old one is in storage; I'll bring that in for you too."

Maddie walked to the file cabinet and began to take out all the files and paperwork with a little more finesse than she'd used with the desk. "You're odd, you know that? Drive a fancy car, decorate the restaurant to look like some place out of a magazine, but don't care a lick about your office. I just can't figure you out."

His fingers typed something on the keyboard, his eyes never leaving the monitor. "I think you need to mind your own business and file."

She dropped another armful of files onto the growing stack. "Now, that is something I have no problem doing."

The typing ceased. "I meant to talk to you about your clothes."

Maddie jerked her head around to look at him. "Excuse me? Now who needs to mind his own business?"

His face flushed. "What I mean is, the dress code. You won't be dealing with customers, obviously, but you'll be in and out of the dining area, so you're representing the Emporium as well."

She glanced down at her faded jean Capris, white shirt, and thin black and white striped vest. Shopping was definitely in order, but this was the best outfit she owned. Of course, she'd picked it out to wear as a hair stylist, thinking it looked trendy with a bit of funk to it. "Please don't tell me you have some all-black dress code or something."

"Business casual. Which means no jeans, shorts, or tennis shoes."

Fabulous. "I guess I have to do some shopping then, huh?"

"Don't you females like that sort of thing?"

The ones who had money did. But not a female who now had to sleep in her car for a while longer instead of splurging on a hotel for a few nights as previously planned.

Her first paycheck couldn't come soon enough. "Speaking of shopping, how often do your employees get paid around here?"

"Every two weeks, a week behind. We just started a pay period on Monday, so your first check will be two weeks from

Friday." He steeled his eyes on hers. "Don't tell me you need an advance already."

Yes, as a matter of fact, she did. "No, just planning ahead."

*Mental To Do List - Tuesday:*

- Buy clothes to appease egotistical boss
- Decorate backseat of Tracker, aka home-sweet-home
- Get massive amounts of deodorant
- Figure out how to sponge bathe at Walmart
- Call Kyle
- Call social worker—see if there's even a chance; otherwise I might as well just quit now

◈

Maddie tucked her cheap pay-by-the-minute cell phone between her cheek and shoulder as she pushed the Walmart cart toward the women's clothing section. "Be straight with me, Corina. Do I have a shot?"

A deep sigh on the other end of the line wasn't encouraging. "It's not over 'til it's over. I'm not going to lie to you. The Blakelys definitely have a leg up. He's been with them almost four years."

"What does *he* want?"

"He doesn't know. And I'm not sure it's wise to tell him until things are a little more certain."

Maddie located the size 6 section of the clearance rack, but only found one pair of pants that fit Reuben's stupid rules. "Why not? If he knows, he'll tell the Blakelys he wants to live with me, and that'll be the end of it."

"A judge might see it as you trying to manipulate and coerce him. Kyle's a tough kid, but for the most part he's always been pretty good and stayed out of trouble. I could see this pushing him over the edge, especially if it falls through and he can't come live with you."

"Which is why I need to get him out of the city."

"How's it going there, by the way? The salon job working out?"

"I, uh, actually found something different. Better. Working in an office, kinda like my receptionist job but full-time."

"What happened this time, Maddie? Cutting hair was your dream job."

No need airing all the details. "I just got a better opportunity. Thought you'd be proud of me."

"Have you found a place to stay yet?"

Yeah, Hotel-de-la-Tracker. "I've got it handled. No worries."

"Maddie, you know I think the world of you. You've come a long way from that sixteen-year-old I picked up from the police station. But at the end of the day, I have to recommend who I think is best for Kyle."

"It'll be me, Corina. I'm what's best for him."

# 6

*God, I need a place to live. I don't mean to be selfish, but . . . I hurt.* Maddie peeled her legs off the cracked vinyl backseat of her Tracker and set her wobbly appendages on the asphalt parking lot.

She'd survived more than a week of sleeping in her car. Only nine days left until she got paid, then maybe she could start looking for an immobile place to live.

Maddie reached her arms into the air and stretched. The responding pop in her shoulders echoed through the air. Sweet, sweet relief. After she finished cracking her aching joints, she shut the door and got in the.driver's seat.

She drove to the McDonald's across the way, then shoved her toothpaste, toothbrush, and hairbrush into her oversized Coach purse. The bag was a knockoff she'd gotten for a steal from a roadside vendor—aka homeless dude—a few years back, but it made her feel cool anyway.

She grabbed a fruit n' yogurt parfait, scarfed it down, then went to the bathroom to freshen up.

After changing into her last clean Reuben-approved outfit and making a note to visit the laundromat that night, she pulled out her toiletry bag.

After brushing her teeth, she squirted bathroom soap onto some toilet paper, wet it down, and washed her face and armpits.

At least she'd figured out what to do for her hair. She'd found every salon in the Sandwich area—minus one—and had mapped out a schedule for haircut/washes so she never visited one twice. She could go three days between washes, the third day being a definite hair-up day, which happened to be today.

Maddie pulled her hairbrush from her bag. A hairstylist she might be, but even she wasn't sure she could make something presentable out of the mop of hair that hung kinked and knotted at her neck. *God, I know I've already asked many times, but just in case you were busy before, I—*

The bathroom door swung open wide. A little girl in pigtails skipped into the room and slid to a stop. "Hi."

Maddie eyed her as she pulled the brush through a tangle. "Hi."

The girl tilted her head to the side, studying Maddie. "It's the first day of no school, so my mom surprised us with Mickey D's for breakfast. Why are *you* here?"

Maddie glanced at her, then back at the mirror. Cute kid, but she needed to hurry if she was going to make it to the Emporium on time. "Breakfast, same as you."

The girl wrinkled her forehead. "Why ya brushin' your hair then? My mom makes me brush mine before I leave the house. Didn't your momma teach you that?"

Maddie's heart squeezed a little at the thought of her mom. "My mom did teach me that. She was very good at doing hair, kinda like your mom is good at fixing yours up nice and pretty."

The girl beamed. "Thanks. I love pigtails. They flop around and help me be not so hot when I play outside. But you still didn't tell me why you're brushin' your hair."

Maddie shrugged. Might as well be honest with the little squirt. "I just moved into town and don't have a place to stay yet. Since I don't have my own bathroom to do my hair in, I'm borrowing McDonald's."

"Where do you sleep then?"

Twenty questions was getting old. Maddie decided to do a switcheroo. "I didn't catch your name."

"It's Sara. What's your name?"

"Maddie."

"So, where did you sleep, Maddie?"

Switcheroo fail. "In my car, but it's just temporary."

Sara's jaw dropped. "You're homeless?"

"Well, sorta. . . . "

The little girl turned around, swung open the door, and ran back into the dining room without using the bathroom.

Maddie shrugged. Maybe homeless people scared her. She'd seen enough of them in her old neighborhood to last her a lifetime. It humbled her that she now qualified for the title.

After pulling the brush through her thin brown hair a few more times, she pulled the hair behind her head and tested the length. The front half tumbled out of her hand. Great. Her "little trims" had officially blown her ponytail plan.

No doubt Reuben-the-style-freak would call her out on bad hygiene. Good thing he couldn't see her legs which were beginning to look junglelike.

Maddie glanced at her watch. A quarter to eight. She stuffed her supplies back into her purse and headed out the door. When she stepped out, she ran smack dab into someone. "Oh, sorry, didn't see you there."

The surprised woman took a step back and seemed to take in Maddie's appearance in a glance.

Maybe she wasn't the cleanest and most put together, but Maddie didn't think she looked *that* bad. She put a hand to her stomach and discreetly checked to make sure she'd zipped her khakis.

Check.

The woman, who Maddie guessed was about thirty, glanced toward the dining room, then back with a concerned smile on her lips. "Hi. I'm Allie Crum." She held out her hand.

Maddie accepted the handshake. "Um, it's nice to meet you. Sorry I ran into you there."

"No biggy. Actually, Sara came out and insisted I talk to you. Is everything okay?"

*God, I know I need help. But complete embarrassment isn't quite how I pictured it. Finding a winning lottery ticket on the floor would work just fine. . . .*

Maddie gasped when Allie pulled her into a hug.

Humiliation complete. Pushing the overly kind woman away would be rude. But accepting an unsolicited hug gave her the creeps.

The woman patted her back while Maddie tried to figure out if she should return the hug or just stand there feeling stupid. "Sara told me about your situation." Mercifully, she released Maddie and held her at arm's length. "How can I help? I know you don't know me, but we are a Christian family and believe in helping those in need."

Humiliation, thy name is Maddie. "I'm fine. Really. I just moved to town and haven't found a place to stay yet. My homelessness is temporary." She hoped. As long as Reuben paid her on time or didn't decide to fire her, which he'd threatened a few times. She should have been nicer to him. Schmoozed a little. But a brownnoser, she was not.

"Still, the moment Sara came out and told me about you, I felt God telling me I need to help. My hubby and I have been teaching our kids about helping those in need and how God wants us to serve those less fortunate. I'm so proud of Sara for listening. Please. Let us do something."

Tears sprung to Maddie's eyes. When had she gone out of her way to help someone else like that, especially a stranger? She'd focused on Kyle and working to get guardianship of him for the last two years. Nothing else had mattered.

"I guess if you know of a cheap apartment I could rent or something, that'd be nice. I'm working at The Sandwich Emporium, so I haven't had a lot of time to look."

Allie's face lit up brighter than mustard on wheat bread. "The Emporium? Really? Oh my goodness, this is *perfect*. We were just going to stop in and visit Reuben after this."

"You know Reuben?"

"Of course. He's my brother."

# 7

Maddie turned her fifteen-year-old piece of junk into the parking lot behind Allie's brand spanking new minivan. Poor city trash verses the wealthy suburban mother. An unlikely pair for sure.

Facing Reuben this morning wasn't going to be pleasant. The man was so hip on "appearances," he was sure to explode when he found out his new assistant was taking sponge baths at McDonald's.

It could be worse though. She could've made herself a lovely sign and parked herself out on the curb.

Maddie hoped Allie would feel the need to keep the news private. But there'd been no time to discuss the matter as the woman had flurried around, introducing her to the trio of children, Cole, Sara, and little Beth, who sat in the McDonald's booth.

By the time Maddie got into her car, she was more than a little flustered.

She planned to run in ahead of Allie's crew and corner Reuben with an at-a-glance summary so he'd understand. Even as she formulated her plan of attack, Reuben opened the door to the restaurant, ruining everything. Sara jumped from the van and ran to him, pointing a finger in Maddie's direction and exaggerating her facial expressions.

Given Reuben's scowl, he wasn't pleased.

When Allie joined the group and started talking as well, Maddie figured she better get out and defend herself. Or, she could just play the sympathy card and see how far that took her. She'd test the mood first.

When she joined the group, Reuben stared at her. "We need to talk."

Definitely the defense card. She'd also try the naive approach but didn't put much stock in it working. "Yes, we do. There is that desk issue we've never fixed." She turned to Allie and smiled. "An office assistant needs her own desk and computer, don't you think?"

Allie looked from Reuben to Maddie, her brow crunched in confusion. "Wait. She's your . . . assistant?"

Reuben shuffled his feet and hooked his thumbs into his front pockets. "I originally hired her as a waitress, but Maddie here pointed out my desperate need to get organized, and given the growth of the company, I agreed."

"You're right, of course. An assistant is just what you need. Maybe you'll actually have time for your family once in a while now." Allie turned toward Maddie. "Now, about a place for you to live. I have a few ideas. I'll make some calls and let you know what I find. But even if you have to use our spare bedroom, you will *not* be sleeping in a car again."

With that, Allie squeezed her with another hug then corralled her three munchkins back into the minivan.

Maddie turned to Reuben who stood with his arms across his chest. When had she seen this stance before? Oh, yes, about a hundred times in the last week.

"Are you going to yell at me? Because if you are, you can save your breath. I'm not listening."

His voice ratcheted up a few decibels. "Why would I yell at you? It's not like you humiliated me or anything. My sister thinks I'm hiring a homeless person as an assistant. I guess in some ways that's good. She probably views me as good Samaritan of the year, but my reputation's on the line, too."

"Oh. I'm sorry. I wouldn't want to hurt that ego of yours the size of the Sears Tower. Next time I sleep in my car I'll think of *you* first."

Maddie didn't wait for a reply but headed into the empty restaurant and straight to his office. As tempting as it was to slam the door, she refrained. Knowing her luck it would come off its hinges.

She turned to see Reuben standing behind her, his eyes a little less fiery and his mouth touched with concern rather than fury.

"Have you really been sleeping in your car?"

She shrugged. "Haven't had time to find a place yet."

"Why didn't you tell me?"

"Oh, yeah, that would be a stellar conversation. 'Hey, boss, I'm livin' in my car, wanna help a girl out?' "

He shoved his fingers through his hair, but stopped short, probably at the loss of his long hair. "Do you need money, or time off to find something?"

"Just let me do my job and pay me on time. That's all I ask. I'm not a charity case."

He pulled a hundred dollar bill out of his wallet. "Think of it as a sign-on bonus. And you will let me help find you a place to stay. Allie won't let me hear the end of it if I don't."

Maddie's back stiffened. She hated handouts. But if it was a bonus, she could take that. She plucked the bill from his hand. "Only if you let me show you how to properly style that new haircut of yours."

Reuben patted his hair. "It wouldn't spike like Judy did it, so I just used some hair gel and combed it back. I thought it looked okay."

Maddie rolled her eyes. She'd been holding her tongue for over a week. "It does if you want to try out for a part in the musical *Grease*." She stepped closer to him and lifted her hands to mess with his hair. The dark blond clumps were glued to his scalp. "Geez, what'd you do, dump the bottle on it?"

He shrugged. "I used to only need a squirt of hairspray. Styling gel isn't my thing."

"Well, you're in luck, because it is mine. Now sit."

She pushed him by the shoulders into his chair, then walked over to the small fridge in the corner and grabbed a bottle of water. "This will be a temporary fix, but at least I can show you how to do it in the morning."

He shrieked when she began to dump the water over his head. "What are you doing?"

"Trying to wet it down a bit. I can't do a thing with all this gel."

Maddie fished a hairbrush out of her purse and went to work. Five minutes later she stood in front of him, putting the finishing touches on the spike. "And that's how you do it. It should be rather simple, because the object of this hairstyle is to be a little crazy with it. Messy is *in* when it comes to spikes."

She handed him a compact so he could see for himself.

He nodded after a quick glance in the mirror. "You're right. It's much better, thank you."

"You're welcome." Maddie turned to put the hairbrush back but froze when Reuben spoke.

"I'm sorry for getting you fired. You really are good at what you do. If you want, we can go back today, and I'll tell Judy everything so you can have your job back."

This couldn't be happening now. "So you're firing me?"

"No, the assistant job is still yours if you want it."

Maddie stared at the brush in her hand. *God, what am I supposed to do?* This job held promise of a future, but what happened if she screwed it up, or in a month or two when Reuben thought he was organized enough, he decided he didn't need her anymore?

Hairstyling was what she was trained for and experienced in. A safe bet.

Maddie glanced back at Reuben and reached up to adjust another piece of his hair that had gone astray, then opened her mouth to answer.

The sound of a throat clearing interrupted her response.

Livy stood at the entrance of the office, hands on her hips, fire spewing from her eyes.

# 8

Reuben stepped away from Maddie and around the desk to where Livy stood. "I was wondering when I'd see you this morning. Everything okay?"

She squinted her eyes at him. "No, no everything is not okay. I walk in and find you nice and cozy with your new waitress-turned-assistant. What's going on, Reuben?"

This was not going well. "Livy, sit down. Let me explain."

"What's there to explain? I won't let you weasel yourself out of this, Reuben. You're cheating on me, aren't you?"

"No, I'm not." Reuben raised his voice louder than necessary, but this was getting out of hand. "Now sit down so I can tell you what happened."

Livy sat in the chair, but her eyes hurled knives in Maddie's direction. Reuben nodded at Maddie to sit as well, but she remained standing.

"If you don't mind, I'm going to get a little fresh air to clear my head." Before Reuben could respond, she stepped around them and out of the office, closing the door behind her.

He turned back to Livy, who sat, arms clenched to her sides. As calmly as he could, he started at the beginning with the fateful haircut and ended with the interrupted apology and offer of restitution. By the end of the tale, Livy had relaxed.

"I can't believe you did such a thing. Of course you'll go and talk to Judy."

Reuben grimaced. As much as he wanted to make this whole mess right, the idea of an assistant had grown on him. "I'll talk to Judy, but the choice is Maddie's. I still think I need an assistant. Besides, Judy's a bear to work with."

Livy scowled at him. "Reuben, she's very kind."

"Are we talking about the same person your mom has refused to speak to for the last fifteen years and you refuse to let touch your hair?"

Livy stood up. "Well, I'm sure she'll pick to go back to her little hairdressing thing, but I agree. You still need an assistant. Would you like me to place an ad?"

"No. I want to hear from Maddie first, and if she declines, I need to pray about it some more." Especially since he'd jumped into this whole thing without consulting the Big Guy.

"Plus, we need to talk." Reuben walked around the desk and pulled Livy up by her hands, then put his arms on her waist and pulled her close. "I never want you thinking I'd cheat on you."

"You have to admit, seeing a woman running her fingers through your hair was a little incriminating."

Reuben bent and kissed her soundly. She returned it, desire oozing from her body as she pressed against him. He pushed her back. "Patience, Liv."

She put a hand to his cheek. "We still need to talk."

Wasn't it the guy who was supposed to be pushing the boundaries? "And we will. Just give me a few more weeks to get some of the red tape behind me, okay?"

Livy smiled and kissed him again. "I'm holding you to it."

When she left the room, Reuben exhaled a breath. Later he'd explore why he was always tense when she was in the room. Right now, he needed to find where his new assistant had run off to.

❧

Reuben walked to the end of the porch that lined the front of the restaurant and glanced around the side.

Maddie stood, her back leaned against the cement wall, head bowed.

He leaned against the railing for a moment, observing her from his perch. Her short brown hair hung lifeless above her shoulders, her full bangs rod-straight instead of the slight curve they usually were. How she managed to look presentable all the other days was beyond him.

When her head popped up and she saw him, he threw a leg over the rail and jumped to the other side. "How you doing?"

She shifted her head to the side and pressed a fist against her eyes. He hadn't thought a tough girl like her would cry, but maybe he'd been wrong. She turned back and smiled at him. "A better question is, how is your girlfriend doing?"

"She's fine. I explained, and she lectured me, like I deserved. I meant what I said in there. I'll go back and tell them my part in the fiasco right now if that's what you want."

Maddie picked at her pink-colored fingernail, then cocked her head to the side to look at him. "Are you a Christian, Reuben?"

No wonder she didn't know, given his rotten attitude with her thus far. "Yeah, although not a perfect one, obviously."

She smiled. "I'll say."

"I deserved that."

"Well, if you're a Christian and give stock in what God commands, then He says you need to give me a huge raise and sign over the title of your big fancy car to me." Her goofy smile gave away her sarcasm.

"I think you're listening to the devil there, Madison."

"You're doing it again. My name is Maddie, remember? Madison is so . . . Wisconsin."

"All right. So, Maddie, have you decided which job you're going to take?"

She pushed off the side of the building and turned to him. "I guess I can suffer through having you for a boss. But I still want my own desk and twirly chair."

# 9

A knock sounded on the door, and Allie poked her head in. "Am I interrupting?"

Reuben waved her in. "Not at all."

Maddie looked up from her spot on the floor where she'd spread out her latest filing project: financial statements. She didn't mind this project as much. As strapped for money as she was, math was always her strong suit. Numbers were so . . . sure. Dependable. Not full of a bunch of guesses like science.

Allie glanced from Reuben to Maddie. "You weren't kidding about needing a desk, huh?"

Maddie jerked her thumb toward her boss. "Try convincing him that."

"I quit trying to convince my brother of anything a long time ago. More stubborn than Dad used to be."

Reuben stood. "What did you need, Allie? We're busy."

The tension could be cut with a steak knife. Allie put her hands on her hips. "Loosen up, Reub. The kids wanted to eat here for a late lunch, and I needed to chat with Maddie. Can you spare her, oh mighty one?"

Maddie hadn't realized it was so late. She stood and stretched her arms. "I think lunch is a great idea. Even workaholics need to eat, Reuben." And the restaurant sounded better than the PB&J sandwich and Cheetos she had waiting for her in the Tracker.

He pushed out from his desk. "Fine. It's time you get a taste of the Emporium anyway instead of hiding out in your car the whole lunch break."

She stuck out her tongue at him. "I've just been going home for lunch, remember?"

Turning and following where Allie had already exited, she didn't wait for a reply.

Maddie headed into the dining room, which buzzed with the end-of-lunch crowd. She waved to Livy, who was busy with a table and merely nodded a cool acknowledgment. More than once Maddie thanked God she wasn't out serving. No doubt she'd have already decorated half the laps in the room.

She sat down at the table Allie and the kids occupied, and was surprised a moment later when Reuben sat down next to her. He didn't say a word.

Tilly, a middle-aged waitress with wild, curly red hair, sauntered over to take their order. "Good afternoon. Can I start you out with some drinks?"

Reuben's lips tipped up for the first time since Maddie had known him. "Tilly's trying to impress her boss with her professional waitress talk."

The apron-clad woman slapped Reuben on the shoulder. "Careful what you say. I might pull a Maddie and dump your food on your lap."

Heat flooded Maddie's neck. Not exactly flattering to have her name known as the town klutz.

Reuben looked at her and frowned. Was he still irritated at her blunder? Surely not. He snapped out of it a moment later and nodded to Tilly. "I'll remember that. Yes, drinks would be great. I'll take a Coke."

They went around the table giving their drink orders, and when Tilly left to fill them, the kids all started talking at once, clamoring for Allie's attention. After they'd decided what sandwiches they wanted, Allie, who sat across the table, leaned forward, a cheesy grin lighting up her face. "I think I found you the perfect place to stay."

*God, have I ever told you how awesome you are? Really, I don't care if it's a hole in the wall as long as I can have a bathroom.*

"It's only been a few hours. How did you find something this fast?"

Allie opened her mouth to speak but was interrupted by Tilly.

"Here we are, folks. A water for Maddie, Coke for Reuben and Allie, and chocolate milk for the three youngsters."

Beth, who Maddie guessed to be about three, squealed and bobbed up and down in her booster seat. "Milk, Milk! Chocolate!"

Allie hushed her. "Patience, Beth." She nodded at Cole. "Help your sister get her straw in the lid, please."

The ten-year-old obeyed and even tickled his sister in the process. He was about Kyle's age. Maddie's heart squeezed as she watched him, even though she knew her brother well enough to know that his response would have been, "Do it yourself." He was the stereotypical defensive foster kid, just like she used to be before Jesus got hold of her.

"Maddie?"

She blinked her eyes and looked at Reuben. "What?"

"Tilly asked if you're ready to order."

She hadn't even looked at the menu. "Do you recommend something?"

He smirked. "The Reuben is our specialty."

Maddie wrinkled up her nose. "Corned beef. Gross."

"Suit yourself. You're missing out."

"You go ahead and order while I decided."

She perused the menu, trying to find something cheap, but found that impossible. The Sandwich Emporium was no regular sandwich joint. No deli meat here. Instead, they had chicken breast on gourmet bread, prime rib on their French dip, and sandwiches listed that she'd never heard of with ingredients that she couldn't even recognize.

After living on McDonald's and sandwiches made in her backseat, spending fifteen bucks on a sandwich gave her chills.

Reuben leaned over, his lips almost touching her ears as he whispered. "It's on the house. Order what you want. Consider it a perk."

She lifted her head, determined not to turn red at the thought of mooching off her boss. "I'll have the French dip with baked potato, sour cream, no butter, and vegetables as my side."

After Tillie left, Maddie tried not to drool at the thought of a hot meal. Instead, she turned her attention back to housing. "Allie, you were saying? About finding an apartment to rent?"

A twinkle sparked in her new friend's eyes. "Well, it's not exactly an apartment."

"A house then?" She'd dreamed of finding a small two-bedroom house with a fenced-in yard. An impossible dream on her budget, but it would knock Corina's socks off when she came to visit.

Allie shook her head. "It's a room, kind of a guesthouse sort of thing."

Reuben choked on his pop. After clearing his throat, he shot a warning glance at Allie. "It won't work."

Allie smiled in response. Clearly she was used to getting what she wanted, although Maddie agreed with Reuben this time. She needed more than a room to bring Kyle home to.

"I already talked to both Mom and Gary. They think it's a great idea."

Maddie looked between the bickering siblings. "What's going on? I don't understand."

Sara, who sat beside Maddie, took her hand and squealed. "You're gonna live with Grandma!"

# 10

*God, I know your intentions are good and all. But . . . my boss's parent's house? Really? If you fell asleep and made a mistake, I completely understand. You're a busy guy. I'll give you a break and let you fix this. . . .*

Little Sara looked like she'd just been handed front-row tickets to see Justin Bieber.

Allie's face beamed with a wide smile. "I know this isn't what you were expecting, but my mom and stepdad have a guest-house separate from the main house. It's small, only one room with a bathroom, but it has a kitchenette and is completely livable and furnished. My dad built it when my grandparents were still living. Mom says you're more than welcome to use it for as long as you need."

Maddie ventured a look at Reuben. He sat with an arm on the table and hand on his Coke. His mouth resembled a downward sloped banana.

"Allie, really, thanks for the offer. I'm just not sure—"

The good Samaritan shook her head. "I won't accept no for an answer, and neither will Reuben. You're *not* sleeping in your car another night."

Reuben shifted in his seat. "Allie's right. It's a good, temporary solution."

No missing his emphasis on the word *temporary*. She dittoed that. "Okay, I'll accept. But I insist on paying them a decent rent."

Allie shook her head. "Good luck getting Gary to accept. He'd rather you just put a few extra bills in the offering or buy a few Bibles for the Gideons."

Where had these people come from? She'd stepped out of the McDonald's bathroom into benevolent land. People didn't do things this way on the streets of Chicago. Not the ones she frequented anyway. Even the churchgoers where she attended on and off the past year were Scrooges compared to these people.

But now that she thought about it, there were a few who offered to help. She'd just rolled her eyes at the time.

"I'll do that then. Thank you."

Sara clapped her hands together. "Yeah! Grandma has the neatest house ever. And you're gonna love her. She makes the bestest chocolate-chip cookies."

～❧～

Five-o'clock came and went. God didn't change his mind.

Maddie pulled up to the two-story Cape Cod and cut off the engine. In front of her, Allie and her crew climbed out of her van. In her rear-view mirror, she saw Reuben exiting his Beamer.

Taking a breath, she grabbed her bag from the backseat and headed toward Allie.

"Reub, why don't you show Maddie the guesthouse while I let Mom and Gary know we're here?" Allie picked Bethany up and balanced her on her hip. "The key is under the flowerpot."

Reuben tried to take Maddie's bag from her, but she shuffled it to her other hand, out of his reach. He frowned at her, but started toward the garage. "Tell Mom to give us a minute. I'll bring Maddie in when we're done."

Maddie followed Reuben up the driveway and along a paved sidewalk beside the garage.

She stopped when she reached the backyard. The setup reminded her of a picture-perfect backyard on a sitcom. Overflowing flower beds lined the house and deck and a small building that stood off to the side. "Nice place."

Reuben cleared his throat and nodded his head toward the building. "This way."

She felt like Hansel and Gretel, being lured into the seemingly wonderful cottage, complete with latticework and shingled siding but missing the edible rooftop. She braced herself for the witch inside stirring a big pot of boiling goo over an open fire.

Or maybe Reuben aka Hansel was the witch. That'd be a twist on the story.

Reuben reached down to retrieve the key. "Grandma and Grandpa lived the rest of their years here, and now every missionary visitor or other special speaker at church makes use of it. You're the first long-term guest."

"It's temporary, remember?"

He looked back at her as he opened the door. "Yes, I do."

Something in his eyes and the softening of his voice told her he wanted to say more. She wasn't sure whether to be disappointed or relieved when he didn't.

They walked into the room, and no witch waited for them. Maddie dropped her bag on the floor and tried to hold back a Sara-like squeal. The room was perfect. A queen-sized bed with a white headboard and matching dresser and side table sat on one side. On the other side was, as promised, a kitchenette, complete with a small stove, fridge, and sink. A loveseat, recliner, and TV created a cozy living area in the middle.

"What do you think?"

Maddie stopped midswirl. She'd been spinning in the middle of the room while he'd picked up her bag and set it by the bed. He must think her a silly teenager. She waited a moment until the room stopped racing, then tugged at her white, button-up shirt that had gone awry during her jig. "It will do for now. Thank you."

He raised his eyebrows. "Is something wrong?"

"Oh, nothing. It's very nice, and I'm more thankful than you can ever know. But it's important I get into my own place soon if I want to have any hope at—"

Maddie stopped herself. She hadn't told him about Kyle yet and wasn't sure she should. Her past was behind her and best forgotten until she was able to do something about it.

"Hope at what?"

A knock sounded at the door, and an older lady peeked into the cottage. "Yoo-hoo. Anybody home?"

Saved by the mom. Maddie smiled as the fiftyish woman, her brown hair sprinkled with gray, waltzed into the room and crushed her in a hug. Like mother, like daughter.

"It's nice to meet you, Mrs. Callahan."

The woman held her at arm's length, her hands patting Maddie's arms. "Actually, I remarried after Reuben's father passed away, so I'm Mrs. Luther now. You just call me Betty, though. No need for formalities here. Now, has Reuben given you the tour yet?"

Reuben shook his head. "No, Mom. We just got here."

"Well, my oh my, we'll just have to change that now won't we." She ushered Maddie toward the small table while Reuben took a seat in the recliner, looking a bit too relieved at having his duty taken from him. "Over here is the kitchen. It has all the pots and pans and cooking utensils you can think of, and probably a few you've never seen before. My momma, God rest her soul, was quite the cook in her day. The microwave over there is an addition since she went to be with Jesus. She couldn't stand the thought of nuking anything, even leftovers."

Tempted to kiss the microwave, Maddie refrained. She and cooking did not get along. "Charbroiled" had a whole new meaning in her kitchen.

"And of course, Reuben's already breaking in the recliner for you, and over there is the bedroom area. We thought about making separate rooms, but Dad preferred it this way, him being in a wheelchair and all."

"I'm so sorry for your loss."

Betty turned and smiled at her. "No need. It's been over a year now, and they're dancing with Jesus now, having a grand ol' time."

Maddie smiled. "Maybe my mom's joining them, too."

Behind her, Reuben cleared his throat. "Mom, I needed to finish discussing some things with Maddie. Do you mind if we meet you inside in a bit?"

His mother's frown betrayed her opinion of his request. "That's fine, but don't be long. I already have supper on the table."

"Mrs. Luther, you didn't have to do that. I'd just planned to—"

The older woman put her hands on her modest-sized hips. "There's not an ounce of food in this little place, and no one on my property is allowed to go hungry as long as there's a bread crumb left in my house. You finish your work chat with Reuben and come join the family. I won't hear another word about it. And remember, please call me Betty." She spun on her heels and walked out before Maddie could open her mouth again.

Reuben popped the footrest on the recliner. "Come have a seat. We're gonna have a business meeting. It's much more roomier in here anyway."

He looked too cute sitting there with his hands behind his neck and his legs stretched out.

Ugh, where had that thought come from? Her boss was mean, overbearing, and male. Cuteness was not allowed. Ever.

*God, please make a hideous mole grow or something, okay?*

"Not exactly a professional setting, but okay." She sat down on the couch opposite of him, kicked off her shoes, and curled her legs up behind her. "What do you want to talk about?"

"You."

"So not a business topic, Boss-man."

Reuben shifted the chair into an upward position and focused on her. "I need to know more about you if we're going to work together. People will ask questions, and right now I have no answers. We're going to go into dinner in a few minutes, and I'd rather not have any more surprises."

"You're talking about Kyle, aren't you?"

Reuben nodded. "Yeah, about Kyle. You do know my mom is pretty strict on morals, right? You living here with a guy isn't going to happen. She has a kind heart, but not that kind."

Living with a guy? What was he talking about?

Ohhhhhh. He thought Kyle was a boyfriend. Actually, that wasn't a bad assumption for him to have. Kept him at a safe distance.

"Kyle won't live with me until I find a place of our own, so don't worry about that."

Reuben shifted in his seat, obviously uncomfortable with the topic.

Fact was, the thought of living with a guy, ever, was pretty taboo for her too. And according to her handy-dandy Bible, she doubted God would appreciate the misunderstanding. Time to divert. "Anything else you want to know? My favorite color perhaps? Don't want you be caught blind with that bit of sensational news."

His eyes caught hold of hers, and try as she may, she couldn't look away. "Why were you living out of your car? The truth."

She held her tongue for a moment. Her past was between her and God, and no one else. "I didn't come from a fabulous family like yours, Reuben. My mom's dead and my dad's a scumbag. I moved here to start over but counted on getting tips to get me by, not on getting fired on my first day. I'm not down to my last penny but didn't want to waste money on a hotel until I got a paycheck."

"I asked if you needed an advance."

"I'm not a charity case. I can do this myself."

Reuben pushed down the footstool and stood. "You have Kyle, right? Why didn't he help?"

He extended a hand to her. She ignored it and stood up herself. It'd been a year since she'd felt the grasp of a man's hand, and she didn't care for a repeat.

"Kyle is none of your business, boss or not."

Reuben stuffed his hands into his front pockets. "Agreed." He looked toward the door and back at her. "Mom's going to wonder where we went."

Maddie slipped on her shoes and nodded. "You're right, and I don't want to keep her waiting. She's already going to too much trouble."

"She enjoys it. Don't get all apologetic on her and ruin her fun. Think of yourself as a stray cat she found and wants to nurse back to health."

"Just as long as she doesn't try to declaw me."

Reuben's lips twitched. "That's the first thing on the list. Gotta make sure you don't scratch up my car."

She rolled her eyes. The man and his oversized toy. "Your precious car will be just fine."

He turned and walked toward the door, and Maddie followed. Her eyes were drawn to Reuben's khaki slacks, more specifically to his hindquarters. Were they . . . moving?

She averted her eyes. Good Christian women didn't look at men's behinds. Or did they? No, surely it was a sin to notice how nice it looked and how he must work out to have . . .

*God, please help me. I know I'm lusting kinda. . . . Is this where I'm supposed to pluck out my eye?*

The movement drew her eyes again. "Uh, Reuben?"

"Hold on a sec." He reached for his pocket and pulled out his phone.

Maddie ducked her head. God would forgive sins of ignorance, right?

When she looked up, Reuben was tapping on the screen with his thumbs. He looked up at her. "That was Livy. I just want to tell her I'll call her back later."

"That's fine. Do you want me to go in without you?" Please say no. The thought of walking into a strange house by herself made her want to hop back in her car and drive over a cliff. Well, maybe not that dramatic, but she really didn't want to.

"No, I just texted her. You were saying?" He put the phone back in his pocket and held the door open for her.

Maddie shook her head. "Not a thing." She exited and started down the walk leading to the back patio before he could question her.

Maddie lifted her fork to her mouth to savor her last bite of the most delicious lasagna she'd ever tasted. She'd be a stray cat more often if it meant she could eat like this. Especially in this picture-perfect setting. Their dining room looked like something out of a sitcom, with the farmhouse table and Reuben's stepdad, who'd introduced himself as Gary Luther, sitting at the head. A hutch filled with china lined one wall with the swinging door that led to the kitchen next to it.

Gary set his fork on his empty plate and patted his slightly paunched stomach. "Betty, love, you've done it again. I believe I might have to unbuckle my belt after that one."

Maddie shifted in her chair. She hated belts. They reminded her of her father.

"Oh, hush. You say that every time, and you're not even wearing one. But I'm glad you enjoyed it." The hostess stood and took his plate. "Anyone else done?"

Maddie chewed her last bite and stood up as well. "Let me help you with the dishes, Betty."

"Absolutely not. Guests of mine are not put to work."

Reuben stood and took the plate from his mom's hands. "You cooked. Go sit and I'll help clean up."

Betty patted his cheek. "You're so sweet, my dear." She let him take the dish, but still picked up leftovers from the table, then leaned over and nudged Maddie with her elbow. "You know they say you can tell what kind of husband a man will be by how he treats his mother. My Reuben's going to make a wife very happy someday."

Maddie didn't love the direction of this conversation. "I'm sure Livy will appreciate that."

Not the thing to say, given the silence that flooded the room for several awkward moments.

Allie cleared her throat and took the plate from Reuben's hands, her eyes boring into his. "As chivalrous as my brother is, I agree with Mom. Guests, men, and children need to leave the room. The faster we get done with this, the sooner we get dessert." She shot Maddie a grin and winked.

Maddie gulped and forced a smile. She'd examine the whole Livy-awkward thing later. Right now, sleep sounded so much nicer than even dessert, but she needed to be sociable. These people had gone out of their way to be hospitable. Making nice was the least she could do.

In the living room, she sat down on the couch and crossed her legs at her ankles. Her body screamed for sleep, and she stifled a yawn. Reuben joined her, sitting on the opposite side of the sofa.

Gary lounged in a brown leather recliner next to a large stone fireplace. "I hear you're working for Reub now. You a waitress?"

Reuben cast a glance at Maddie, his eyes conveying an apology. "No, Maddie's my new assistant. With the new restaurants next year, I needed help with the office work. It'll let me be able to be on-site more when the building starts."

Gary nodded. "Good idea. How's it coming with the business plans?"

Reuben's face hardened, much like it did with her at times. What had Gary done to illicit such a response? "Everything's fine. Nothing for you to worry about."

The hurt in Gary's eyes was disguised unsuccessfully by his smile. "Not worried. I'm sure you have it handled. You're a good businessman. Your dad would be proud."

Betty walked into the room, followed by Allie, both oblivious to the tension that could be cut with a steak knife. "The kids are upstairs playing so we can all visit for a bit." She sat in the burgundy Queen Anne chair on the other side of the fireplace, and Allie joined Reuben and Maddie on the couch, sitting between them, much to Maddie's relief.

Reuben shifted in his seat and stretched an arm across the back of the couch. "Mom, let's not play twenty questions tonight."

Ditto that. Those words were the best she'd heard all night.

"Oh, posh, I wasn't planning on grilling her, Reuben. Just a little conversation is all." Betty crossed her legs, her blue jeans a sharp contrast to the Victorian-style chair. "Maddie, Allie said you grew up in Chicago?"

"Yes ma'am. I lived there all my life and just graduated from cosmetology school last spring."

Her eyebrows raised. "Really? How wonderful! Too bad Reuben already snatched you up. I hear Judy's looking for another stylist at the—".

"Mom." Reuben's sharp voice stopped his mother short. "Maddie's already met Judy."

"Oh, I see." Betty narrowed her eyes at Reuben, then shifted in her chair and looked again at Maddie. "What of your family, dear? Are they still in Chicago?"

"Mom." Reuben barked again.

While it was sweet that he wanted to rescue her, she didn't need him butting in and making scene. "My mother passed away several years ago, and my dad has some problems. I'm not sure where he's at right now."

The room was quiet, interrupted only by the gargling of Gary's stomach. Betty cast him a stern look. "Don't tell me you're hungry again."

"Nope, just digesting. But dessert does sound good."

Allie hopped up from her place between Reuben and Maddie. "That's a wonderful idea. Mom, I'll help you get it ready. Maddie, I hope you like strawberry shortcake?"

"Sounds delicious. I suppose you won't let me help with this either?"

Betty tsked. "Not on your life. We'll be back in a jiffy."

The two walked out of the room, and Gary folded in the footrest and stood up as well. "If you'll excuse me, I'm going to go see if I can sneak a bite from the cook. Wish me luck."

When the room was empty except for Reuben and Maddie, she ventured a glance his way. He sat, his head leaned back on the couch and his eyes closed.

"That's quite a family you have."

He turned his head toward her and he opened one eye. "That's the understatement of the century. They're good people though. I'm sorry about—"

She held up a hand to stop him. "Don't. You had the same questions. But you do need to tell them about the Cut 'N' Style incident before they hear it from the gossip channels."

He groaned. "I was surprised they hadn't heard already. I'll tell my mom tonight, though."

She raised her eyebrows. She'd assumed he'd put up a fight about it. "My version or yours?"

Reuben shifted guiltily. "Neither. I'll give a brief summary that incriminates neither of us."

Maddie wanted to push the issue but let it slide. "So how long have Gary and your mom been married?"

"A year and a half." His voice sounded stilted to her ears, holding a false vibrato.

"Do you like him? Gary, I mean?"

Reuben opened an eye again and glanced at her. "Why do you ask?"

"You didn't seem thrilled with him."

"Now who needs to mind her own business?"

"Touché."

Maddie thought back to the string of "stepmoms" her dad had brought home. Each one got progressively worse until the last one. Rachel. She'd been normal but had seen her dad's true colors. Just not fast enough.

Then Maddie's fragile world had crumbled.

She shivered at the vivid memories. Ones she wished would fizzle up and die. But still they came. The pictures of her dad, his hands balled in anger, growling at Rachel. The poor woman had shielded Maddie as best she could, but the beating still came for both of them.

A hand pressed against her shoulder, and she jerked away. Maddie opened her eyes to see Reuben next to her, his eyes full of concern.

"You okay?" His low voice brought her back to the present. She was in a warm house surrounded by decent people. No one would hurt her.

She took a breath. "Yes. Just bad memories is all."

"Wanna talk about it?"

It was the first question he'd asked her that seemed like he actually might have a caring bone somewhere under that thick skin.

It almost made her want to answer him, but she shook her head instead. "No, I—"

Betty's singsong voice floated down the hallway. "Here comes dessert." She entered the room moments later, carrying a large platter, which held several plates of shortcake covered in strawberries.

Allie trailed behind her carrying a can of whipped cream and a handful of forks. "Anyone hungry?"

As if on cue, Gary plodded in behind them. "That'd be me." He approached Betty from behind and gave her a side hug. "You've outdone yourself tonight, Babe."

The older woman pushed him away with her hip. "Go sit down, you big mooch. I already told you, our guest gets served first."

He smacked a kiss on her cheek anyway and headed back to his recliner.

After everyone was served, Maddie munched on the most delicious strawberry shortcake she'd ever tasted. The home-made cake was moist and the strawberries ripe and sweet.

The conversation flowed again once everyone finished their dessert and had their mouths free, but thankfully it focused on mundane topics like the latest weather patterns and city poli-tics. Maddie groaned when Reuben mentioned that the mayor took the tea-dousing incident well. She hadn't known he'd been the mayor. No wonder Reuben had been so mad.

As much as Maddie was enjoying herself, the bed in her new digs called her name, and rather loudly at that. Reuben now sat next to her, and several times she tried to catch his eye to give him a hint of her exhausted condition, but he was talking about his business plans to his mom, so nothing could distract him.

Maybe if she closed her eyes for just a second, she'd get enough oomph to last another half hour. Maybe. . . .

# 11

$M$addie stretched and yawned. She snuggled into the soft pillow and smiled.

Her eyes popped open a moment later, and an unfamiliar room filled her view. She sat up, dazed and more than a little confused.

Where was she?

The evening before trickled back into her memory. A place to stay . . . dinner with the family . . . dessert . . . and then she was so tired. . . .

Did she fall asleep?

Maddie raked her fingers through her hair and looked at her shirt, the same one she'd been wearing the night before. She wiggled her toes. No socks. She didn't remember taking them off.

Surely Reuben hadn't carried her to bed. A moment later she saw her socks lying on the floor. Would he have taken them off? The thought of his fingers on her toes made her stomach tighten.

That meant he'd handled her dirty socks.

The tightening morphed into nausea.

Or was it just hunger? She saw a trip to McDonald's in her future again. *Note for To-Do list: Go to grocery store.*

She scanned the cheery room and saw a box on the small kitchen table.

Throwing back the covers, Maddie padded to the kitchenette and picked up a small note sitting on top of the box.

*M, Hope you slept well. Mom put a few things together to tide you over. C-u at the restaurant in the a.m.—R*

Maddie dropped the note and opened the box to find sugar, flour, salt, cereal, bananas, and bread. She reached over and opened the fridge. Three containers of leftovers filled one shelf and a pitcher of tea and gallon of milk sat on another.

*God, you and I are going to have to have a serious talk about your chosen methods of provision.*

She'd left Chicago to prove she could make it on her own. No judge would ever let her have Kyle while she was on welfare, church-style.

Every inch of her wanted to take the box and throw it in the trash.

Her stomach growled, protesting the idea.

It was right. No use wasting perfectly edible food. Maddie rummaged through the cupboards for a bowl then poured the cereal and drenched it in milk.

When she'd sipped the last drop of Frosted Flakes–flavored milk, she set it in the sink and headed for her suitcase. Her Bible taunted her from its spot on top of her clothes.

*Okay, God. I know, I know.*

She'd skipped the last two days, no doubt part of the reason for God's unseemly behavior of late.

"And where would you like me to read today, oh Wise One?"

Maddie flipped through the Bible, undecided if she should continue on in the book of John or if she should go someplace new. Her flipping stopped in the Old Testament. "Moses, God? Okay, you're the boss."

She glanced at the door. Anyone who heard her converse with God would think her nuts and probably sacrilegious. But she and God had an agreement. She'd be real with Him if He'd be real with her. It fit them just fine, and no lightning bolts had been flung. Yet.

The verses in front of her blurred together, so she blinked and focused in at the beginning of the chapter. The story was vaguely familiar. She remembered her mom reading to her about the plagues and God parting the Red Sea for Moses and the Israelites, but after that everything blurred.

She read to herself for a few minutes, but when she got to chapter sixteen of Exodus, she gasped. After all God had done for them, how dare those selfish people complain. Didn't they remember the sea, the plagues? To think they didn't even trust God with something as silly as bread.

Her faith may be new, but at least she didn't pout to God all the time.

"And the Lord said to Moses, 'Behold, I will rain bread from Heaven for you—' "

Maddie blinked and reread the passage. Rain bread? Probably just a metaphor. She kept reading. God promised quail as well. Not too shabby of a meal. Sounded like something they'd serve at one of those fancy downtown Chicago restaurants. She was surprised Reuben hadn't figured out how to make a quail sandwich yet.

Her mouth flung open as she continued to read. Quail covered the ground? Dew turned into bread?

Maddie glanced over at her dining room table, which still held the remnants of God's provision to her. The same provision she'd resented and almost thrown away.

She closed her eyes.

She'd behaved no better than the greedy Israelites.

⁓◌⁓

"Good morning, love of my life."

Reuben looked up from his laptop to see Livy leaning against the office door. He glanced at the clock, which read eight-thirty. "Good morning to you too. You're up bright and early." She rarely arrived at the restaurant before ten.

She shrugged. "I had a few things I wanted to get done so I thought I'd get a head start. Plus, it gave me a chance to see you." The sashay of her hips as she walked to his desk hinted at an ulterior motive.

He cleared his throat. "We still on for dinner tonight?"

Livy walked around his desk and hopped up, sitting directly on top of the papers he'd been working on. He tried not to be annoyed.

"Of course we are. I have the evening shift covered here."

"Sounds great." Now if she'd just move so he could finish his work. . . .

Her legs began to travel back and forth, like a child dangling her feet on a swing. But this was his desk. In his office.

"How's the new girl working out?" Her tone carried a casual note, almost too casual.

"She's doing fine. Speaking of, I thought I should mention—"

Reuben heard the office door open, but Livy blocked his view.

"I'm sorry, I didn't know someone was in here. I'll come back."

*Maddie!* She was a half hour late, but he'd expected that. He stood up and held a hand to Livy and pulled her off the desk. Her bottom lip curled in a pout.

"No, come in. Livy just came in early to get caught up on work. Didn't you, honey?"

His girlfriend frowned. "But you were saying—"

"We can finish talking tonight, okay?" She needed to know about Maddie's living arrangements, but now was not the time. It would take a little smooth talking, without his assistant present, to get her to understand.

Livy reached up and planted a kiss directly on his lips, lingering longer than appropriate with an audience. His cheeks blazed hotter than the Panini grill in the kitchen when she released him and winked. "See you later, hun."

His gaze flickered from the sculptured body of the blonde who just exited the room to the petite, wisp of a girl who stood before him. They were as different as peanut butter and jelly, but went together about as well as grease and water. Livy's long, flowing locks curled to perfection contrasted sharply with Maddie's chocolate brown hair cut in a short bob with bangs. He wanted to sweep the hair from her forehead and tuck it behind her ears.

Maddie's lips curled into a smile, and she set her purse in the corner. "Sorry I'm late, boss."

Reuben wanted to tell her that she should have slept in longer, but encouraging an employee to be late wasn't the smartest thing to do. Rated right up there with carrying her to bed the night before. But his mother had insisted.

He'd been fine until halfway to the cottage, she'd wrapped her arms around his neck and snuggled into him. A very unbossly feeling had filled his gut.

And unless he'd like to lose his girlfriend and get slapped with a sexual harassment lawsuit, it was a feeling he needed to squash immediately.

"No problem. Just call next time, okay?" As he moved to sit back down, the phone rang. He reached to answer it, but Maddie was faster.

"Reuben Callahan's office, can I help you?" She winked at him as she cradled the phone against her shoulder. "Mmmhmmm. I see. Actually, I'm his administrative assistant." A pause, and she laughed. "Yes, I'm sure of that. I tell you what. Let me take a look at his schedule and give you a call back."

She jotted something down on a Post-it note and laughed into the phone again. "Yes sir. Thank you for calling. I'll get back to you."

Maddie returned the phone to the desk and smiled at him. "Mr. Limberg needs to reschedule your Thursday two-o'clock meeting. Where's your schedule?"

Reuben fished out a small four-by-six planner overflowing with Post-it notes from under a three-ring binder and handed it to her. "Everything's in there. Somewhere."

She shook her head. "I can't believe you don't have an electronic calendar. You can just use your e-mail software, you know."

Did she think he was a complete idiot? "I just haven't had the time to set it up."

"I can do for you. I am your assistant, after all."

"Later. I need my computer right now."

"Fine." She picked up a stack of paperwork and began putting them in piles. "You know, you still owe me a desk."

"I got you a place to sleep last night. Beggars can't be choosers."

Her hands paused, and her eyes met his. "Allie and your parents got me a place to stay, if memory serves me correctly. You just came along for the ride."

Reuben bit down the bitter pill her words flung at him. Gary was not his parent, but if he corrected her, he'd sound petty. "We'll go tomorrow."

"You've said that every day for the past week. I say we go today."

"No time."

She was silent, and he glanced up, his eyes meeting her rock solid gaze. "You're just going to have to make time, then. They'll never be a day when you have absolutely nothing you could be doing."

The irritating thing was, she had a point. Still, he needed to finish reviewing these invoices and send them off to the accountant. "Tomorrow. I promise."

"Why don't I just go myself? Give me a price limit, and I'll stay under it. I'm a bargain shopper, I promise."

Not that he wouldn't mind handing off the task, but he *did* mind handing out his credit card. "The cashier might give you a funny look when you try to use my credit card."

Her lips tilted upward. "I could lower my voice real low and pretend." She tucked her chin and cleared her throat. "Like this."

Reuben bit down the chuckle that threatened to escape. Most days Maddie rankled his every nerve. But she was growing on him. "Okay, so maybe you could pull it off. But I'll go anyway, just in case. Tomorrow."

"Today. After lunch."

Irritating female. "Three o'clock."

She nodded, a cheesy grin lighting up her face. "Deal."

Reuben settled back into his desk while Maddie continued to shuffle paperwork. He stole glances at her every few minutes but forced his eyes back on the work at hand. She'd need her own office if this was going to work long-term.

And he still had serious reservations about that too. He needed an assistant, no doubt, but Maddie was not the typical employee. She challenged his every word and her edges were as rough as sandpaper.

And the woman was clumsy. There wasn't a day that passed that she didn't trip over something or drop a stapler.

She'd look at him with those dark, troubled eyes and dare him to reprimand her.

He'd give anything to know who had hurt her so much that she'd built a mile-high wall around her, armed with sharp, verbal jabs.

"Reuben?"

He snapped his head up to see Maddie's questioning glance. "Yes?"

"You okay? I called your name like five times."

"Sorry. Just concentrating."

Her eyebrows arched high behind her dark bangs, and when he looked down to see doodled circles on the invoices in front of him, he turned them over and stood. "Changed my mind. Let's go now."

"Okay, but I've got a few questions first."

Questions were good. As long as they weren't anything like the awful *What are you thinking about?* one Livy always flung his way. "Shoot."

"First, I have a few other office supplies I need. You don't have a supply stash I don't know about do you?"

He was good to find a pen that still had ink in it. Office supplies were never top on his list. "What you see is what you get. Make a list on the way."

"Second question." She set her elbow on the desk, and put her chin in her hand and smiled. "Do you always doodle so pretty on your invoices?"

He grabbed his keys from the desk. "Just go get in the car."

⋘⋙

Maddie stifled a yawn and looked at her watch. Past ten-thirty, and Tilly had already come in to say good-bye and let them know that they were the last ones there. "You do know you have to pay me overtime, right?"

Reuben's face flared red as he put his muscle into tightening the last screw. He looked so cute sitting on the floor putting together the desk. She'd tried to convince him to let the store assemble it and deliver, but he'd insisted he could handle it.

Then they'd gotten back to the restaurant to find everything in chaos and Livy in a dither. Two waitresses had called in sick for the lunch shift and a cook had shown up late.

Reuben didn't start on the assembly until well after six. Four hours, his canceled date, and a ticked-off girlfriend later. . . .

The macho man wiped his brow on his sleeve. "You can leave early tomorrow to make up for it."

"What a great boss you are, Mr. Tightwad."

"At least we understand each other." He tossed the screwdriver back into the toolbox and pulled himself up. She should give him a hand up. It would've been the polite thing to do.

Thank goodness she didn't do polite. Because even though she wanted nothing to do with men, Reuben was proving dangerous.

Just that morning she'd noticed his cologne again. And liked it.

And watching his determined self put together that dumb desk even if it killed him. It was just plain hot, even when he did slip back into jerkdom.

*God, help me.*

Men were dangerous, and she couldn't afford to slip up here.

"Here, help me shove this back, will ya?" Having long since given up on his button-up dress shirt, he put a hand to the front of his white T-shirt and gave it a few pulls, unsticking the sweat-soaked cotton from his chest. A smell strong enough to make a skunk gag slammed up Maddie's nose.

She tried not to cough. The man's deodorant must have worn off, either that or he'd forgotten to put any on.

Romantic notions officially went down the tubes, where they belonged.

*Thank you, God, for making men sweat profusely and stink like dirty gym socks after doing simple tasks.*

Maddie grinned. She was getting this ungreedy thing after all.

"You gonna help or not?"

"Yeah, sorry." She took one side of the desk and helped him slide it into the spot they'd cleared earlier. Her own desk. She was official. A step up from the salon booth at the Cut 'N' Style, and even better than the counter she'd sat behind in the college's office.

"I'll have another phone installed soon. Mine already links to the phone in the kitchen, so we'll just add another line."

Left up to him, it'd be a year before that happened. "Sounds good. Should I call the phone company in the morning?"

The look on his face was worth a shopping spree at Target. "You can do that for me?"

Maddie ran a finger over the wood veneer of her desk. "I *am* your assistant."

"I know. I just didn't think. . . . Never mind. You do that, and I'll work on getting my old laptop up and running for you soon."

Did he think her a complete technological idiot? "If you bring it in, I can do that too."

"You know computers?" He asked as if the concept was the strangest he'd ever heard of.

"I'm a product of the technology age same as you, Mister, if not more so. At the age you were fiddling with CDs, I was burning music from iTunes to the iPod Rachel got me for Christmas."

"Who's Rachel?"

She hadn't meant to go there. Rachel wasn't a topic up for discussion. Ever. Maddie turned her attention to the desk and put the box of pens they'd purchased in the top drawer. "Just a girl my dad used to date." But she was so much more than that.

Reuben yawned. "I don't know about you, but I'm ready to head out."

Maddie grabbed her purse while Reuben flipped off the light and followed him out of the office. Halfway across the dark dining room, she ran into his back. "Reuben—"

He hushed her and put a hand behind him as if to shield her. "I saw something."

Her arms prickled like tiny ants using her skin as a dance floor to do the cha-cha. "What'd you see?"

Reuben nodded toward the front window. "I thought I saw a person in the window looking in. Or maybe just a shadow."

A shadow could be anything, right? A stray dog, lost kitty, homeless guy, a big dude with a bazooka ready to blow his way into the restaurant. A girl didn't grow up on the streets of Chicago without a healthy dose of fear of bad guys.

Reuben motioned her to get back into the office. Not a chance. She hid her face behind his back and grabbed a handful of his shirt. Maybe she'd watched *Scooby-Doo* too much as a kid, but usually it's the person that goes to the "safe" place who finds the ghost. No, she'd stay here so Reuben could protect her. Just like Fred did for Velma and Daphne.

Her protector grunted, then dropped to his knees on the floor. Maddie followed suit and crawled up beside him. "Are you sure you saw something?" She whispered as quiet as she could.

He put a finger to his lips and nodded his head, then started to crawl toward the back wall where the waitress station hid them from view. A second later he shoved a cell phone into her hand. "I'm gonna get a closer look. If I yell or anything happens, call 9-1-1, got it?"

Maddie looked from the Blackberry to her boss. "Why don't we just call them now and let the police come and look?"

"Because it might be nothing. I don't want everyone talking about how I called the police because I was afraid of the dark and thought I saw a monster."

Maddie's stomach lurched. "A monster?"

Reuben took her free hand in his and squeezed. "Not really a monster, but you know how rumors get twisted. Remember, if something happens, call the police."

She nodded. The plan did not sound like a good one. By the time she heard something, it might be too late. But Reuben already jumped ship . . . er . . . waitress counter, and left her to fend for herself. Some protector he was.

*Dear God, please send your lightning to strike down whatever bad thing is out there. Unless it really is a stray kitty or dog, then please don't kill it and help it find a nice loving home. I really do like puppies. Maybe I could get one someday for when Kyle comes home. . . .*

A crash and a yell sounded from the dining room. Maddie shrieked and curled into a ball under the counter. With hands shaking, she punched in the three most important numbers she knew.

# 12

Reuben put his fingers to his temples. The blue and red lights blinded him, and the sirens dumped fuel onto his already frazzled nerves. "No officer. I don't know what it was. It looked like a person peeking in the window. Since everything was dark, I couldn't really tell."

"So no one attacked you?" The cop stood poised to take additional notes.

Would the guy stop asking the same question over and over? "No. Like I already said, I just tripped over the table."

He scribbled something into his notebook then snapped it shut. "Well, I'm afraid there's nothing we can do then. There's no sign someone tried to break in, nothing stolen, and no physical harm." He nodded toward Reuben's foot. "Well, not the criminal kind anyway."

Reuben winced as a paramedic finished wrapping his ankle. What a crazy mess. People must be thinking the worst. And there were quite a few of them across the street, gawkers trying to get a peek at the action.

He tried to move his ankle, but the throbbing pain stopped him. "It isn't broken, is it?"

"Nope, just a good sprain. You'll wanna keep off it for a few days, and I'd suggest seeing a doctor in the morning since you won't let me take you to the hospital to be sure."

A run to the ER would just add salt to the already gaping wound that was his pride. "Thanks for the offer, but I'll be okay."

Reuben glanced at Maddie, who stood against the ambulance door. Her lips were pressed into a straight line as her eyes searched the area as if she were looking for someone.

The paramedic helped him off the gurney. "You really need crutches, sir. At least make sure someone drives you home."

The officer grunted. "And that's an order. Can't be driving with a bum right ankle. You already caused enough stir tonight, no need to add a car accident to your list. In fact, I'll get one of the men to take you—"

"Really, it's okay." No way was he going home in a squad car.

Maddie pushed off from her spot and put her hands to her waist. "I'll take him home."

Riding with her wasn't on the top of his list of things he wanted to do right now either, but no other option presented itself. Unless he wanted to call Allie or his mom, and that just wasn't happening. And Livy was already hot about him canceling their date. She'd probably just kick him in the other ankle.

With the help of the cop and Maddie, he squeezed into the front seat of her Tracker. His ankle smarted as he settled into the cramped quarters, and he tried to ignore the rips in the black and red seats. The vehicle brought him directly back to his high school days when a Tracker was actually *cool* to drive.

Maddie jumped into the driver's seat. "Ready?"

"Yes." So much more could be said, but he was afraid he'd yell. Loudly.

"You'll have to give directions."

He navigated while she drove under the speed limit. Halfway there, he couldn't stand it anymore. "What are you, a turtle?"

She frowned. "I just don't want to hurt you more."

"Your driving wouldn't hurt a squirrel if you ran into one."

The Tracker accelerated two miles an hour.

Maddie pulled into his driveway a few minutes later and rushed around to his side to open the door.

He took hold of her arm and heaved himself out of the seat. Biting his lip against the stabbing pain, he attempted to walk by himself but only lasted two steps.

Maddie slipped an arm around his back. "Lean on me. I'll help you."

"I think you've helped enough tonight." A sharp prick stung his side. "Did you just pinch me?"

"Yes, I did. Stop being a jerk."

He hobbled beside her up the sidewalk to the front porch. "Me? You're the one who caused all this."

Maddie huffed. "Don't you blame your ankle on me. You're the one who wanted to be all macho and brave the shadow yourself."

It sounded lame when she put it that way. The shadow? Had he really snuck across the dining room because of a little shadow? "You're still the one who called the police."

"Yes. *After* I heard a crash and you yelling."

"I'd tripped over a table for crying out loud. What did you think happened?" They reached the top of the steps, and he grabbed his keys out of his pocket.

"Oh, I don't know. My boss tells me to call the police if I hear anything weird, then said boss starts to howl louder than a beagle on a scent. What do *you* think I should assume?"

Irritating female. Especially because she was right. Reuben unlocked the door and allowed her to help him to the couch.

He fell back, resting for the first time that day. His muscles would be ticked at him in the morning. Maddie helped him lift his feet onto the couch and prop his ankle on a cushion.

She turned away. "I'll turn on the light."

"No." He barked louder than he meant to, but the thought of light filtering through his eyes to his already pounding skull made him jumpy. He tapped a finger to his forehead. "Head hurts."

"Right. Well, if you don't need anything else. . . . "

"Thank you, Maddie." He couldn't see her features through the darkness, but he did hear her shift back toward him and could make out her silhouette from the dim moonlight filtering through the front window.

"Don't get all sappy on me, boss."

He reached up and snatched her hand. "No. Really, thank you. I was a jerk a while ago and here you are, trying to take care of me. You've gone above and beyond."

She squeezed his palm then wiggled her fingers to withdraw, but he held tight. Now he wished he'd allowed her to turn on the light so he could see her face, those brown eyes that made him want to figure out what was going on behind them.

Maddie coughed. "Do you want me to call somebody to stay with you? Your mom? Allie? Livy?"

"No. I don't want to wake Mom or Allie, and Livy and I . . . it wouldn't look right for her to be here this late. Word's gonna get around town anyway about all the ruckus. No use giving them anything else to wag their tongues about."

Maddie tugged at her hand again, and this time he released it. The gossip queens would have a conniption fit if they found out he'd held hands with his assistant, in the dark, in his house, alone.

What was he saying? It wasn't like he kissed her or anything. Not that she wasn't kissable. Those adorable lips of hers that puckered when she was deep in thought or twisted to one side when she was being silly, they'd be so easy to kiss—for some other man who was interested in such a thing.

Not him of course.

"Livy seems nice. When you gonna pop the question?"

Maddie's voice crammed sense back into his wayward mind. "There you go again, putting your nose where it doesn't belong."

"You do realize you're the biggest topic in the town gossip chain, right?"

No, he didn't. "How would you know that?"

"I have ears. I don't participate, because obviously I don't care, but there's Camp B and Camp E, and not much in between."

"I don't know what you're talking about." The woman was making no sense at all. People didn't care about him and Livy. Their relationship was private.

"Camp B are those who are betting on a breakup. No chance of the relationship surviving. Camp E are the ones who are convinced you'll elope like your mom did. No one foresees a traditional wedding happening though. Except for Livy."

"And you found this out after being here, what, a little over a week?"

"More like in the first forty-eight hours, give or take. You're quite the popular man, Reuben. And for what it's worth, Camp B is made up mostly of single women."

Interesting. "What camp are you in?"

"Camp I, for sure."

"And that stands for?"

"Camp I don't give a rip as long as you pay me on time."

Her sentiment should please him. So why did he feel a twinge of disappointment? "You win. Camp I is definitely my favorite. And I'll add a billion dollars to your next check if you'll pick me up in the morning."

She nodded. "Sure. Who's your doctor?"

"Why do you need to know?"

"Because I also need to schedule you an appointment in the morning."

Reuben sighed. Were all assistants so bossy?

# 13

"Mom, stop hovering." Reuben adjusted the ice pack on his ankle. The doctor had confirmed the sprain and told him to lay low for a few days. Before he could argue, Maddie had cleared his schedule. Having an assistant was proving to be quite nice.

Mothers, on the other hand, were irritating.

"I just want to make sure you have everything you need. Now, here are some books I got from the library, some *Sports Illustrated* magazines I wrestled away from Gary, and your favorite, chocolate brownies."

She pulled the Tupperware out of her bag to reveal the gooey chocolate squares. Never mind. Moms rocked. "Can I have one now?" He reached a hand toward the box only to have it swatted away.

"No you don't. Not 'til you eat your lunch."

Reuben started to protest, but then saw her fishing something else out of the bag of wonders. He leaned over to peek. "What've you got there?"

She popped the lid on a compartmental container. "Just a little chicken and dumplings I had left over."

His favorite. He took it from his mom and sniffed. These were no leftovers. These were fresh-from-the-oven, melt-in-your-mouth, sent-down-from-heaven dumplings.

"Have I ever mentioned that you're the best mom in the world?"

She kissed his forehead then handed him a fork. "You didn't have to, sweetie. I can see it in your eyes. Now, eat up. Livy will be here soon."

The chunk of chicken he'd just started to swallow lodged in his throat. He coughed but it remained stubborn.

"Oh dear, are you okay?" His mom grabbed him by the arm and sat him up, then proceeded to beat him on the back.

The chicken shifted, and he swallowed. Air. Relief. "Sorry, swallowed wrong."

She put her hands to her hips and shook her head, her gray-streaked ponytail swinging like a bell. "Don't ever scare me like that again!"

He laid back onto the couch. "Livy's on her way?"

She busied herself with organizing the books and magazines on the coffee table. "Yes. I called her when I left. She wasn't happy that she hadn't heard from you. Said she didn't even know what had happened or that you were hurt."

How could he be so stupid? Of course he should've called and let her know before she found out from someone else. She must be ticked. "I didn't even think to call her. Maddie handled everything else and I just—"

"Is everything okay with you two?"

Reuben blinked. Where had that come from? "Maddie and me?"

She arched her eyebrows and crossed her arms. "You and Livy."

Good question. "Yes, of course. Why do you ask?"

She sat on the edge of the coffee table and leaned over to pat a hand on his knee. "It's not a good sign when your girlfriend is the last to know you're hurt."

"I told you, I just didn't think about it. But you're right. I should've had Maddie call her too."

From her sour expression, the answer didn't please her. "Reuben, as your mother, you know I reserve the right to ask personal questions even though you won't like them, right?"

This couldn't be good. His mother usually whipped out whatever question she wanted, no matter how personal, without batting an eye. For her to feel the need to use a preamble frightened him. Reuben nodded while unsure if he wanted to hear what came next.

"Are you going to ask Livy to marry you or not?"

First Maddie, then his mother. "With the new restaurants opening, we haven't had time to talk about it. Maybe I just need to ask her and get it out of the way."

The moment he said the words, regret stabbed at him.

A spark lit in his mother's eye brighter than the fireworks that would light up the sky in just a few weeks. "A marriage is not something you 'get out of the way,' Reuben. It's a lifelong commitment to—"

He interrupted her before she could launch into her tirade on the aspects of a quality marriage. "I know, Mom. Just a poor choice of words."

Like she was one to talk nowadays anyway. She married Gary when Dad was barely cold in the ground.

He didn't blame her for that though. Gary was the one who'd manipulated her into it.

His mom stood and set the tub of brownies on the coffee table. "I just want you to pray long and hard about it, dear. The way I see it, your words hit the bull's-eye."

He narrowed his eyes. "What's that supposed to mean?"

"Only that—"

The opening of the front door interrupted. "Yoo-hoo!"

The object of their conversation glided into the room, a pouty frown on her lips. "Oh Reuben, why didn't you call me?"

His neck flushed hot under his T-shirt collar. "It's been a crazy morning. I'm sorry, Liv."

"I mean last night when it happened. You could've been hurt, Reub. Did someone really try to break in?"

"I doubt it. Probably just a kid or something. All I saw was the shadow." It sounded even more moronic now. He had been scared by a shadow in the dark. What kind of man was he anyway?

All he'd thought about at the time was keeping Maddie safe. But he wasn't about to relay that information to Livy.

"Well, you should have at least called me so I could take you home."

"Maddie was there, so she dropped me off."

Livy's mouth tightened and his mom took a step back. "I need to be going, Reuben. Call me if you need anything, all right?"

"Yes, Mother. And thanks for the food."

After the door shut, Livy walked over to the couch and knelt beside him. Before he could utter a word, she took his face in her hands and pressed a kiss to his lips.

He kissed her in return, as he had many times in the last ten years. No sparks flew, but that was normal. They'd known each other so long they were almost like a married couple.

Almost.

She broke the kiss then inched back. "Next time, call me. I know she's your assistant, but I want to be the one who takes care of you."

"I will, I promise. It was just late and I didn't want to wake—"

Another kiss broke off his words. When her hands began to trail down his shirt and her shiny blonde hair fell across his cheek, his body rebelled and responded to her touch. He broke the kiss. "Livy—"

She leaned down to his ear and whispered. "We need to talk."

He gripped her shoulders and pushed her back an inch. "I already told you, Liv—"

She rocked back on her knees. "Yes, I know. You're busy. But we have time now. I need to know what you want, if there's a future. I love you, Reub."

Guilt crushed him when a tear rolled down her cheek. "I know you do. And I love you too."

Livy used her fist to erase the errant tear, then leaned forward. Her emerald eyes shone bright. "Then let's do it. Get married. We can elope, go to Vegas this weekend, I don't really care. As long as I'm with you."

He leaned up on one elbow and caught her cheek in his other hand. "Okay. We'll get married."

She squeezed him as if he were a bottle of ketchup down to its last drop. "I'll book our tickets to Vegas tonight."

# 14

*B*lood pounded in Reuben's ear while he was smothered by his now fiancée.

What had he just agreed to?

The words had slipped out of his mouth, a product of his intense desire not to see the woman who'd been a part of his life for the past decade cry because of him. But he couldn't just up and marry her. Not right now at least.

He wasn't a spur-of-the-moment type guy. And he definitely wasn't a Vegas type guy.

He had to fix this. Before plane tickets were booked.

Should he tell her he'd marry her, but just not in Vegas? Plan a church wedding for a year from now? It'd give him time to get used to the idea anyway.

Or he could call the whole thing off for a final time. Everything they'd been the last decade could stop this very moment. Livy would be mad. Hurt. Distraught.

Reuben wasn't sure what he would be. Relieved?

But what if he regretted it the next day? What if he woke up and realized Livy was no longer his? What if the thought of never being with her hit him once she was gone for good?

They'd taken breaks in the past. When he went to college. And after a few especially bad fights since then.

This was different though. Defining.

That she worked for him now only added to the mess. If they broke up, would she quit? And if she didn't quit, could he handle working next to her?

He blinked, the direction of his thoughts dawning on him like a blinding light. He couldn't break up with her. What was he thinking? They were Reuben and Livy. A team. The invincibles. He remembered the summer they coined the term for themselves.

The day before he had left to go to college Livy had cried herself dry in his arms on his parent's front porch swing. "It'll be okay, Liv. I'll be back at Thanksgiving."

She sniffled. "But that's months away. I'll miss you."

He kissed her forehead. "We'll be okay. You love me, and I love you. That's all that matters. Four years, and I'll be done with school. Then I'll never have to leave you again."

She looked up at him with those dangerous green eyes. "You promise you won't leave me for some gorgeous girl who flirts with you at college?"

He shuddered at even the thought. "I promise. You and me, we're a team. Reuben and Livy. Together, we're invincible, love. No one can come between us."

She leaned up and pecked him on the lips. "I like that. We're the invicibles."

Two months later, she'd called it off. Said she couldn't wait around for him forever.

But when he returned six years later, Bachelor's and Master's degrees in hand, she'd been single. They'd naturally drifted back together. She'd joked that even though time had passed, they proved their relationship really was invincible.

Livy was safe. Nice. Beautiful. The perfect wife for an up-and-coming businessman. She'd been there for him after his dad died, and when Gary successfully brainwashed his mom.

Sparks weren't everything. Relationships needed to be more solid than that.

He pulled back and looked her in the eyes. "You deserve better than Vegas, Livy."

"As long as I have you, that's all that matters."

"No. We'll do it right. A church wedding, big dress, nice flowers, the works."

She shook her head, her blonde hair swishing around her shoulders. "That'll take too long. I want to marry you now. Plus that's expensive. Neither of us can afford a big wedding, and my mom certainly can't handle the expense."

"It doesn't have to be extravagant. We'll set a date for next summer, save our pennies between now and then. No more BMWs."

Her mouth pulled down into a familiar pout. "But that's a year from now. I don't want to wait that long."

He needed a distraction. "We can go ring shopping on Sunday."

Her perfectly red lips tipped into a smile. "Fine. But I think a winter wedding would be better. Maybe January."

"We'll see. Are we on for Sunday though?"

She leaned forward and pressed a quick kiss to his mouth. "You betcha. Now, I need to get back to the Emporium and get ready for the dinner rush."

Business. Back to a conversation he could handle. "How was lunch?"

"Busy."

Good. They needed busy. The thought of finances made his head ache again. And now he had a wedding to pay for too. Livy's mother lived on disability, so it'd be up to him.

And knowing his designer-loving fiancée, he doubted the idea of a scaled-down wedding would last too long.

"I'll be back in tomorrow."

She kissed him one last time and left.

Reuben reached for the Tupperware of brownies, hoping to get his mind off what just happened.

Engaged. To Livy. It shouldn't sound so odd. Everyone knew they'd eventually get married. It was assumed.

He bit into one of his mother's triple-fudge, Sandwich-famous brownies that normally melted in his mouth.

Today, given the way his stomach revolted, it might as well be liverwurst.

❧

Maddie glanced at Reuben's laptop screen. Finally, five o'clock.

She'd felt odd taking over his computer, but it was the stubborn man's own fault. If he'd gotten her desk earlier and brought in his old computer, she wouldn't have to borrow his.

Closing the top of the computer, she glanced at the closed door, then pulled out her cell phone and dialed Mrs. Blakely's number. She hadn't talked to Kyle in almost a week, and it was killing her.

The older woman answered. "Blakely residence."

"It's Maddie. Kyle around?"

A moment of silence was followed by a sigh. "Hold on, I'll get him."

At least she didn't try to cut her out. That was something. "Thanks."

She heard a muffled Mrs. Blakely yell for Kyle, then a hushed dialogue she couldn't make out. A minute later, a familiar voice drifted through the line. "Hey, sis."

"Hey. How's everything?"

"Fine I guess." His voice sounded like a shrug.

"You like being out of school?"

"I dunno. I'm just stuck in this dumb house. I wanna go skateboarding but the Sergeant won't let me."

Maddie winced at the nickname she'd coined for the woman after her first visit to Kyle's foster home. Unfortunately, it fit well the woman who liked to manage her household with direct commands and required yes ma'am's in return. "She can't hear you, can she?"

"I'm not stupid. She went outside to prune her precious garden."

The woman tried to grow vegetables every year, but had a red thumb. Her rows of peas produced a pod or two if she was lucky. "Still, it's not nice to call names."

"Whatever. You're the one who started it."

Mothering your little brother wasn't the easiest thing in the world. Still, she determined to do her best. "Everyone makes mistakes, even me, little squirt."

"Now who's calling someone names?"

Maddie smiled. "That's different. I said it with love."

"I did too. I love calling her Sergeant."

Time to change the subject on what would prove to be a losing battle. "Any big plans for the summer?"

"Watch TV. Eat. I dunno."

Typical Kyle. "I should see if you could come visit me sometime."

"Would they let me do that?"

The thought had been a spur of the moment one, one she should have kept to herself until she talked to Corina. "Maybe. Let me ask. But this is between you and me, okay?"

"Sarge won't care. She'll be happy to be rid of me."

The drillmaster might care more than Kyle realized. "Just keep it quiet and don't get your hopes too high, okay?"

"Fine. Hey, I gotta go. Sid and I were gonna play some Xbox when he got home, and he just walked in the door."

Sid, Mr. Blakely, was the one thing that made having her brother away from her tolerable. He played video games with Kyle like an overgrown kid himself, and was the only person who could get Sarge to loosen the reigns a hair.

"Okay, I'll talk to you next week, 'kay?"

"Sure. Bye."

She listened to the dial tone for a second before hanging up and blinking away tears that threatened to fall.

Kyle was the only thing she had left. She refused to lose him.

While she'd been probably the worst role model possible the last few years, she had changed. God had gotten hold of her, and now everything in her wanted to make up for all she'd put him through.

A knock on the door brought her to her feet. She rubbed the bottom of her eyes to make sure they were clear. "Come in."

Tilly poked her head in. "Hey, do you know if Reuben was coming in at all tonight?"

"No, he can't be on his foot for a few days. Do you need something?"

The older woman laughed. "Nothing you can help with, I'm sure."

Maddie straightened her back. She wasn't a perfect waitress, but she wasn't stupid either. "Try me."

"Can you cook?"

❦

This did not bode well.

Maddie stared at the apron as if it were a snake hanging from Tilly's finger. And, really, it might as well have been, given her dismal cooking skills. She'd have preferred waitressing to cooking.

Yet she hated that everyone thought her completely inept. "I'd love to but—"

The woman tossed the apron back on the counter. "Thought so. I'll just call Reuben."

"Wait. Why do you need another cook?"

A man behind the biggest grill she'd ever seen looked over his shoulder. Matt, if she remembered his name correctly. "Can't do everything myself, and Ricardo called in and quit. Livy usually picks up the slack, but she left home sick about a half hour ago." He flipped a chicken breast and basted it with some orange, peppery looking sauce.

She turned back to Tilly, whose upturned eyebrow did nothing to calm her nerves. "Isn't there someone else we can call in?"

"Already tried the part-timer we have. Left him a voicemail. Listen, I'll just call Reuben. He'll be crankier than a crab if no one lets him know."

Maddie threw the apron over her head and tied the white strings in the back. Reuben didn't need to be in here standing on that foot all night.

Besides, how hard could it be? "Where do I start?"

❦

Maddie replaced the handset and sat back in Reuben's office chair, then allowed a feeble smile to escape her lips.

She'd caused more disasters tonight than she'd ever done in her life.

But according to Matt, he couldn't have done it without her, regardless of the fact that she'd overseasoned a few chickens and charbroiled a beef brisket.

And he promised that dropping the bottle of salt, lid open, onto the fries had been his fault, not hers.

To redeem herself, she'd made a call to Ricardo, the cook who quit, and convinced him to come back after Tilly let her know his reason for leaving.

Standing up, she froze when her back made the loudest moaning sound she'd ever heard a part of her body make. It culminated in a defining *crack*. Ahhhhh.

One would think she'd be used to being on her feet for hours on end, being that her chosen profession had been hairstyling. But at least then she could raise the chair to a comfortable level.

But that kitchen was brutal. She'd had to bend, twist, and reach for three hours straight. She'd offered to kiss Matt's tennis shoes when he told her it had died down enough for him to handle on his own.

If she never saw another sandwich in her life, she'd be forever grateful.

A knock sounded on the door. "Come in."

Reuben opened the door and hobbled into the room on crutches.

She stood up and rushed to help him. "What are you doing here? The doctor said you need to stay off your feet."

He sat in the chair in front of the desk, and Maddie took the crutches and leaned them against the wall. She hopped up on the edge of his desk, letting her feet dangle. Her only other choice was to sit in his office chair, and she'd rather crawl under the desk than to do that with him present.

"Allie drove me. I called Livy to see how the night went only to find out she went home sick and left Tilly in charge. So I called here and found out my cook quit and my assistant decided to try lend a hand instead of call me."

Maddie jutted her chin out and held her head high. "We handled things. And I called Ricardo and convinced him to come back."

Reuben's eyes flashed. "You did what? You should have called me, Maddie."

She swallowed the excess spit in her mouth. "He was upset. I calmed him down."

He raised his eyebrows, not looking pleased with the abbreviated version.

She straightened her back, feeling like smelly sauerkraut in a Reuben and Livy sandwich. "All I know is that Ricardo agreed to come back in tomorrow on two conditions."

Reuben clenched his fist. "If you promised him a raise, you're fired."

"I told him Livy would stop calling him Paco."

"Huh?"

"Evidently she has trouble remembering his name?" She'd believe that when someone convinced her that peanut butter and tuna actually tasted good together.

"I'll talk with her. What was the other condition?"

"A raise. I told him he'd need to talk to you about that, but that if he didn't come in tomorrow, there was no need. He said he'd be here."

Reuben put a hand to his forehead. "Great, just great."

"Other than that, everything's fine. You should have stayed home."

"You're stubborn, you know that?"

"Absolutely."

He shook his head then sent her a crooked smile. "So, you're my expert fill-in cook now?"

She shuddered at the thought. "Let's just say, you probably took a loss today considering all the food I messed up. Matt said it wasn't that bad, but he's a good liar."

He leaned forward and pressed a hand to her knee. "Thank you, Maddie, for trying. But next time, call me."

She brushed off his hand and stood up. "Hands off, Mister. Haven't you ever heard of sexual harassment? I could have a hidden camera here and nail you with a big ol' lawsuit."

"Good luck with that. Restaurant owners aren't really rolling in the dough, you know."

Maddie stuck out her tongue at him and handed him his crutches. "No prob. I'll just take the Beamer."

"As long as you take the car payment too, it's a deal."

"Never mind, it's all yours." She gave him a hand up. When he took his crutches, she wiped her hand on her slacks, hoping to rid the pin-pricks that remained.

He settled the crutches under his armpits and looked back at her. "You have dinner yet?"

"I sampled while I cooked. Now I'm just ready to crash. You're paying me overtime for tonight, you know that, right?"

"Shoot. I was hoping to treat you to dinner as payment."

Dinner with her boss. No thanks.

Maddie turned and grabbed her purse faster than she thought possible and made a dash to the door, ignoring the fact that she was leaving her hobbling boss in her dust. "Well, goodnight."

She slung open the door, waved to Allie who sat at a table sipping a drink, and hurried outside and into her Tracker.

Slamming the door, she dropped her head to the steering wheel.

Her heart was such a rebel. The dinner invitation was just that. Dinner. At her place of employment. Nothing more.

Then why was her heart racing like it had just run a marathon?

It made zero sense. Guys were all jerks, her boss being one of the leaders. And he wasn't even available, which made it even worse.

She put a hand to her traitor heart.

*Please God! You made my heart, you can convince it to change its mind, right?*

# 15

Reuben brooded the whole way home. He liked control, but right now, *helpless* described his situation quite well.

He couldn't even drive himself to and from the restaurant. How sad was that? And on a day when everything fell apart, he hadn't been there to keep things running. His assistant, who by the conversation he'd had with Matt, was a terrible cook, had to step in.

She was lucky he didn't send her packing for not calling him. Matt and Tilly had both been lectured about it too.

Livy better be glad she was home puking, because a large part of him wanted to fire her too, engagement or not. Paco? Really?

"A penny for your thoughts."

Reuben glanced at Allie, who stepped on the brake for a red light. "I was wondering if we'd get lucky and have any customers tomorrow."

"Matt said he'd fixed most of her mistakes. It can't be all that bad, Reub."

Yes, it could. "Word gets around fast in a small town; you know that."

"Have you talked to Livy?"

Reuben had briefed his sister on the situation, and she'd been none too happy at Livy either. "Not yet. I intend to call her when I get home."

"What will you say?"

Good question. He hadn't figured that out just yet. How do you lecture an employee when you're engaged to her? "I'll just tell her to be nicer to Ricardo."

His sister's cleared throat and silence reeked of disagreement.

"What? You don't like my tactic?"

She steered through the left turn onto his street. "It's not that."

"Then what?"

The minivan stopped in his driveway, and she turned off the engine. "Why do you let her do this, Reuben? She walks all over you and it's like you're oblivious."

Reuben's chest tightened. No woman walked over him. He was his own man. And his sister needed to keep her nose out of it. "I asked her to marry me today."

Allie twisted in her seat and made a show of pulling on her ear. "Excuse me? I don't think I heard you right. You asked her to *marry* you?"

He nodded, knowing that his answer would only add kindling to the blaze. "Yes, and you're going to be happy for me, whether you like it or not."

Her eyebrows arched, almost reaching her hairline. "You can't command someone to be happy for you. Not even you are that powerful, little brother."

He refused to listen to her. No one appointed her, or his mother, for that matter, in charge of his life, and they had no right to barge in and give opinions wherever they wanted. Reuben opened his door and got out, not caring that he didn't have his crutches.

Using his hand on the red metal hood to support himself, he hopped around the front of the minivan, then used the tip of his foot to hop the rest of the way down the long sidewalk to the steps. Allie ran behind him, holding his crutches.

"Reub, you'll get hurt. At least use these to get up the steps."

"No. I can do it myself." Some strange sense of pride made him do it. He needed control. He didn't need a crutch, or his sister, or even his assistant.

He reached the last step, but his foot slipped and he began swaying backward. He flung his hands to the front, hoping to grab onto something, but there was only air.

Hands gripped his back and caught his fall, pushing him back to an upright position. He didn't turn around to acknowledge them, just made the last jump and unlocked the door.

He tried to close the door behind him, but a crutch blocked the way.

"No, Reuben. I'm coming in whether you like it or not."

Fine. Have it her way. He hopped to the couch and collapsed onto the leather cushion. He thought himself a fairly in-shape guy, but if a few hops took his breath away, he needed to up his visits to the gym. Now that he thought about it, he'd missed his visits to the gym in the last few months. He'd remedy that as soon as he was back on two feet.

Allie settled on the other end of the couch. "I'm sorry I made you mad."

"No you're not."

She frowned. "Yes, I am."

"You're sorry that I'm mad, but not sorry for what you said."

A smile touched her lips. "Okay, you've got me there. But you have to know, I love you, Reuben. You're my only brother, and I hate to see you make a mistake and end up miserable for the rest of your life."

"You and Livy have always been friends. How can you say that?" Even as he said it, he knew the answer. His sister and his fiancée hadn't "hung out" in years.

He'd never been brave enough to ask why.

"You know as well as I do that I don't count Livy as a best bud anymore."

Though not sure he wanted to know, he asked the question that'd been on his mind for the last five years. "What went wrong, Al? Between you and Livy?"

She fiddled with the hem of her shirt. "We just didn't see eye to eye."

"On what?"

Reuben didn't care for the way she looked everywhere in the room but at him.

When her eyes finally met his, she bit her lip. "Lots of things. Livy changed."

"How?"

She shook her head. "It's in the past."

"I'm a big boy, Allie. I can handle the truth."

"You remember the summer Stew and I met, right?"

"I do. I was really excited for you." He remembered her excited e-mails, about how Stew was so good with five-year-old Cole and didn't care about her past mistakes. She'd gotten pregnant her senior year of high school, and while she decided to keep the baby, Cole's daddy had jumped ship. Finding a guy who looked past all that and saw the real Allie had been huge for her.

He'd proposed after only two months, and she'd said yes.

"Well, Livy wasn't nearly as excited."

Dread wrapped itself around Reuben's belly. "Why not?"

"I think partially because she was single and jealous. She was still pining over you even though you hadn't been together for a while." Allie sat down on the chair across from the couch and stared at her fingers. "She kissed him, Reuben."

The blurted out confession slapped him in the face. "What? When?"

"She was jealous when she found out he was going to ask me to marry him after only two months. She ranted at me for making such a stupid decision, then started ignoring me completely. Then she called Stew one night, said her car was in the shop and she needed a ride. When he dropped her off, she gave him a little-too-friendly thank-you kiss on the lips.

"Stew pushed her away and made her get out of the car, then confessed to me later. I confronted her, and she apologized and begged me not to tell anyone. That she didn't know what had come over her. I agreed, but things have never been the same."

Reuben swallowed the fury burning in him and reached forward and squeezed her hand. "You should have told me."

"To be honest, part of me is mad at you, too."

"At me? Why?"

Allie stood and put her hands on her hips. "Livy isn't the girl for you, Reuben. You've been so wrapped up in the restaurant, not to mention this whole stupid vendetta against Gary, that you can't even see it."

Reuben sat speechless.

She picked up her purse and gave him one last parting glance. "It's time to take a hard look in the mirror, Reub, before you end up married and miserable."

"I'm happy about this, Allie."

"Are you?"

He sighed. "Just promise you won't tell anyone yet. I want to wait a little while before we announce it."

Reuben took a breath and knocked on the door of the small Cape Cod. Ring shopping. He could do this.

The door opened in front of him, and Reuben's mouth dropped.

"Livy, you look . . . amazing." That was an understatement. Her golden hair curled and rested on her bare shoulders. The pink strapless dress she wore floated above her knees, and the only jewelry she wore was a necklace with a single pendent that dangled dangerously close to no-man's land.

That was, no-unmarried-man's land.

He tried not to squirm in his jeans and navy polo shirt he'd thrown on after church.

"Reuben, I was just finishing getting ready."

He stepped over the threshold into the foyer. "Is your mom home?"

The object of his query stepped from the kitchen, leaning heavily on her cane. "Right here, young man."

Livy bounced back up the stairs as Gertrude hobbled to her normal chair in the living room. Given no other choice, he followed and took a seat on the floral sofa. "How you feeling, Gertrude?"

"Fair. The doctor's trying out some new medicines. Still waiting to see what's worse, arthritis or the side effects. But enough about me and my ailments. How's the restaurant business these days?"

Reuben leaned forward and set his elbows on his knees. "Great. Two more restaurants should open by the end of next year."

"Are you planning more after this?"

He nodded. "Absolutely. This is just the beginning of phase two."

"And what's phase three?"

Reuben grinned. "National." Just voicing the words made him shake with excitement. By then he'd have a whole corporate staff here in Sandwich and a big office building to house them in.

Their dream, his and his dad's, was so close he could smell it.

"Sounds like you have it all planned out. It's good to know my daughter will be well provided for." The bland tone betrayed her true feelings. Reuben knew she'd never really liked him, although she'd never offered a reason for her upturned nose.

"Livy's very important to me. I'll take care of her." It was the pure and honest truth. Despite their differences of late, he'd do anything to protect her, provide for her.

"I know you would, dear. I did want to ask you about this new assistant you've hired. A hairdresser, Livy says?"

Reuben shifted on the sofa. He didn't want to discuss Maddie tonight. "I was bogged down with paperwork, it seemed like the right thing to do. She's working out great. A godsend really."

Gertrude tapped her cane on the hardwood floor. "And what all does she do for you? I mean, assistant, that can be so *many* different things these days."

Surely she wasn't insinuating what he thought she was. "Normal things. Mostly administrative tasks like filing, and eventually I want to hand over payroll and invoicing too."

Her eyebrows shot up. "Mostly? Does she assist in your personal life too?"

"Not really. She did help out when I was laid up earlier this week, and she lectures me about not eating breakfast, but so does everyone else." He didn't add that she'd started a ritual of bringing him something to eat every morning. Friday, it'd been a blueberry muffin and orange juice. Granted, it looked like it'd come premade from the supermarket, but still. It's the thought that counts.

"Speaking of your ankle, how exactly did you hurt it?"

Reuben eyed the stairs. Shouldn't Livy be ready by now? She looked ready to him earlier. Maybe she was putting on a sweater.

He looked back at Gertrude, who tapped her cane again. "I, uh, tripped over a chair in the restaurant."

"How awful." Did he detect a gleeful tone? "You need to be more careful. And Maddie was there to help you, was she?"

Reuben stilled. From the sound of it, Gertrude had already heard the whole story. Why was she grilling him then?

The click of sandals on the steps saved him. "Ready to go, Reuben?"

He held out his elbow to her. "Shall we?"

She accepted and snuggled close to his arm. "We shall." She turned back to her mother. "Don't wait up."

Reuben escorted her to the car and held open her door. Instead of getting in, she turned and kissed him. "Thank you. I'm so excited to pick out a ring and make this official."

He only nodded, not sure how to broach the topic on his mind. Getting into the driver's seat, he started the car but instead of shifting into gear, he turned toward her. "I wanted to talk to you about the announcement."

She grabbed his hand in hers and smiled. "Well, I already told my mother of course, but I thought we'd stop by and tell your mom and show her the ring, and Allie too of course. And we'll need engagement pictures to put in the newspaper soon."

This from the girl ready to fly to Vegas this weekend. "Actually, I think we should wait a little while before announcing it."

Her hand tightened on his. "Nonsense. There's no reason to wait." Her eyebrows furrowed together. "You aren't having second thoughts, are you?"

"Of course not. I just want it to be special. Maybe announce it when we get together for the Fourth of July."

Her face lit up like a kid in a chocolate shop. "That's perfect!"

Reuben half-listened to her talk about different kinds of wedding flowers on the drive to the jewelry shop.

An hour later, he ignored the protest of his wallet as he put a hefty deposit down on a ring the size of Texas.

# 16

$S$itting cross-legged on her quilt-covered bed, Maddie opened the *The Sandwich Daily* and flipped to the classifieds.

The guesthouse had been wonderful these past two weeks, and she couldn't get much cheaper than free.

Charity wouldn't get her Kyle, though. She needed to make it on her own two feet without the help of the Luther/Callahan clan.

Yet rentals she could afford weren't leaping off the page either.

She leaned back and flopped onto a pillow and covered her face with her hands.

"God, what now? Corina's going to freak out when she finds I'm mooching off people. You promised you had my back. Need to see a little of that back saving, please."

Her cell vibrating interrupted her conversation with the Almighty. Her heart squeezed when she saw the Blakely's number. Kyle rarely called on a Saturday night, but she'd take any chance to talk to him she could get. "Hello?"

"Guess what?"

She settled back into the pillow and smiled at Kyle's higher than normal pitch. "What?"

"The Blakelys want to adopt me."

Maddie's breath froze in her lungs. "They told you that?" She'd thought they wouldn't tell him until it was more of a sure thing. Or at least, that's why Corina had told *her* not to say anything. She'd assumed it went both ways.

"Yeah, just tonight. Wanted to know what I thought about it."

Maddie curled up her knees to her chest and took a slow breath. "What do you think about it?"

"It's cool, I guess. I mean, Sarge isn't my favorite, but Sid is fun."

She swallowed the lump the size of an orange in her throat. "I see."

"Hey, have you, uh, heard from Dad at all?"

That wasn't what she expected. Kyle almost never talked about their father, and neither of them had seen him in over four years. "No."

"Just curious."

"You thinking about him lately?"

"He was a big fat jerk."

Maddie turned to her side and fiddled with the edge of the pillowcase. "Yeah, I know."

"Do you remember before mom died? He wasn't so bad then."

She fisted a chunk of pillow like it was a stress ball. "He was always mean, Kyle. Mom just mellowed him a little."

"Yeah, I guess."

Memories flooded her. Her dad would yell over a mess, and her mom would do her best to calm him down. Mom was a peacekeeper and was good at it. When she died, the peace left too. "Why are you thinking about all this now?"

"Sid said if they adopted me, I could call him dad and Sarge mom."

Maddie sat up. "He didn't."

"Yeah, I thought it was dumb too. I had a mom. And I hate my dad, why would I want another one?"

The sister in her wanted to scream AMEN. She squelched it though, as she doubted it was the proper motherly thing to do. "Did you tell them that?"

"Naw. I just said I'd think about it and went to my room. They didn't seem happy when I left, but I don't care."

She needed to talk to Corina. Now. "It'll all be okay, Kyle. I promise."

"Don't make promises you can't keep, big Sis."

୧୭

What day was it?

Oh, yeah, Sunday. Maddie rubbed her sore eyes, pulled her knees up in bed, and hugged the quilt closer to her body. She never wanted to get out of this bed. She could die there and wouldn't really care.

Kyle was right. Her promises were empty. She'd called Corina, hoping for some good news.

There wasn't any. Everything was looking great for the Blakleys and pretty hopeless for Maddie.

It would help if she could show a stable job and housing, but even with that, the marks against her record were going to make it almost impossible.

Maybe they were right. She was damaged goods anyway and could barely hold down a job. No use even trying.

A knock on the door interrupted her self-loathing.

She ignored it, hoping whoever was there would go away, but the pounding persisted. Slipping her feet into slippers and pulling her thin robe over her spaghetti-strap cotton night-gown, she padded over to the door and opened it.

Maddie clenched the robe tighter. Reuben stood on her doorstep.

He leaned a shoulder against the door jam, looking mouth-watering hot in his dark jeans and light blue, short-sleeve dress shirt that he left untucked. His hair was all wrong yet again, but he still looked gorgeous.

*He's engaged, Maddie. Control the drool.* "You didn't want me to work on Sunday, did you?" She opened the door wider and stepped aside, her silent method of inviting him in if he wanted.

He accepted and walked past her, shoving his hands in his pocket. "No, we're closed on Sundays, you know that." Without asking, he took a seat on the couch and patted the spot next to him.

Maddie debated. She hated him seeing her like this, barely dressed and hair probably a crazy mess. But it wouldn't do to excuse herself to shower and change with him here. Not only would it be rude but also he might think it an invitation.

Which it wasn't. At all. She wasn't that type of girl anymore.

She settled down on the opposite side of the couch, putting as much room between them as possible without making her discomfort obvious. "What are you doing here?"

Reuben drew one leg up and laid a foot on his knee. "I was coming to invite you to church, but I've changed my mind."

Maddie picked at her thin, cotton robe. "Can't blame you there."

"What's wrong, Maddie?"

She shrugged. "Just slept in. You didn't catch me at my best."

One side of his mouth curled into a shy smile. "I wasn't talking about your appearance. You look . . . " He shook his head. "What I mean is, your face."

Scrunching up her nose, she put a hand to her cheek. "Not much I can do about the way my face looks."

"Your face is adorable, Maddie. But it's also all red and splotchy and your eyes look like you've either been crying or had a few too many drinks last night."

"Yeah, not really a drinker anymore."

"So you used to be?"

She glared at him. Her past indiscretions were the last thing she wanted to discuss with her boss. "I got some bad news is all."

"Care to talk about it?"

She shook her head. Curling back up into bed and sleeping away the pain sounded much better than spilling her guts to her cute boss.

Reuben chuckled. "I'm glad you think I'm cute, but I'm not sure why that should keep you from telling me what's bothering you."

Mortification took on a whole new definition when it sunk into Maddie's head that she'd spoken her thoughts aloud. Why in the world did she do that? "I didn't mean—"

"Hey now, don't tell me you didn't mean that I'm cute. That would mean you think I'm ugly, and you don't want to be telling your boss that, do you?"

Yeah, actually, she'd prefer that over the alternative. But in an effort to keep her job, she just shook her head.

"What's wrong Maddie? If you don't tell me I'll . . . I'll tell Allie something's wrong and she'll weasel it out of you."

Allie could wring the truth out of a psychotic murderer. Might as well fess up now on her own terms. "I talked to Kyle's caseworker last night."

He frowned. "Wait, your boyfriend has a caseworker? Is he . . . ?"

Maddie rolled her eyes. "Kyle's my brother, not my boyfriend. You hadn't figured that out by now?"

Reuben blinked, his forehead wrinkled in confusion. "So, your brother has a caseworker?"

"He's in foster care."

Reuben frowned. "Were you?"

"Briefly. Mostly in a girls' home though. Too hard to handle, or so said my caseworker."

"Somehow I can see that."

She punched him in the shoulder. "Shut up. I'm reformed now. I'm trying to get custody of my brother so he can come here and live with me."

He looked around. "Here?"

"And there's my problem. His foster parents want to adopt him, and I'm not exactly an example of stability right now to compete."

Reuben stood up and pulled her up by the hand. Maddie fidgeted with her robe. He wouldn't try to hug her, would he? That would be over-the-top awkward.

He released her hand and took a few steps toward the door. "Get dressed."

She blinked. "Excuse me?"

"I'm headed in to talk to Mom. Get dressed and come to church with us."

She put her hands on her hips. "Aren't you Mr. Demanding."

He turned around when he reached the door. "You don't go to church?"

"I haven't been in the last month or so, but I planned to find a church eventually." She just didn't care to be ordered around like a three-year-old by her boss on her day off. The guy had a serious attitude problem.

"I'm sorry. Let me start over. Maddie, I would be honored if you joined my family and me at church today. If you'd rather not, I completely understand, but given your current state of frustration, I think God's house is the perfect place to be."

She rolled her eyes and lowered her voice in an over-the-top imitation of Reuben. "'Hey, we're going to church, do you wanna come?' would have worked just as well. But, yes, since you asked so politely, give me fifteen minutes."

His eyes traveled down to her toes and back up again, probably wondering how she could make a miracle and be presentable in such little time. She tugged the robe tighter.

Mercifully, he didn't comment, but nodded and headed out the door. Maddie raced to lock the door, glanced at the clock, then spent the next ten minutes taking the fastest shower she'd ever managed in her life. She lifted a breezy, cotton dress, the only one she owned, over her head and let its length settle to an inch above the floor. After a little twirl in front of the mirror to make sure the funky-print fabric had settled right, she made quick work of her hair, dabbed on a touch of lip-gloss, and grabbed her purse before heading out the door.

As she walked the path between the guesthouse and the big house, she slipped her phone from her purse.

Seventeen minutes. Not too shabby.

She paused at the French door, unsure if she should knock or walk right in. She'd never had to go in without someone walking with her. But knocking on the back door seemed goofy.

She turned the handle and began to push when the door jerked from her hand.

"Good morning, Maddie. I hear you're joining us today." Livy stood, decked out in a spaghetti strap dress that showed an inch or so more cleavage than Maddie thought appropriate for church.

And, good night, did the woman have a lot to show! She put Maddie's own 34B to shame.

"I am, if that's okay with you. I mean, I didn't realize you were here."

Livy stepped out onto the porch and closed the door behind her. "Everyone's still getting ready now, and I'm sure they don't want a guest in the house at the moment. Why don't we sit out here and chat for a bit?"

Her pride bruised from the blatant reprimand and Livy's overemphasis on the words *family* and *guest*, Maddie sat down in a patio chair, wishing again that she'd never gotten out of bed. Why had she let Reuben talk her into this?

Oh, now she remembered. He'd looked so gorgeous that she couldn't say no.

A totally horrible thought to have about a guy, especially when he was her boss and his girlfriend sat right next to her. *God, please forgive me.*

"So, I hear you used to work at the Cut 'N' Style?"

This could not end well. "For a short time, yes."

"How short?" Her lips curled into a crooked smile.

All the defense mechanisms she'd had in her arsenal in Chicago, ones she thought she'd shed when she gave her life to Jesus, came marching back, reporting for duty. *God, I want to show her love. But I really don't like her. I really don't.*

"Reuben offered me the job at The Sandwich Emporium the same day I started the Cut 'N' Style. I'm sure he's told you the story."

Livy raised an eyebrow. "In fact, he did. He was really quite upset about his hair. That style was his pride and joy, you know, besides his car of course. He also mentioned how you tried to blame it all on him too. Really very sad, especially after all he's done for you."

Maddie stood, tipping the patio chair over in the process. "Excuse me, but you have no right—"

Betty opened the door and stepped out. "Is everything all right out here?"

Livy stood up and winked at Maddie. "Of course, Mrs. Luther. Maddie can just be a little clumsy is all. We're getting to be real good friends, aren't we?" She took a step toward her and gave her a one-armed hug. "See? Bosom buddies."

Reuben stepped out from behind his mom and walked over to the twosome. "I'm glad to see you both getting along so well." He put his arm around Livy and squeezed. "Now, let's get to church."

# 17

*God, you cut newbies some slack, right?*

She sure hoped so, because not one word of the pastor's sermon had yet to make it past her eardrum to her brain.

Who could blame her? She sat sandwiched between Reuben and Livy, but how that happened was still a blur.

She faintly recalled being ushered down the aisle and walking with the flow of traffic into the pew. And *maybe* she recollected Reuben scooting in next to her and pointing out key people like the pastor and youth pastor and a deacon or two. But then she'd turned to see Livy standing on the other side of her, her face redder than that horrible lipstick she was wearing.

Jealousy had dripped from Livy like sweat on a pig.

She had nothing to worry about, though. Reuben sure wasn't going to pass up someone as gorgeous as Livy for a stick figure like herself.

As Maddie had moved to scoot down the pew so the couple could sit together, the music began and the congregation stood. She'd been so enraptured by Reuben's beautiful, if a little off-tune, tenor, that she must have forgotten to scoot upon sitting.

Because now, her right thigh rubbed against her boss and her left against his steaming mad girlfriend.

She should change her name to bologna.

"Are you trusting God today?" The pastor's sharply spoken words yanked her back to the present. An interesting question.

Yes. She trusted Him. He would provide . . . somehow.

"If you just thought in your head, 'Yes,' what about that bill you're struggling to pay?"

She really did need to give Reuben's mom some rent money.

"That problem that keeps you awake at night?"

Maddie bit her lip. She'd barely slept ten minutes all night worrying about Kyle.

"That relationship that needs mending?"

The bodies on each side of her shifted.

"So let me ask you this one more time with those things in mind. Are you trusting God today?"

*Okay, God. I get it. I need to trust you with Kyle.*

"Recognizing the need to trust God is the first step. But the next step is even harder."

Oh, for goodness sake. It seemed hard enough just the way it was.

"If you trust him, you'll put your money, or your action, where your mouth is. God requires more than lip-service faith, ladies and gentleman. He requires obedience. Remember the man who came to Jesus and asked him to heal his servant? Jesus said, 'Take me to him.' But the man replied, 'Lord, I don't deserve for you to come to my home. But just say the word, and my servant will be healed.'"

Maddie squirmed in her seat. Oh why had she chosen today to come to church for the first time? One more week would have been just dandy.

The pastor leveled his gaze across the room. Maddie pretended to have a renewed interest in the hymnal in front of her.

"That took some guts, folks. That man trusted Jesus enough to know that he could heal his servant without even entering his home. He walked back, knowing his servant was healed. That's the kind of trust we need to have in God. The kind that seeks God's will and believes God's word is powerful and trustworthy. So, I ask you again. Do you trust God today?"

Maddie blinked away a tear. She wanted to trust. Really. But Kyle was different. He was her brother, her only living relative besides her worthless father. God was certainly big and powerful and could do whatever He wished with the situation. But deep in her soul, she feared He would drop the ball. That He would let her down just like everyone else had.

"I'll ask you one last time before we end the service. Do you trust Him?"

Would she go to hell if she said no?

⌒∽

Reuben passed the butter to his mother and took the bowl of mashed potatoes from Livy. The movements represented a normal Sunday lunch with his family, except today, Maddie sat across from him, attracting his eyes more often than was appropriate. Livy sat beside him, her gaze drilling into the side of his head as if surveying for oil, and his conscience screamed at him, especially after that grueling sermon.

He trusted God with his life, sure. But how often had he worried about the restaurant expansion? About his relationship with Livy? About his mom and her new husband?

Not to mention the question that hung over his head about his dad.

The answer was easy. Give it all to God. The execution was the part that tripped him up.

His mother leaned toward him and patted his arm. "Reuben, any more news on the restaurants?"

"Not really. Still working out the details." That things were stalled due to financing wasn't something he was broadcasting yet.

"I'm praying those details work themselves out soon. You have the potential to go really big with this." Gary spoke up from the other end of the table where he sat next to Allie and Stewart, Reuben's brother-in-law and best friend. The children all sat at the "kids" table in the kitchen.

Who did the guy think he was? Like he knew about business and the potential of anything. All he did everyday was piddle around the house and mooch off Reuben's father's years of hard work. And then he sat there, at the head of the table, like he was replacing him.

No one could replace Matthew Callahan.

Reuben's mom smiled at Gary from across the table. "That's so sweet of you, dear."

Reuben stabbed another piece of chicken with his fork. Did his mom have to be all mushy in public? Did she have no respect? She always called Dad "dear" and to hear it out of her lips for Gary was just gross. Next they'd probably start making out in the kitchen.

He'd give up on Sunday dinners if that ever happened.

Allie broke the silence when she turned toward their guest of honor. "So, Maddie, Reuben treating you okay at the Emporium? Not being too much of a grump?"

Maddie nodded. "He's greatly improved, thank you."

Improved? Had he been that bad? "Hey now. That implies I was less than perfect before, an accusation I resent."

His mother wagged her fork at him. "Now, Reuben, no fibbing at the dinner table. We all know the real story of how you got your haircut."

He narrowed his eyes at Maddie. Livy was the only one he'd confided the complete truth to, and he trusted her not to say anything. "The haircut story?"

"Don't go blaming Maddie. Miss Agnes from the Cut 'N' Style told me the whole story. You should be ashamed of yourself, although," she looked over at the poor girl with tomato-red cheeks, "I think you're much better off working for Reuben over here than Judy the Grouch."

"Mom!" She never said a mean word about another human being.

"Just stating a fact. Now, Maddie, I've been meaning to ask. Everything okay with the cottage? If you need anything, just holler."

Maddie shook her head and started to speak, but Reuben interrupted her. "Actually, she needed to discuss that with you." He ignored the telepathic message his assistant was sending him across the table with the sharp shake of her head and narrowed eyes. "She's going to start looking for a different place tomorrow."

His mother's eyes darted back and forth between Reuben and Maddie. "Is something wrong?"

Maddie cast Reuben a look hot enough to melt provolone cheese. "Nothing's wrong. The room is perfect. But other circumstances have come up that require me to have a place just a little bigger."

Livy stood up and tossed her napkin on her plate. "I need to go. I'm sorry . . . I forgot, uh, something I had to do this afternoon."

The table was silent as she pushed back her chair and raced from the room. Reuben rose and followed her through the living room and out the front door. He caught up with her next to her little Mazda.

"Livy, what's wrong?"

She spun around, fire leaping from her eyes. "What's wrong? Really, Reuben? You have the nerve to ask me that?"

Females. Why did they expect men to know exactly what they were thinking, especially when they made no sense whatsoever?

"I really don't know, Livy. We were having a normal Sunday dinner and—"

She stomped her foot. "Normal? You'd call that normal? You couldn't keep your eyes off her."

Now she was talking crazy. "Off who?"

"Maddie! I'm not stupid, Reub. I have eyes. First you set her up with a place to live, now you're helping her find something bigger? What's really going on, Reuben?"

Heat twisted in his gut. "You have no idea what you're saying. I don't like Maddie, and I don't cheat. And I don't go around kissing other people's fiancée's either."

The moment the words escaped his mouth he regretted them. He'd told himself it didn't matter. It happened years ago. Livy had grown up since then. But his lips had a mind of their own.

Livy put a hand to her chest, her eyes bulging. "Excuse me?"

Now he was just plain mad. "I know about you and Stew."

Her eyes narrowed. "Who told you that? Since when do you listen to gossip, Reuben Callahan?"

"I wouldn't call my sister, the wife of the guy you seduced, a gossip."

She took a step closer to him. "You're just trying to change the subject. This isn't about me."

"Maddie and I have nothing going on, Livy. She's my assistant, and that's it."

"How can I believe you?"

He crossed his arms across his chest. "How can I believe you about Stewart? He was engaged to my sister, Liv."

Her eye twitched. "I guess we have a problem then."

"Yeah, I guess we do. Because I'm not marrying a woman who thinks I'm a cheater."

Livy's chin lifted an inch. "Are you breaking up with me? Just like that?"

A good question. Not one he could answer right now. "No, but I think we need to figure all this out before we announce something like an engagement."

She nodded. "Agreed." She turned to her car and opened up the driver's door. Before she sat down, her eyes flickered to his. "Reuben? Do you still love me?"

The same question he'd been asking himself since picking out the ring. "Yes, I do love you, Liv."

She stared at him another moment, then got in her car and sped away.

Reuben stuffed his hands in his pockets and made his way back up the driveway. As he ascended the steps of his mother's porch, the real question tugged on his mind.

He may love her, but was he still *in* love with her?

# 18

*Thank you, God, for friends like Allie. And for places like the Yum-Yum shop on a sunny Saturday afternoon. And for ridiculously good chocolate ice cream.*

Maddie took another bite of chocolate goodness and smiled at her new best friend. She tried to forget that said friend was sister of her boss and the guy her heart seemed to have a wee little crush on. That was one secret her new friend could *never* find out about, and one her brain had determined to put a stop to.

"I know I asked you this a few weeks ago, but there were too many observers for you to be honest. How do you really like working for Reuben?"

Revise that. One secret she *prayed* Allie would never find out about. She'd been at the restaurant for a month now, and her boss was one topic she determined not to dwell on. "I like it just fine. The man's a little unorganized, but I'm working on that."

Allie took another bite of her ice cream then turned to the kids at the next table over. "Cole, help your sister." A glob of ice cream was ready to fall off Bethany's spoon into her lap at any moment.

The ever-attentive mother turned back once disaster was averted. "So what about Livy?"

Just the name made Maddie want to scream. "Livy?"

Allie shrugged. "Just curious what you think about her."

The descriptions that ran through Maddie's head were the exact opposite of Christianlike words. None acceptable to speak aloud, ever, much less in the presence of children. Plus, she wasn't sure of Allie's relationship to the woman. Maybe they were friends too and this was a bait. Highly doubtful though. "She's . . . interesting."

Allie's face turned into a smirk. "I can tell you skipped church last week, otherwise you wouldn't let a fib roll off your tongue like that."

Maddie's opinion of her new friend inched up a few notches. "Your kids are in hearing distance. You don't want me to voice my true feelings, believe me."

She winked at her. "Now, Maddie. We do need to love people, even our enemies."

"I wouldn't say she's an enemy. I just don't think she cares for me that much."

Allie lifted another spoonful of vanilla ice cream and licked it from her spoon. She pointed the utensil at Maddie. "You know why she doesn't like you, right?"

"I guess she was mad that Reuben didn't consult her about hiring me. And I don't blame her really. She is the manager and his girlfriend."

The spoon wagged in her face. "No. The real reason is that she's intimidated by you."

In Maddie's dreams. "Why? I have nothing compared to her. Gorgeous, curvy, successful blonde versus short, flat, broke brunette. Ding, ding, we have a winner."

"You, my friend, suffer from a bad self-esteem. You're beautiful and don't even know it. Besides, your looks don't matter to her. You have the one thing that Livy always wanted and never really had, and she can't stand it."

"Fine, I'll bite. What is this wonderful thing I possess that she's envious of?"

Allie eyed the kids' table and leaned forward, whispering in a conspiratorial voice. "Reuben's attention."

Maddie coughed, causing the ice cream she'd stuffed into her mouth to spray all over the table. Allie tossed her a napkin as she dodged the ice cream pellets.

When she'd wiped her mouth and the table, Maddie shoved her bowl aside. "That's ridiculous."

"I'm his sister, Maddie. I know things. Reuben's business is his life, and you're working with him all day, five days a week. Before if he needed something, he'd go to Livy. Now, he has you."

Just great. No wonder Livy had been giving her a cold shoulder. If she got one more icy stare, she might have to invest in a parka even though it was the last week of June. "I'm his assistant. I'd think Livy would be happy to have more time on her hands."

"You don't know her at all, do you? The woman's green with envy."

Maddie pulled her bowl back and twirled her spoon in the ice cream. "Why doesn't Reuben do something then? They hardly ever go out, not that there's time, I guess. I mean, I'm no relationship expert, but there isn't a lot of depth there, especially if she's jealous over someone like me."

Allie took a lick from her spoon and shrugged. "Livy's just a habit for him. They've known each other forever and I think they just decided, why not get married? Or should I say, Reuben decided. Livy's been head over heels for years."

Maddie stopped her swirling. "Are you saying they're engaged?"

Allie widened her eyes. "Shhhh. You didn't hear that from me, okay? They haven't announced it. I think Reub's waiting till the Fourth of July to make it public."

Maddie sat back and took a bite of chocolate yumminess.

At least she could understand Livy's motivation for the cool shoulder a little better now. Maddie couldn't imagine loving a man and being with him for that long, knowing that his heart wasn't in it. How terrible. But why hadn't Livy given up years ago? And why was she still marrying him?

"Love."

Her head popped up. "What?"

Allie gave her a quizzical look. "You asked why Livy was still marrying him, and I was saying it was because she loves him. Unrequited love causes a woman to do strange things."

Maddie bit her tongue. She needed to control it better. But it all made sense now. "Like be really mean to someone she thinks is a threat?"

"Exactly."

"But I'm not a threat, Allie. I have no desire to steal any man's attention, much less Reuben's." She set her forehead in her palms. "What am I supposed to do now? I feel like a flimsy piece of turkey sandwiched between stale bread."

Allie ran a hand through her long, brown hair. The Callahan family members were all blessed with naturally wavy hair, unlike Maddie's paper-thin mane. Another curse from her father.

"Let me get this straight. You think my brother is like stale bread?"

So the analogy wasn't perfect. "Your brother isn't quite as stale as Livy, but he can be a grump. And demanding. And rude."

Allie whistled. "You've got it bad, don't you?"

"What are you talking about?"

"You're falling for him too, aren't you?"

When sandwiches fly. "I'm not falling for any man. I just want to do my job, and that's it."

She stuffed a heaping spoonful of ice cream into her mouth and swallowed it whole. An instant tightening gripped her skull.

*God, if you get a chance, please tell Eve that eating off the tree of knowledge was so not a good idea. I mean, the whole childbirth pain is bad enough from what I hear, but now I have to suffer friends who can read minds, too. So not fair.*

# 19

*God, why did you make Mondays?*

Maddie jumped out of her Tracker and popped the hood. Smoke billowed out from underneath, and she turned her head to escape the puffy gray air. Several choice words came to mind. Her mouth ached to let them rip, something she'd tried very hard in the last six months not to do.

*You're punishing me for that whole trust thing, aren't you?* It had to be it. God was enacting revenge because of her lack of trust confession. She deserved it, too. Especially after skipping church yesterday.

Maddie balled up her fists and stomped her foot. What she wouldn't give for a nice punching bag right about now. She returned to the driver's side and fished her cell phone out of her purse. A flip of the phone told her that her day was not getting better. The battery was dead.

She threw the worthless device back in the bottomless pit of a purse and slammed her fist into the side of the door in frustration. Her knuckles caught the metal door, the pain of the impact reverberating through her arm. She cradled her hand against her, squeezing her eyes shut. A trickle of hot tears escaped the dam and slid down her cheek.

A honk caught her attention, and she wiped the tears before glancing back to see Reuben's stepdad headed her way. The guy was massive, standing well over six feet. He reminded her of a football player but with gray hair and the beginning of a potbelly. He shouldn't scare her. He was as nice as they came. But already her skin became clammy and her throat tightened. She'd been fine when Betty was with them . . . but alone?

His fingers hooked through his belt loops as he walked toward her. "You've got some car trouble?"

No. Trackers just like to spew smoke on occasion. "Yes, it looks like it." She ran her fingers through her hair. Such a crummy start to a beautiful day. Normally she'd be basking in the sunshine and admiring the cloudless blue sky, but all she could focus on were the gray clouds pouring from her vehicle, the red swelling of her knuckles, and the gigantic man standing next to her.

Maddie stepped aside as Gary leaned under the hood and wiggled a few things and made a few grunts. After a minute, he wiped his hands on his jeans and turned back to her. "Looks like you got a broken radiator hose. You on your way to the Emporium?"

She nodded, then looked at her watch. Ten minutes late already. Reuben was going to have a cow.

"You just go hop into my truck and I'll give you a lift. Don't worry about a thing, I'll have it taken to the shop and get this fixed up for you in no time."

"Oh, no, I couldn't impose on you like that." *Please, God, don't make me ride with another scary man.*

He put a large hand on her head and ruffled her hair as if she were ten. "Not an imposition at all. I'm retired and believe me, Betty will be happy to have me out of her hair for a while today."

The fatherish gesture caught her off guard and lessened her fear a tad, but she set her shoulders back and nodded, determined to not let it affect her. "Thanks. I appreciate it."

He thumped her on the back as they walked to his oversized black Ford truck, and Maddie blinked back tears as she climbed in. Was this how having a dad who actually gave a hoot about her felt like? One who didn't take immense glee in backhanding her every time he got angry?

⁓❧

Maddie restrained herself from tipping her head to one side and beating her ear to make sure it was working properly. Surely she misunderstood. Maybe the car drama earlier had messed with her ability to comprehend. "You broke up?"

Reuben shook his head and continued to type on the computer keyboard, hunt and peck style. "That's not what I said. We're just taking a breather."

Thus far in their very short working relationship, she'd attempted to stay platonic with her boss, besides the whole school-girl crush thing. Sure, when he'd been hurt, she'd taken him to the doctor, arranged for his transportation and follow-up. But that's what assistants did, right? She still knew zero details regarding his relationship with the blonde bimbo—er—wonderful restaurant manager.

In that spirit, all she'd asked was if Livy was okay lately, since she hadn't seen her and Reuben spare more than a handful of words in the past week. And given her conversation with Allie two days prior, it seemed a little odd.

She turned back to her own computer. "How long have you been dating, anyway?"

"On and off since high school."

Maddie twirled back around in her chair. "So, what, like ten years?" Was she baiting him since she already knew the answer via Allie? Yes. But otherwise he would know she'd been talking behind his back. And she was insanely curious as to what was going on.

Reuben only nodded, his eyes still glued to the computer screen.

The dude must have serious commitment issues, especially if he needed to "take a break" after ten years. Or maybe Allie was right and he didn't really love his new fiancée. "Was this hiatus your idea or Livy's?"

He shrugged. "Mutual."

Even an idiot could tell there was much more to this story than he was letting on. She wouldn't have even gone there at all except that she'd gotten a phone call from Livy that morning asking to talk with her privately tonight. Not an evening she particularly looked forward to having.

No use riling him up about it though. She turned back to her computer and continued on the newest task her boss handed over to her: payroll. They used a company to process it, but from the looks of things, Reuben did nothing more than call in the pay and horde the information he got back: no double-checks, no filing of payroll journals.

She'd already been on the phone three times today with his accountant to ensure everything was flowing to him correctly. What a mess.

"What, no more questions?"

Maddie swiveled around again to find her boss sitting back in his chair, his hands clasped across his chest, his eyebrows raised.

"Uh, not really. It sounded like you didn't want to talk about it." She smiled and winked at him. "I'd like to keep my new job, you know. No sense grilling the boss about his personal life and making him mad."

Reuben leaned forward and set his elbows on his desk. "Have I told you that you're doing a marvelous job and I have no idea what I'd have done if you hadn't botched up my haircut?"

She tossed a pencil at him, which he caught midair. "That was not my fault. We've been over that already. Speaking of, you're still doing your hair all wrong." His hair that was supposed to be spiked lay limp to the side. He looked like he had on a bad toupee.

He ran his fingers over his head. "I can never get it to go right. Does it look that bad?"

"No, you just look much more handso—uh, professional the other way."

His eyes twinkled at her blunder.

Maddie turned back to her computer so he couldn't see her embarrassment. As she typed something completely unintelligible onto the screen, she attempted an air of normalcy even though her heart rejected her attempts and thudded in her chest. "You need to go ask Judy to give you some of the special hair gel for that. It will solve all your problems."

Maddie stilled her fingers when she sensed a presence behind her and a weight leaning on the back of her chair. She glanced back to see him leaning over her shoulder, his arms resting on the back of her chair. Hadn't the guy every heard of personal space? Her tingling skin didn't mind. Although it really should. "Do you need something?"

"Just curious about what you're trying to get at with all that stuff on the screen."

Heat flooded her face as she pivoted her gaze back to her screen, which read "al;sdkfjaoij;rlkj;alsdfj1o98okjd" in the document she'd been typing on.

Her hair smelled good.

Which meant he was way closer to her than he should be. What had he been thinking?

He knew the answer to that before he thought it. His flattered self had kicked into manly high gear at the thought of Maddie having a crush on him. He was more convinced than ever that she did. The red cheeks, the slip of calling him handsome, the fake typing on the computer.

He took a few steps back, turned the guest chair in front of his desk around and sat. A safe, comfortable, non-lawsuit worthy distance. "Have you heard anything more about your brother?"

Her pink cheeks drained of their color. "No. Everything is up in the air right now. No formal paperwork has been filed, so that's a little hope."

"I was serious about finding you a new place. Something with two bedrooms. You have a job now, you're doing fabulous and unless you steal from me or something, I wouldn't think of firing you. I'd be happy to tell the case worker that as well."

Her smile didn't meet her eyes. "Thanks. At this point, I don't know how much help it'll be. They're looking at what's best for him in the long run, and I'm not exactly the posterchild of stability."

"Have you talked to Kyle to see what he thinks about all this?"

Maddie shook her head. "Caseworker says it would look bad, like I'm trying to get to his head or something. I requested a weekend visit for him to come see me, and she thought she could get it approved, so that's a plus. Do you think your mom would mind if he stayed with me?"

His mother was likely to organize a parade and fireworks to welcome the boy. "She won't mind. But I'm curious, I always figured that they give relatives a major consideration."

Maddie shrugged. "They probably do. But my case is a little different."

He might be opening Pandora's box, but he couldn't stand not asking. "Why?"

"Well, since I aged out of the foster care system for one. But let's just say, I didn't have a stellar history either."

"Like?"

"I was a teenage girl in the slums of Chicago. Your imagination can fill in the blank."

The blank was a large one with many options, some worse than others. Reuben refused to even guess. "What made you change?"

"A teacher. After I graduated, I worked odd jobs for a year or so, then enrolled in cosmetology school at the insistence of our social worker. My mom always loved to do hair before she died, used to be a hairdresser when I was really little, so I guess it runs in the family. Anyway, my teacher was a Christian. I thought it hokey at first, but my mom was a Christian, even though we never went to church, so it intrigued me."

A Christian who didn't go to church? Odd. "Why didn't you go to church?"

"My dad didn't want us to. Anyway, Ms. Johnson showed me that Jesus loves me, so there was at least one dad who wasn't a jerk. I gave my heart to Jesus, and the rest is history."

"How long ago was that?"

"Seven months."

"Wow. So you're really just a baby Christian then." He regretted the phrase as soon as he used it. It sounded so immature, almost degrading.

"I'm still learning, but I doubt I'll never know it all"

He nodded. "I've been a Christian since I was four, and I'm still learning."

Her nose wrinkled in the most adorable way. "Did you say four? As in, four years old?"

"You have a problem with that?"

"But . . . how did you even know what to do? That you even needed to?"

The faded memory still lingered of that bittersweet day. "I was a very astute toddler. My grandmother passed away that year, and everyone told me that she was in heaven. I wanted to make sure I'd go there too, so I prayed with my Dad the night of her funeral."

Maddie shifted in her seat. "I feel like I'm in the presence of Mister Experienced Saint."

He sat forward, leaning his elbows on his knees. If she only knew. . . . "I am so far from being a saint, it isn't even funny. Christian's aren't perfect, Maddie. You should know that by now even in the short time you've been one."

"I'm different. My life has been full of crap for years now, and old habits are hard to kick. But you? What's the worst thing you've done? Steal gum from Walmart?"

"Actually, no, a Snickers candy bar."

Her lips flickered with a satisfied grin. "See? What did I tell you?"

He shook his head. "I struggle with sin every day. It may not be physical harm stuff, or doing drugs, but a sin is a sin."

"Give me an example."

"Of what?"

"What have you been tempted with today, let's say?"

Her eyebrows were raised and her bangs fell ever closer to her eyes. Her mouth twisted in a sideways move, such a classic Maddie face, daring him to prove her wrong.

Oh, yeah, he was definitely tempted today. In a way that was so disturbing he got up and walked to his office chair and refused to look at her again. "I'm tempted to fire you if you don't let me get back to work, that's what."

Maddie laughed. "You're such a liar."

In more ways than she knew. "You're right. I'm gonna go grab some lunch. Do you want something?"

She shook her head. "No, I need to call your dad to see if there's any update on my Tracker."

He'd wanted a diversion, but explaining Gary wasn't what he had in mind. "He's not my dad."

Maddie twirled in her seat to face him. "I'm sorry. I guess I knew that but—"

"My dad died two years ago." Thanks to the man who conveniently filled his shoes six months later.

"Again, I'm sorry. I have to call Gary anyway. If it's ready, do you mind if I take a long lunch to go get it?"

"Of course not. Let me know if you need a ride." Although he fully planned on making Gary do the honors. The man wasn't good for much. He could at least do that.

⁂

Maddie had always heard of people having panic attacks, but never had she been close to experiencing one until she heard the quote from the mechanic.

"How can that be? I thought it was just a radiator hose."

The man with the blue, oil-stained work shirt with A&J Automotive printed on the pocket shook his head. "Yep. But that was only the beginning of your problems." He began listing engine parts she'd never heard of and detailing their paltry condition. "So, in all, it'll come to about $1,100 with tax."

It'd take every cent currently in her checking account, minus about twenty dollars. All the money she'd been saving for a deposit on a rental. "Is there anything that can wait?"

The older man rubbed his chin. "Well, we could probably wait on a few things and save you a couple hundred dollars, but I wouldn't go more than a month or so before getting those taken care of."

Gary took her elbow and led her to a chair. "You all right, Maddie? Your face went pretty white there for a minute."

She nodded, not certain of her voice at the moment. A few hundred dollars would help the short-term, but there was no way she'd get to move now.

*God, are you listening? Do you see what's happening? I gotta tell you, I'm totally confused. I was trying to trust you and. . . .*

"Miss, what would you like me to do?"

Gary answered before she could. "Go ahead and fix it all."

Her heart thudded in her chest and her hands shook. "No, no. The minimum is fine. I'll bring it by later for the rest."

A hand rested on hers and squeezed. "Chuck, I'll take care of the difference. Just make sure it's safe for her to drive, okay?"

The mechanic nodded at him. "Yes sir. I should have it ready by tomorrow."

Maddie stared at his back as the grease-covered man walked away, her eyes wide and her mind racing to figure out what to say. She hated being a charity case. Already she was mooching lodging off of the family, not to mention a made-up job. "Gary, I can't let you do that. I have money."

"I know you do. But I want to help."

She blinked a tear away. Every inch of her wanted to protest, to tell him no, she could make it on her own without help. But the excuse sounded flimsy. Gary knew now that she was a big fat failure. "Thank you."

"I'll take you back to the restaurant. I'm sure Reuben will bring you home tonight."

Oh, goody. Just what she wanted.

She wasn't sure which one she dreaded more, bumming a ride from her boss or her looming talk with Livy this evening.

~∞~

When she arrived back at the restaurant, the mood had shifted. Livy was there, her eyes following Maddie as she walked to the office.

Reuben ignored her when she entered the office, which was just fine, except she needed to tell him about her car and the ride she would need that evening. She'd never felt so humbled in her life, except maybe for when social services came banging on their door and took her and Kyle away. The neighbors, including her friends, had watched as the lady ushered them into the back of the state minivan, her dad yelling curse words from the front door.

She sat in her seat and turned on her computer monitor.

"I'm leaving in about a half hour."

*Please, God, let him be coming back before the end of the day.*
"Where are you going?"

"To the architect's. He's up in Joliet, so I'll be gone all afternoon. You can hold down the fort, right?"

She forced her head in an up and down motion. "Yes, but I was hoping I could bum a ride from you tonight. The problem ended up being more complicated than they thought."

He stood up and grabbed a briefcase beside the desk. "Livy has Monday nights off, so she can swing you by home."

Wonderful. Just absolutely peachy. "Are you sure she won't mind?"

He hesitated a moment, but nodded his head. "Positive. I'll mention it to her on my way out. Oh, and I left a few things for you to get done on your desk."

He walked out of the office without even a wave good-bye.

⁓📖⁓

"I'm glad this worked out for me to take you home. I'd wanted to talk to you anyway."

Maddie shifted in her seat, praying the ride would finish quickly. Just a few more blocks. "Yes, you mentioned that when you called last night." The phone call had been completely out of the blue. She wasn't even sure how Livy knew her cell number.

"I'm sure you've heard that Reuben and I had a little tiff."

Or a big one. "Yes, Reuben mentioned something briefly."

"What he probably didn't mention was that it's all your fault."

Maddie blinked. Her fault? That wasn't how Reuben explained it. "I'm not sure I understand."

Livy pulled into the driveway and shifted the car into Park. "I have eyes, Maddie. I can see that you're attracted to Reuben."

"It's not like that at all. I promise." Kinda. Sorta.

Livy reached a hand across the center console and squeezed Maddie's. "First, I want you to know that I understand. It's perfectly natural at your age to have a crush on an older guy, especially your boss. You didn't have a good childhood and you're looking for that male figure to fill the void."

Maddie crinkled up her brow. She didn't know she was doing all that . . . and what was the "at your age" stuff? Livy was five, maybe seven years older than her, but acted like a spoiled two-year-old half of the time. Not exactly the older, wiser woman Maddie wanted to take advice from.

The would-be psychologist continued. "Listen, you don't have to say anything. But I just want to make sure you realize the problems this is causing."

"Livy, I'm not—"

She held up her hand. "Just hear me out. Reuben's been working his heart out trying to grow the Emporium into something big. I've been patient, knowing that as a man he has needs regarding his career. He needs to feel like he can provide for me, that he's worth something. But we're finally to the point where we can take our relationship to the next level, and in comes this girl, barely out of high school, who has a major crush on him.

"Of course this is going to make him go a bit crazy. But you have to know that you aren't what's best for him, Maddie. He needs a woman who knows him, who's experienced, who can be his helpmate. Not some flighty child who still, really, hasn't found herself yet."

Her eyes softened. "We all know how poorly the two times you tried to help in the restaurant turned out. Both times you cost Reuben a lot of money and long-time customers. Not to mention the added payroll expense. The only reason he hasn't fired you is that he feels bad for you."

Tears stung Maddie's eyes. Had she really become a burden? Useless?

"Just think about it. In the end, I'm sure it would be best for us all if you could just go back to cutting hair and let Reuben run his business exactly as he had been."

"I can't go back. Judy fired me."

Livy's lips lifted into a sly smile. "I've already talked to Judy and have it taken care of. You can start back tomorrow if you'd like."

She shook her head. As crazy as her childhood had been, even she knew that just up and leaving wasn't appropriate. "No, I'd need to give Reuben notice. I can't just leave him like that."

"That's sweet of you, but really, do you think he needs you, Maddie? You do realize he's just handing over busy work because he feels sorry for you, right?"

No, she hadn't realized. She'd thought he appreciated her help, that he needed it. But obviously it'd all been an illusion that she created in her mind.

"You're right. I'll call Judy in the morning."

Livy nodded. "And I'll talk to Reuben. I'm sure he'll be relieved."

Maddie let herself out of the car and dragged her feet toward the cottage behind the garage. As she walked, a calm breeze rustled her hair, a stark contrast to the storm raging inside her heart.

She reached her door, then looked back at the house. Through the French door, she could see Betty and Gary laughing, having dinner together at the kitchen table. They were such a sweet couple, and from what she'd heard, they'd gone through a lot of pain in their lives, having lost their spouses. How nice that they had each other to lean on.

She pushed open the door and didn't bother to turn on a light or change her clothes. She just walked over to the bed and curled into a ball on top of the quilt.

*God, are you there? Can you hear me? I know you work hard on Sundays, so maybe you take Mondays off or something? Because this day stunk really bad. Worse than a skunk. Was I really leading*

*Reuben astray? I didn't mean to. You know good and well I didn't want to like him.*

Silence filled the room. No answer. No apology from God for his oversight. No explanation for the crazy events of the day.

Maybe he'd be back in business in the morning.

# 20

*G*od was taking an extended vacation.

"Thanks for the ride, Betty."

The older woman sat in the driver's seat, her mouth drooped into a frown. "I still don't understand why you're going back to the Cut 'N' Style."

Maddie wasn't sure she understood either, but the bottom line was she needed a job, and even if Livy was wrong and Reuben did need her, her presence created a strain on Reuben's impending marriage. She may be a lot of things, but a marriage wrecker wasn't one of them. "I just think it's better this way. Reuben doesn't really need me anyway, and Judy was nice enough to give me my old job back."

"What did Reuben have to say about this?"

Maddie looked at her fingers. She hoped Livy had told him, and prayed that she was right, that he wouldn't mind her not giving notice. "Livy is going to tell him."

Betty folded her arms. "What does that parasite have to do with anything?"

"Did you just call her what I think you did?"

Betty's hand covered her mouth as a flush rose up her neck to her cheeks. "I'm sorry. I didn't mean to say that out loud."

That Reuben's mother didn't like his choice of women was an interesting turn of events, but Maddie determined not to interfere anymore. Her ex-boss's relationships weren't her business. "I told Livy last night about my decision, and she offered to relay the information, is all."

Betty's eyebrows rose. "Are you sure she didn't have more to do with this?"

How does one not lie but still not tell the truth? "I made the decision, Betty."

The older woman studied her for a moment, then nodded. "Fair enough. But I want you to come to the big house for dinner tonight, you hear? Nothing fancy, just a goulash."

The tip of her tongue almost refused, but instead she gave in. "I'd enjoy that, thank you."

She stepped out of the car, thanked Betty, and walked toward the Cut 'N' Style. Major déjà vu. Had it been over a month since her first humiliating day here?

The door jingled as she opened it, and the pungent scent of perm solution and shampoo wafted under her nose. For the last two years, she'd loved that smell. But now, she fought the urge to sneeze.

Judy walked from the back room, her hands on her ample hips. "Look who's come crawling back for her job."

Not exactly. "I appreciate the opportunity, Judy."

"Rules will be the same as last time. A complaint in the first week and you're fired. You'll get walk-ins only and the rest of the time you can sweep up after the other stylists and clean."

She nodded. Oh, why couldn't it have worked out with Reuben? Maybe she should have asked him first, talked it out. But no. Livy was right. He only acted out of guilt and a sense of responsibility, not out of true need.

She set her purse under the counter. Her heart soared when she glanced at the mirror to see Kyle's picture and the Bible verse still taped exactly where she'd left them. A few times she'd almost given in and come back to get them, but fear that Judy had torn them up and trashed them kept her from making the trip downtown.

The morning passed by uneventfully. The only walk-in was a mother bringing her two-year-old for a trim. She'd managed to make the cut presentable after being bitten, kicked, and screamed at for almost twenty minutes. The little girl's mom had been apologetic, and Judy had tossed her a bandage for the teeth marks that bled.

The door jingled at a little after eleven, and Maddie turned around to see Reuben standing there, fire in his eyes.

Miss Agnes tried to hail him over to the reception desk, but his eyes never left Maddie.

"You left." His voice was low and firm.

The customers who waited for the other stylists took extreme interest in him as he strode closer to her. She fingered the broom in her hand, glad she had it between them and that there was an audience. "You didn't need me."

"Says who?"

"Me." And Livy, but that was irrelevant.

Judy stepped from behind her. "Reuben, you need a cut again so soon?"

He narrowed his eyes. "No, I just need a word with your new stylist."

She looked at her watch. "Well, you'll have to wait a few more hours until her shift is over."

His jaw worked over a few times, and Maddie knew a moment of doubt. What if he had wanted her? Needed her? Or had it just been a silly crush like Livy noted, that would only cause him to stumble?

"I need a cut then, and I request Maddie."

A hush fell over the salon. Judy looked from Reuben to Maddie. "Fine. But you'll pay for it this time. If I'd known it was your fault before, I never would have given you a freebie. In fact, I should charge you double."

He didn't respond, just strode over to the chair and sat down with a huff.

*God, I have no idea what to do right now.*

As soon as she prayed it, the answer seemed too simple. Duh. Cut the man's hair. She slid into routine, wrapping the cape around his neck, her fingers brushing against his skin. She jerked her hand back as if his skin was poisonous. In some ways, it held more danger than a snake.

She walked around and leaned against the counter. "How would you like it cut, sir?"

He raised his eyebrows. "I trust you to make it look good."

Everything in her wanted to say, "It looks good just how it is," but she refrained. Instead, she walked behind him and started to trim the perfectly fine haircut. The salon behind her finally started to buzz again with independent conversations, so she bit her cheek and started into her normal, friendly discourse. "So everything going okay for you today?"

"No."

She bit her lip trying not to smile. "I'm sorry to hear that."

"My assistant quit on me with no notice today. Didn't even bother to tell me either."

Her fingers stilled. "Didn't Livy relay the message?"

"She did, but not until she came in for the day, about three hours after I expected you, and two hours after I gave in and called my mother who told me where you were."

Her heart sank. Now he thought her a good-for-nothing employee. "I'm sorry. Livy said not to worry about telling you, that she'd do it."

"Which leads me to another question. What were you doing talking to Livy about your employment? You work for me, Maddie."

She sighed. In hindsight, he was right. But at the time it seemed like her only option. Livy made it all sound like perfect sense. "She's the manager at the restaurant."

He shifted in his seat, and Maddie held tight to the scissors. Did the man want a repeat of their last disaster?

"Like I said, you work for me."

"Worked."

"Work. I'm offering you another job."

She walked around in front of him, set the scissors safely on the counter, and turned to look at him again. Big mistake. He looked way too cute sitting there, face set in stone, his body covered in a cape and his hair all wet and crazy. Take about twenty years off of him and he reminded her of a stubborn seven-year-old who didn't want a haircut. "After I just quit?"

"This will be part time. To help with your funds. Gary told me about your car costing so much, and I already know about Kyle. I don't know what you think, Maddie, but I really did need your help. Even if you just come for a few hours after your shift here."

The proper answer would be no. But the money would be a help. She glanced behind her to look at Kyle's picture. He was her priority right now. Not Reuben. Not Livy. She clenched her fists. No one would get her mind off the goal.

"Okay. I'll come back. But my hours here vary. So sometimes it will be in the morning."

He nodded. "Even better. Just let me know the week before what your schedule will be."

"Deal."

He smiled at her, and her traitor heart skipped a beat. "So are you going to finish my hair?"

"I'm done cutting it, but I can style it if you like and sell you a miracle gel that will make all the difference."

He sat back in the chair. "Sold."

She squirted a glob of gel into her hand, walked back behind him, and plunged her fingers into his hair.

Their simultaneous intake of breath reminded her that running fingers through his hair was indeed a very, very bad idea.

❧

Reuben flung open the restaurant door as hard as the metal door allowed and stalked back to the kitchen, ignoring the whispered glances of customers, to where Livy stood barking orders to the cook.

"We need to talk."

She turned around, her lips curving into a smile but the action not quite reaching her eyes. "It's the lunch hour, Reuben. Can't it wait?"

He took a breath to keep from yelling out his reply. "Now."

Not waiting for her to argue, he turned around and stomped out of the kitchen. Never had he been so angry as he'd been after talking to his mother that morning. Maddie was the best thing that'd happened to him in a long time. He'd made more progress in the last month than he had in the last year. With her taking care of the administrative work and keeping him organized, he actually had a snowball's chance in Mexico of having two grand openings next year.

He reached his office and slammed the door closed behind him. The dining room probably bustled with gossip about him, but at the moment he didn't care. At all. Let them print it in the newspaper for all he cared. "Extra, Extra! Is The Sandwich Emporium owner on the verge of going postal?"

He paced between his desk and Maddie's, unable to sit down. He needed to hit something. Hard.

The door opened, and Livy entered, her face as innocent as a puppy who'd just peed on the carpet. "You wanted to see me, Reub?"

He stopped his pacing and pointed to the chair in front of his desk. "Sit."

She complied and sat, crossing her legs at the ankles. Her hair was pulled into a bun, something he'd never seen her do until today. What was she trying to do, practice being queen?

He moved to sit in his office chair, needing to put the desk between them. He wasn't afraid he'd hit her. His dad would climb right out of his grave and pummel him if he ever hit a woman. But shouting in her face wasn't beyond his temperament at the moment.

"Why'd you do it?"

Livy folded her hands in her lap. "Do what?"

"Fire Maddie."

Sparks flew from her eyes. "Excuse me? Is that what she told you?"

Not exactly. But no one could convince him that she had no hand in it. "I want to hear your side of the story."

She shrugged her shoulders. "I took her home last night, and we got to talking. I'd mentioned that Judy was still short-handed, and Reuben, you should have seen her eyes light up. I could tell her heart was there.

"And I know you, honey. I know you wouldn't want anyone to sacrifice a dream on your behalf. I'd heard Judy mention that she'd take Maddie back in a flash, so I relayed the information. The girl was so tickled, I thought she'd jump out of her seat. I told her she should really give you a little notice, but she asked that I tell you for her."

Maybe he got the sense from being in the sandwich business for so long, but Reuben could usually spot bologna a mile away. This time though, he had two very different stories and had no clue which to believe. "So you're telling me this was Maddie's idea? And only because she wanted to work at the salon?"

She nodded. "Exactly. I wouldn't come in between you and your direct report, Reuben. That would be just plain rude of me."

"I'm glad you feel that way. Because I hired her back."

Livy's eyes widened, her face blushed a fuchsia pink, and her lips parted. "I, uh, how? I mean, she was so happy about working at the salon. Why would you want her here when she's unhappy?"

"We compromised. She'll work full-time at the salon, and a few extra hours here everyday. I know she could use the money. It's a win-win all the way around."

She bolted from her seat and straightened her shoulders. "I'm glad it worked out. If we're through, it's still the rush hour."

Reuben nodded and watched her go.

Something smelled fishy, and it wasn't the grilled tuna sandwich Police Chief Garrison ordered every Tuesday.

# 21

*T*he goulash was amazing, Betty."

Her landlord waved down the compliment as she loaded the dishes into the stainless steel dishwasher. "Nonsense. Plain ol' goulash can't be called amazing. But I'm glad you enjoyed it."

Maddie opened her mouth to explain more but snapped it shut. The truth was, the goulash tasted good and reminded her of a similar dish her mom used to make, but the company is what made the meal special. She never ceased to be awed by the friendly banter back and forth between Betty and Gary, the genuine interest the two seemed to have in Reuben's life.

Even though the man himself seemed to resent it. He'd remained quiet the entire meal.

Allie and her crew weren't in attendance that evening, which Maddie feared would make the evening intolerable. On the contrary, the dinner made her heart yearn for the family life she'd never had, for the relationship with her brother that would turn nonexistent if she didn't get custody of him soon.

Even though she had zero clue how she could pull it off, she was determined not to let him go.

"Reuben told me about the situation with Kyle."

Maddie's hands stilled on the Tupperware container she was sealing leftovers in. "Then you understand that my need to move isn't personal?"

The dishwasher started whirring and Betty joined her by the counter. "I never thought it was. In fact, Gary and I have been keeping an eye out for places for you to rent. You know us retired folks; too much time on our hands makes us dangerous."

Maddie smiled. "I doubt that, more like makes you god-sends. Seriously, thanks for understanding and for lending me the use of the cottage. It's the nicest thing anyone has done for me in . . . well, in a very long time."

"It's our pleasure. You've been delightful company and we'll miss you. But you'll still come over for dinners, right?"

That sounded heavenly. "Of course. I couldn't give up a Callahan meal. They're known for their fabulous cooking, you know."

The woman laughed as if she'd just told the most hilarious joke. "Honey, I can make a mean goulash, but my culinary skills don't go much past that. Reuben's father was the real chef in the family."

"What about Reuben?"

"He's pretty good at it himself, although he's got himself so wrapped up in the numbers stuff at the moment that he's lost the joy of owning a restaurant. I try to tell him it's quality over quantity, but he doesn't listen to his Momma."

Interesting. "Well, about the housing. Not sure when I'll be able to find something, but will let you know in advance. I still want to pay you for the time I've been here."

Betty's eyebrows raised an inch and she put a hand on the counter. "Madison Buckner, if you even think about giving me money for my Good Samaritan action, I'll, I'll, well, I don't know what I'll do, but it won't be pretty. You'll be robbing me of a blessing."

Robbing her? She'd stolen quite a few things in her life, but a blessing? "I don't understand."

"The Bible clearly says that those who give and get nothing in return, their reward is given from God. But if I get an earthly reward for my good deeds, well, then why should God give me one too? Not to be mean, but a reward from God is much greater than any money you could give me. And besides that, I don't need the money, and you do."

Who could argue with that logic? "Then I guess I'll settle with a thanks."

"Good, and you're welcome. We're finished in here, so why don't we join the men out in the living room?"

They walked to the front of the house to find Gary reclining in his chair and Reuben flipping through channels. Maddie sat down on the couch, putting a full foot in between herself and Reuben. She would have sat at the other end, but feared it would look too obvious that she was avoiding him. Betty took her regular chair and propped her feet on the ottoman.

Reuben clicked off the TV and turned his attention toward her. "So, Maddie, what are your hours the rest of the week?"

"I work mornings since I wasn't originally on the schedule. I should be at the restaurant by four every day."

He nodded. "That'll work. The architect gave me a preliminary draft of the blueprint for the new restaurants, and I want to show it to you. And I got really behind on things today. The payroll company had to call me because I forgot to approve everyone's hours."

Now that could have been a tragedy. She'd forgotten about finalizing the payroll. "I'm sorry again about leaving like that. I just thought—"

He reached over and laid his hand over hers. "No need to explain. I understand."

She felt the stares of Betty and Gary, so snatched her hand back and pretended to examine a nonexistent hangnail.

Gary cleared his throat. "How's the Tracker running for you?"

*Thank you, God, for a change of topic.* "Great. Thanks again for taking me over there this afternoon. It behaved like a charm on the way home."

"Good, good. And how about that, the bill coming up so much less."

Yes, how about that. It still smelled fishy to her. The mechanic told her the parts ended up being much cheaper than he'd estimated, thus saving her three hundred dollars, the amount of cash Gary was going to front her. She'd been able to pay for the whole thing by draining most but not all of her bank account. Still, she wondered if Gary didn't have a hand in the lower price, a handful of cash, that is.

"Yes, a true answer to prayer."

He nodded, his face unreadable. "Sure was. Now, did Betty tell you about the place we found today?"

She looked from Betty, who wore a conspiratorial grin, to Gary, who was the picture of triumphant, to Reuben, whose face reeked of guilt as he took a keen interest in the remote control. "No, she mentioned you'd been looking but not that you found anything."

"I hope you don't mind, but I took the liberty of calling a few of the landlords. One of them happens to be a good friend of mine."

Now, there was a shocker. The Luther/Callahan family seemed to know everyone in town. "Where is it?"

"Actually, it's not too far from Reuben's house. It's in the older section of Lake Holiday, but it's been kept up quite nicely.

Bob had renters in it until a month ago when they bought a bigger house, so he's been debating whether or not to sell it."

Her hopes plummeted. "I'm really not able to buy anything right—"

Reuben interrupted. "He understands that. If you like the place, he'd be willing to rent it out for a while, then give you the option to buy it later if you'd like. No strings attached."

She looked over at him. "You knew about this?"

"Mom called me this afternoon, and I went to look at it before coming here."

Her fist clenched a wad of fabric from her shorts. This was the nicest family she'd ever met. But it was still her life. Her decision. Her plans. Did Reuben expect her just to bow down and obey his commands? Typical male. See a damsel in distress and their ego went into overtime. They had to save her.

Well, she wasn't Cinderella, and she could do this just fine on her own.

"Thank you, but—"

"Do you want to go look at it?" Reuben's eyes lit up like it was Christmas Eve.

"Tonight?"

He withdrew a key from his pocket. "Bob gave me a key so we could stop by whenever you had time."

How could she say no when he'd gone to the trouble of getting her a key? The story of the greedy Israelites came to mind. Was this God's way of providing for her, and she was refusing on principle only because she wanted it a different way?

*God, forgive my selfishness, and thank you for your provision, even if it isn't exactly like I'd like it. If possible though, could you leave Reuben out of the provision thing from now on? I mean, yeah, provide for him, but I'd rather you use someone else, anyone else, to help me out. He's just too . . . handsome. Send an ugly guy, 'kay? Thanks.*

Her hopes deflated the moment they pulled up to the house. There was no way she could afford it. Evidently God answered her prayers, because Reuben sure wasn't helping her provision by showing her this house.

If anything, he was waving carrot cake under a rabbit's nose and then snatching it away. This bunny wanted to just hop away and go back to scrounging for food. It hurt less that way.

She slid out of the front seat of Reuben's Beamer, still wishing Gary had agreed to come. But Reuben had squirmed, and Gary had faked exhaustion. Somehow she didn't believe him given that it was only seven-thirty.

"Reuben, I—"

He walked around the car and swept an arm in front of her. "You first. And trust me, Maddie."

Oddly, she did.

The wood siding was a pale green color, and the two-car garage was lined with a stone façade. Not fancy like Reuben's house a few blocks away, just homey and inviting. They walked up the three steps that led to the small front porch, and Reuben inserted the key into the lock.

She followed him into the house and smiled when the harsh scent of fresh paint mingled with the woodsy fragrance of Pine-Sol tickled her nose.

The living room was empty except for a stone fireplace. A white ceiling fan with gold trim hung down in the middle. The carpet was a faded tan color, and the walls sported a peeling paisley green and mauve wall paper under the chair railing and off-white paint above. Obviously decorated in the eighties, but for her, it just felt like home.

The retro décor gave her hope. Maybe she could afford this place after all.

"So what do you think?" Reuben stood to the side, his hands behind his back, feet apart, letting her take it all in.

"I like it so far. But what about—"

He took a step toward her and placed a hand on the small of her back, silencing her logical reasoning. "Let's just see the rest of the house first, okay?"

She agreed quickly, needing to get his hand away from her back before she gave in to her impulses and jumped into his arms.

*God, I don't like men. I really don't. Please make me stop feeling this stupid attraction to a man I don't want, can't have, but desperately want to kiss. Ugh, yes, there, I admit it. I want to kiss a kinda-engaged man. Send Ye forth the lightning now.*

They walked through the living room to a small dining room off the kitchen. The floor sported ceramic tiles, some chipped here and there but clean. The appliances weren't new by any means, but there was a fridge, stove, and dishwasher. At least she wouldn't have to purchase any of those.

Reuben pointed to the door on the other side of the kitchen. "That leads to the garage. The small door on the left is the pantry."

Maddie bit her bottom lip. A pantry? Why was it that the thought of her very own pantry made her giddy? She could go grocery shopping and not have to move aside cups to fit the food. Woohoo!

And if Kyle came to live with her, she was sure to need plenty of groceries. Even a few years ago, the boy could eat like a cow. His teenage years were sure to do damage to her meager budget.

If, that is, he came to live with her. That was all that mattered right now.

"You okay?" Reuben stood with his arms crossed over his chest, his forehead wrinkled in concern.

She nodded and flashed him a smile. "Yes. Just worrying for nothing. Let's see the rest of the place."

He led her back through the living room and down the hall, showing her three bedrooms, two bathrooms, and a closet in the hallway which held a washer and dryer.

Two more things she wouldn't have to purchase.

When they came back to the living room, she popped a squat on the floor, leaning back on her hands and looking up into his bemused face. "You've done a great job as tour guide. But now we need to face reality. How much does it cost, Reub?"

He smiled, and only then did Maddie realize she'd slipped and called him the nickname many others around here did. "Sorry, I mean, Reuben."

He sat down on the worn carpet and draped his arms over his knees. "No apology needed. It sounded kinda nice. Like we're friends instead of boss and employee." He turned his face to look at her. "We are friends, right, Maddie?"

Her voice refused to work due to the emotion lodged in her throat, so she only nodded.

He winked at her. "Good. I'm your handsome boss and friend. I can handle that."

"My, aren't we a little egotistical today?"

"What? You were the one who called me handsome."

Maddie rolled her eyes. "Did not."

"Did too."

"Whatever. At least I know you're tempted to sin now too."

He shifted to look at her. "What are you talking about?"

"You never did answer me, remember? Pride goeth before a fall. You think you're handsome." She shook her head. "Sinful, sinful, sinful."

"I do not. I was repeating what you started to say, then turned tomato red, if I recall."

"Fine. Then answer me now. The truth. What are you tempted with?"

His eyes locked with hers. "What if I said kissing you?"

Maddie cleared her throat and willed her face not to blush. The man clearly was joking to get a rise out of her. "I'd say I'd have to quit for real this time, because I'd hate to be the one who causes you to sin. Kinda like Bathsheba and David."

His deep laugh lessened the tension. "If I remember the story right, David was the one at fault there."

"True. I don't remember the story very well, but wasn't Bathsheba bathing on the roof or something? Goodness, the woman should've known better than that, especially if the King's window overlooked her house. The little hussy."

His eyebrows rose. "You think she was doing it on purpose? Trying to seduce him?"

"She sure didn't turn him away."

A finger poked her arm. "Would you have turned me away if I tried?"

Desire and caution warred inside of her, causing what felt like a bad case of indigestion. "Of course I would. I'm reformed, remember?"

His eyes sparkled with mischief. "Do we need to test it out to make sure?" He leaned toward her and put a hand to the floor as if he was going to crawl up to her.

She giggled and rolled out of the way and hurried to her feet. "No, I don't think that's necessary. Besides, we never did talk money."

He stood up and shook his head. "Now, Maddie, I'm not the kinda guy that pays for kisses."

She blinked. Did he know? No, he couldn't. He was just teasing. She stuck out her tongue at him to cover her discomfort. "Good, because it'd cost you an arm and a leg for me to kiss the likes of you, all homely and everything, and I'm sure you'd like to keep yours."

He smiled, then turned and walked to the back window. "I am partial to my limbs. Now, how about you take a look at the backyard?"

The man obviously didn't want to talk about the money aspect. She'd humor him for now. "Fine."

He opened the door and let her out first. The backyard took her breath away.

She stepped out onto a wooden deck and took a deep inhale of air. The back lot held a tree smack dab in the middle and beautiful green grass that could use attention from a lawn mower. But there was evidence of a previous garden in the corner and flowers planted along the backside of the house. There wasn't a fence, but trees lined most of the yard.

Closing her eyes, she imagined Kyle climbing the tree with friends, and her lying out on the deck in a patio chair enjoying the evening air. Maybe a barbecue in the nice weather, having birthday parties back here.

Here her dreams could come true. She could have a normal, peaceful life. Her dad forgotten, her past behind her. She could move on.

If the price was right.

A voice sounded in her ear, quoting a number she couldn't quite understand. His lips were so close she could feel breath on her earlobe.

She turned to find Reuben standing directly behind her, barely an inch away. "What'd you say?"

He repeated the number, much lower than she'd even dreamed of hoping.

She blinked. "But . . . how?"

He shrugged. "Tom doesn't want to deal with it right now. He just wants someone who will take care of it and pay the small mortgage he has on it so he doesn't have to dip into savings to pay it. The economy isn't the greatest right now, so he couldn't sell it for a good price anyway. Plus, I told him I'd help you update the place a little over time and keep it in good shape."

A tear escaped her eye, and she held up her hand to brush it away, but Reuben's reflexes were faster. He put a thumb to her cheek and wiped it away, lingering longer than necessary.

Her heart took on a beat of its own, racing faster than her chest could bear. She held a hand over her heart, willing it to slow down and behave itself. But when Reuben took a small step toward her, closing the one inch gap, and covered her hand with his, all attempts to slow it vanished.

She looked up at him, her mouth opening to ask what he was doing, but no words escaped as his lips claimed hers.

And for a moment, nothing else mattered. Only the feeling of Reuben's mouth on hers, his lips probing, moving so sweetly and tenderly. She moved her hands to his shoulders, and he slid his arms around her waist and pulled her closer, molding them into one.

Warning bells sounded in her head. A man was kissing her. Holding her. Touching her. All the memories of the last time she'd been like this swarmed back into her mind, and terror grabbed at her heart. She pushed his shoulders away, but he held tight.

Just like before.

A scream caught in her throat, and Reuben finally lifted his head, his eyebrows knit together in concern. "Maddie?"

She gave him a shove, turned toward the door and ran inside.

# 22

Stew, I'm totally getting sued." Reuben hunched over and allowed the sweat to drip off his brow onto the paved running track. He hadn't run in months because of his crazy schedule, and his gasping for breath told the story.

He'd only agreed to do it now because his brother-in-law had all but forced him to go. That, and he could stand to blow off a few gallons of steam.

Stew put his hands on his hips, struggling for air himself. "I knew . . . " *gasp* "something was" *gasp* "up." He took a few steps and collapsed on the green grass in the middle of the track.

Reuben followed suit. They probably looked like two old farts barely able to run a lap instead of guys in their late twenties who should be pumping iron at the gym. He looked over at Stew, who covered his face with his arm to shield out the hot June sun. "Allie told me by the way."

He peeked out behind his arm. "Told you what?"

"About you and Livy."

The poor guy's face turned redder than it already was. "Reub, I'm sorry."

He waved him quiet. "No need. It wasn't your fault."

"Man, it's no excuse. I should have told you a long time ago myself."

"It was Livy who should have confessed." After Allie first told him, he'd decided to forgive and forget. It had happened years ago.

And after what happened with Maddie, he was no different than her.

Stew sat back up and draped his arms over his knees. "So what's this about being sued?"

Reuben pressed the palms of his hands to his eyes. "I kissed her, Stew."

"Kissed who?" His tone implied this was the craziest thing he'd ever heard.

Which fit the action, because that kiss was the craziest, stupidest, most wonderful thing Reuben had done in his life. "Maddie."

Stews mouth hung open. "No way."

"I don't know what came over me. Lately I can't take my eyes off her."

He let out a snort. "Or your lips?"

Reuben kicked to the side, catching his friend in the leg.

"Ouch."

"I need advice, not sarcasm. She could seriously sue me for this. I'm her boss. There's no way I should be kissing her."

Stew shook his head. "How did she react? I mean, did she kiss you back?"

"She pushed me away and ran."

"Dude, you need to talk to a lawyer or something. This could be bad."

Sound advice, but not what he wanted to hear. Especially since Maddie had barely talked to him since the incident. It'd been two days now, and one would think he had the bubonic plague the way she was treating him. Every time he started to say a word to her, she'd jump out of her seat, claim she had to go to the bathroom, and come back five minutes later and ignore him. He knew women sometimes had issues, but going to the ladies' room ten times in the two hours she'd been there yesterday afternoon seemed a little excessive.

He had visions of her calling different lawyers getting price quotes.

Yet, the frustrating thing was, he'd liked it. He liked *her.* She was funny and tough. She didn't get all fake and sugary when she wanted something like Livy did. When she was mad at him, he knew it.

She stuck her tongue out at him to be goofy.

And talked to herself while filing, even though he was sure she had no idea she did it.

His favorite was her yelling at her computer when it didn't cooperate. She said every word imaginable but a cuss word.

Her faith was refreshing and bold, not stagnant like his had been lately. She read her Bible on her lunch breaks, and made odd analogies using Bible stories that she got only half the facts right on.

Man, he had it bad.

A punch in the arm brought his mind back around. "Ouch. What was that for?"

Stew sat beside him, his legs bent and arms draped over his knees. "You were daydreaming, probably about your assistant."

"It wasn't like that."

"No?"

Reuben punched the ground with his fist. "This could ruin my business, Stew. And what if Livy finds out?" Even though they were technically still on a break, they'd been talking more, and Livy was acting like her old, clingy self.

Stew clapped him on the back. "I don't know what to tell you about that. But I'd apologize to Maddie, bring her chocolate as a peace offering, pretend everything is normal beyond that and pray like crazy."

"I've been praying nonstop for two days."

"Good. Oh, and whatever you do, don't kiss her again."

Reuben nodded, but even while he knew that, he was afraid if presented with the opportunity, he'd do it again in a heartbeat.

***

Maddie clutched the strap of her oversized handbag and hastened her pace into Reuben's office. Anything to avoid Livy's look of disdain or even worse, a conversation. Thankfully, the woman seemed to prefer giving her dirty looks over actually talking to her. Maddie could only wonder how she'd be treated if Livy knew she'd kissed Reuben too.

She shut the door behind her a little harder than necessary, relieved that her boss wasn't at his desk. Maybe she'd get lucky and he wouldn't show up at all today.

This was all his fault anyway. He shouldn't have kissed her. Men were all the same and wanted only one thing. A woman and a bed. And even then they'd settle for a backseat.

She was done putting out for jerks though. God made it clear that sex was only for marriage. Maddie had no desire to be hitched to anyone, let alone a guy who obviously didn't have a problem locking lips with another woman.

He hadn't insinuated he wanted more. But all men did. It was a fact of life.

Sitting down at her desk, she clicked on her computer and started in on the mounds of paperwork in front of her. It didn't seem like Reuben had done a thing since she'd left the previous day, except for adding things to do onto her stack with sticky notes covered in scribbles attached. The guy was administratively clueless. And this job was turning out impossible to do on a part-time basis.

An hour later, she stood up and walked to the cabinet to file some paid invoices when the office door opened. Reuben stepped inside, a hand behind his back, and smiled at her.

Maddie frowned. Something wasn't right. She turned back to her filing, hoping he'd just leave well enough alone.

"Did you have a good morning at the Cut 'N' Style?"

No such luck. "I did. I, uh, was just getting ready to use the ladies' room, if you'll excuse me." She didn't really need to go, but maybe she'd just wash her hands again or something. Anything to avoid conversation.

To her horror, Reuben walked straight to her and put his free hand on her shoulder. Surely he wouldn't try to kiss her here, with Livy right outside. "Reuben—"

"We need to talk."

Weren't women the ones who wanted to talk and guys the ones who tried to avoid it? Reuben was as masculine as they came. Someone needed to remind him of the stereotype. "About what?" *Please, God, I really don't want to talk about the kiss. Or my past. Or Livy. Or marriage. I really, really don't. Please make him just shut up or go away.*

"I'm sorry. I shouldn't have done what I did."

That put things mildly. "Apology accepted. Can I go now?"

"So you're okay with everything?"

She clenched her fist. The man just couldn't leave well enough alone. "No, I'm not okay with it, Reuben. But can we please just forget about it?"

"I'm not sure what else I can say to make this right."

Angry heat pricked at her skin. "You can't, okay? The last time a guy kissed me he ended it with a slap in my face and a fist in my belly, so I guess I should be thankful you weren't quite so rough, but I'm not giddy about talking about the experience."

She turned back to her filing, but her blood was bubbling and she was on a roll. Her voice grew louder as she went, shoving papers into random files with the force of an F-5 tornado. "I thought you were different, a decent guy who cared about women instead of all the other lowlife men I've known who only care about one thing. But no, you went in for the kill anyway. Bravo, Reuben, you proved my theory about men is right on."

She gave the file drawer a shove, slamming it closed, then grabbed her purse. "I'm leaving early."

Reuben took a step toward her. "Maddie, I'm sorry." He shoved a box into her hands. "I brought you chocolate."

Looking at him, her emotions warred inside her. Could a man be that stupid? Really? "You think chocolate makes it better?"

He flushed. "No, I—"

She shook her head. "I can't deal with this today. I just need to go home."

"You'll be back tomorrow though?"

Against her better judgment. "In the morning. Judy asked me to come in the afternoon instead."

"That'll be fine. We can finish talking then."

Dread plopped a seat in the middle of her belly. "Great."

"You do know I'd never hurt you, right?"

She wiped her eye to prevent a tear from falling. "I thought I did, but—"

He took two giant steps toward her and wrapped his arms around her shoulders, pulling her into a hug. "Maddie, I promise, I'll never hurt you. I may act on impulse and do stupid things, but you never need to be afraid of me."

Needing to put distance between her and this man who repulsed her and drew her like a magnetic force field at the same time, Maddie pushed out of his arms, grabbed her purse and the chocolate, and walked out the door.

# 23

*I*ndependence Day was officially one of Maddie's favorite holidays.

Food, fireworks, and a day to celebrate being independent from people who tried to control your life . . . and country.

Yet why was it that on the day she celebrated independence, she felt even more dependent than ever?

She was headed to the Lake Holiday Independence Day Fest.

With the Callahan family.

Joy, oh Joy.

The plan was to meet at Reuben's after church, then head over to the beach together.

Pulling into his driveway beside Allie's minivan, Maddie questioned her sanity. She'd barely said a word to her boss the whole week, yet now she was willingly going to his house to go to a party with him, his family, and his soon-to-be fiancée.

At least she assumed they were still getting engaged. It hadn't been announced, but neither had an official breakup either.

Time would tell.

She took her time walking up the sidewalk. The house wasn't grand, but it had character. You couldn't see the entrance from the road because the sidewalk lined the garage and took a turn to get to steps that led to the front door. The dark wood vertical siding added warmth with a tinge of mystery.

It matched its owner perfectly, except it probably didn't brood when it was mad.

Maddie knocked, and a second later, Allie opened the door looking all motherish with her khaki Bermuda shorts and blue t-shirt sporting a shiny, sequined flag covering the front. A headband with wired red, white, and blue streamers going in all directions and blue socks with white stars completed the look.

Maddie swallowed the giggle that threatened to burst. "Nice outfit."

Allie smiled. "Wait 'til you see the back." She spun around, then looked over her shoulder. "Cool, huh?"

Not quite the word Maddie would use. A large firework burst had been made out of sequins to cover almost the whole back, and written in the bottom with sparkly red fabric glue was, "I'm a firecracker!"

Said firecracker turned back around, all grins. "I made it myself. Cole said he planned to tell everyone he's adopted if I wear it to the picnic. I told him I have his bare baby-butt pictures I can show everyone to prove otherwise, not to mention some fabulous birthing footage on DVD."

That was one movie she'd skip out on too. "Nice ammunition."

"I thought so."

This occasion was the one time she thought God was okay with a little fib. "Well, I don't care what he says, I think it's fantastic. You're certainly creative."

Her friend grinned from one ear to the other. "I'm so glad you think so." She handed Maddie a gift bag. "Because I made you one too."

Maddie swallowed her protest to spare her friend's feelings and peeked in the bag. "Wow. You really shouldn't have gone to all the trouble."

Allie pulled her into the room. "Hurry and go change. The bathroom's down the hall on the left. Livy will be here any minute, then we'll get going."

Never mind. The Fourth was no longer her favorite holiday. She should have realized Livy would be coming too. Duh. "Great."

Since no valid, courteous excuse to turn around and run away came to mind, she lifted the gift bag, smiled, and turned to go clown-up.

She was going to look ridiculous at her first public function. Just peachy.

Reuben's house wasn't exactly familiar, as she'd only been there the one time, and then, it was dark. She walked through the living room with its tall, pointed wood ceilings and down the hallway.

Only one picture graced the hall, and it was a Christmas shot of Allie's kids.

Now which door was the bathroom? On the left, but there were three doors, all closed.

Eeny, Meeny, Miny, Mo.

She opted for the third one and knocked on the door. When no answer came, she reached for the knob, but the door opened before she could turn it, sending her sprawling into the room and into a bare-chested man.

Large arms caught her and set her upright. "Fall much?"

She pushed away and kept her eyes trained on his face, even though her peripheral vision told her that he wore green swim trunks and a pair of flip-flops. "Reuben. I was, uh, looking for the bathroom."

"Wrong door."

Looking past him, she saw that now. An iron queen-sized bed stood in the middle of the room with a solid blue comforter. Clothes were tossed over the footboard and a few more lay scattered on the floor.

"Sorry. Allie said left, but not which one. I chose door number three."

"I believe door number two's what you're looking for."

Maddie put a hand against the doorjamb to steady herself. "Right. Thanks."

Reuben crossed his arms across his broad chest and cocked a half smile. "You need anything else?"

Blinking, she realized she'd been staring at him. "No, sorry, I'm going now. Thanks for the, uh, directions."

Inside the bathroom, she pounded her head on the porcelain sink. What in the world was wrong with her? She turned on the faucet and splashed cold water on her face.

Men were in her past, not her future. Except for Kyle, of course. But she'd teach him to be a good guy, not a jerk like the rest of them.

Her glance met the gift bag decorated with tiny flags.

It didn't really matter anyway, because after she showed up in that number, guys would hardly be flocking around her.

A quick shirt change, and she resembled something off a scrapbook page.

She didn't even look in the mirror on her way out. It would just be too awful.

Allie clapped her hands when she emerged into the living room. "You look fantastic!"

Livy had arrived, and now stood in a pair of shorts that were lucky to come an inch below her tush and a bikini top.

Dump a bucket of water over her and she'd be ready for the cover of the swimsuit edition of *Sports Illustrated*.

Reuben, a black tank top now in place, emerged from the kitchen and jerked to a stop, almost dropping the Coke can in his hand. "Uh, wow. You and Allie . . . match."

Maddie forced a smile, thankful for her one-piece swimsuit underneath that she'd given in and purchased yesterday. The moment Allie wasn't looking, this shirt was coming off.

They all made their way out to Allie's van, which barely fit them all. The three kids took the very back, and Reuben and Livy sat in the middle seat.

Maddie turned to Allie. "How about I just drive separately?"

She shook her head and opened the passenger side door. "Don't worry, there's room, It's an eight-passenger van. Besides, you need a pass to get in. Oh, I'll be right back, I forgot my purse." She turned and scurried back up the walk.

Maddie swiveled to where Reuben sat on the seat, Livy on the other side of him. Both of them looked about ready to bust up laughing.

She glared at them and lowered her voice. "Shut up and scoot over."

A hush filled the van on the drive to the beach on Lake Holiday. Allie attempted to get everyone to join into a riveting rendition of "God Bless America," but she had no takers.

At the beach, Cole took off with friends, Allie took Bethany and Sara to the bathroom, Stew left to help oversee the sack races. And Livy hung on Reuben's arm and smiled. "You look so festive today, Maddie."

"Yeah, well, it's for the country, what can I say." She eyed the direction Allie went and saw her crazy friend disappear into the lodge. Operation ditch-the-shirt commenced. She pulled it over her head and folded it up and set it with the pile of towels and other things they'd deposited on the ground. If someone stole it . . . well, that'd just be too bad.

She glanced at Reuben and Livy, who stood there watching her. "Now, I'm going down to the water. See ya later."

⌒⌒

She had a tattoo.

His feisty, sassy assistant had a tattoo on the small of her back the size of his fist. He watched her slim figure walk down toward the beach, her hips swaying slightly but not exaggerated like Livy's usually were.

A pull on his arm brought him back to earth. "Reuben, I'm hungry."

He shifted his focus and gulped. His eyes needed to behave. Even though he and Livy were tenuous at best and hadn't officially called the engagement back on or completely off, he still didn't need to be ogling another woman at the beach.

Especially when that woman was Maddie.

"All right, what do you want?"

"The barbeque sounds good."

He smiled and wrapped an arm around her. "Fantastic."

On their way over to the food, Livy leaned her head on his shoulder. "At least now we have confirmation."

He glanced down at her. "Of what?"

"Your assistant. I mean, really? A tattoo? A little one on your ankle, maybe, but not that monstrosity. The woman's just trashy, Reuben."

"Maddie isn't trash. She's had a hard life."

She flipped her blonde curls to the other side. "Whatever. I don't want to talk about her anyway. Guess what I picked up yesterday?"

Not the ring. Please not the ring. He'd actually forgotten about the over-sized, over-priced diamond they'd picked out weeks ago that was being resized. "Livy, we haven't had a chance to talk since—"

She cut him off by pulling him to the side and around to face her. "I was wrong that day. I overreacted. Can you forgive me?"

"Of course, but it's not that simple." This isn't where he wanted to have this conversation. Mostly because he still wasn't sure what he was going to say. He needed to tell her about the kiss. And after he did, he doubted there was going to be a lot left to talk about anyway. "Let's just enjoy today, and we can talk about it tomorrow, okay?"

She lifted to her tippy-toes and pecked him on the cheek. "I agree. Today will be our fun special day."

Hmm. That went better than he'd expected. No tears or stomping feet or demands to talk now. But the day was still early.

They met up with Allie and the kids who were already in the BBQ line and inhaled some of the most delicious food on the earth. The group met up with Stew at the beach to begin their traditional sand castle build.

Maddie stood beside Stew, a piece of paper in her hand. "I think we can do it."

Stew put a hand to his chin. "It's risky. Totally could bomb."

She patted him on the back. "I have faith in you, Stew."

Reuben plucked the piece of paper out of her hand and turned it over to see the proposed design, then shook his head. "Not going to work. No way."

Maddie snatched it back. "You're just chicken. No guts, no glory."

"No, I'm realistic. You can't make a Statue of Liberty out of sand."

She hitched a thumb behind her. "That guy over there is making the White House, so we have to step it up a notch."

The woman was going to make Stew crash and burn. And Stew was famous for his sand castles. "Maybe if you just did a picture of it . . . lying down or something."

"Nope, we're doing this baby upright and four feet tall."

"Four . . . what? You've got to be kidding me. That's insane."

Stew nudged Maddie with his elbow. "Maybe Reuben's right."

She gave Reuben a look that would burn sand. "You just go over and do something you're good at . . . maybe the Angelina Jolie lip contest or something. Leave the building to the professionals, okay?"

The group snickered and Reuben rubbed his lips. "I don't have Angelina lips, and I'm not putting on lipstick to prove it, thank you. Livy and I will go check out the Anything that Floats contenders. We'll be back to watch you eat your words."

He tugged Livy along with him as they headed to where groups were preparing contraptions for the water. He'd made one a few years ago. It came in last place, so he had stuck to helping Stew with the sand castle.

It looked like his assistant was helping him with that task too.

Two hours later, after unsuccessfully trying to convince Livy to participate in anything remotely fun, they returned see the castle judging.

And there, close to five feet off the ground, stood a stunning replica of the famous Lady of Liberty.

Beside her stood a beaming Maddie and a puffed up Stew, along with Allie and the kids, getting their picture taken by onlookers.

Livy whistled. "Well, I guess she did it, huh."

If it had been a previous year, and anyone else, he'd have had envy spilling out his ears. But he didn't begrudge Maddie even an ounce of her victory. "Yeah, I guess so."

Maddie started toward them, and Reuben cleared his throat to prepare for the crow he'd be eating any second. "Whadya think, boss man?"

"What can I say, you proved me wrong."

Livy patted his shoulder. "Hey, I think Elvis is going to take the stage soon. I think it's about time for . . ." she winked at him, "you know—"

He tore his eyes off the sand marvel to Livy, who wasn't making a lick of sense. "Time for what?"

She pulled his arm toward the stage and laughed. "Oh, stop it, you know what."

"Livy, I am not getting on stage with Elvis."

She hopped onto the stage and grabbed the microphone. "Attention everyone!"

A sickening pit festered in Reuben's stomach. What was she doing?

"Reuben, come up here. It's time for our announcement." She waved him up.

Hands pushed him from behind, and he had no choice but to comply or look like an idiot. The only announcement he could think of was *not* one he intended to make today. They hadn't talked about it specifically, but surely she didn't think—

"You all know that Reuben and I have dated for a while, and well, Reuben's asked me to marry him, and I've accepted!"

# 24

Maddie covered her mouth to keep it from dropping in shock. While she had wondered what exactly the status of her boss's relationship was, she'd decided it wasn't any of her business.

In a billion years she wasn't expecting this.

Especially after that stupid kiss.

She turned and shoved past Allie and Stew, who both stood with eyes bulging, and walked down the beach to a spot less crowded and plopped onto the sand.

Engaged.

Reuben was engaged.

She shouldn't care. Should be happy for him. Relieved even.

But she wasn't.

Not even close.

He'd just proven her theory about men. They didn't care who they hurt in their quest to conquer women.

Bile rose up in her stomach. She'd been the object of such conquests one too many times, and there was no way she'd let him affect her again.

For the last week, she'd refused to talk to him, yet the memory of his lips stuck with her, hard and fast, like a blood-sucking tick.

Sand oozed through her fingers as she tried to grip a hand-ful. She lifted her hand and threw the tan particles, watching them float limply to the ground in front of her.

She could leave. Start over in a new town, but then her dream of rescuing Kyle would be out of reach.

Or she could stay and be strong. She couldn't cower and run every time a man crossed her path. Reuben was the one who would be sorry for messing with her.

"Maddie?" Allie stood beside her, hands in the pockets of her shorts. "Wanna talk?"

She shrugged. "Nothing really to talk about."

Her friend sat down beside her and elbowed her in the side. "We can talk about how you ditched the shirt as soon as I was out of eyesight."

Oh, yeah. The shirt. "I, uh, was hot."

"Liar, liar, pants on fire."

Maddie chuckled. "Fine. It was hideous, and I didn't want to be seen. That better?"

"Brutally honest. Now that's the Maddie I know."

Lying back on the sand, Maddie stared at the fading blue sky, hardly a cloud visible. Lucky for it. "You're a good friend, Allie."

"What do you think about my new future sister-in-law?"

Poor Allie, having that woman in her family. "She deserves him, that's what I think."

Allie shifted in the sand and stared at her. "Now that was mean."

It was meant to be, but Allie was his sister, and if some women ever dissed Kyle like that, she'd get decked. "I wish them all the happiness in the world in their marriage. How's that?"

"A little better." A crooked smile tipped Allie's lips. "I had kinda hoped. . . ."

"What, your brother and me? No way. I know you thought Livy was jealous, but she can have him. I'll be perfectly happy, ninety years old, rocking on the front porch, all by myself. Maybe Kyle will have some kids and I can be the fun Auntie. I don't need a man to have a life."

Allie lay back in the sand beside her. "Why are you scared of guys?"

Maddie tossed a handful of sand onto her friend. "They have cooties, duh."

"Seriously, Maddie."

Her chest constricted, feeling like gravity was pinning her to the ground, taking her breath. "I don't want to talk about it."

"Sometimes talking is healing for the soul."

Maddie sat up and looked out at kids splashing in the water down the beach. "Sometimes it rips open old scars and makes you bleed to death."

Allie sat up too and squeezed her arm. "I happen to know that God has this amazing first-aid kit just for such occasions. I won't make you talk, but I'm here if you ever want to, 'kay?"

She got up and walked back toward the party, leaving Maddie alone with her past.

⊷❧

*This is a mess, God.*

Reuben made a random right turn down a deserted country road and hit the gas until the speed of his car matched the pace of adrenaline running through his veins.

He was engaged. Like it or not, he hadn't been able to humiliate himself or Livy in front of everyone. And back at the house, she'd kissed him and said she needed to get home, then left without a chance for them to talk.

So now here he was, driving ninety miles an hour past fields of budding corn stalks, trying to figure out the rest of his life.

He pressed on the brake as a stop sign waved in front of him.

The car screeched to a stop.

Much like his life had this last week.

The latest profit numbers from Wade, his accountant, weren't good. Opening another restaurant looked riskier every day.

His assistant hated him and was barely saying a word to him.

He was engaged to a woman who he wasn't sure he was even in love with anymore.

Lovers had quarrels. Annoyed each other. But this was more than just another fight.

He'd kissed Maddie. Until she'd pushed him away, he'd completely enjoyed the experience.

The sparks that had been missing with Livy for so long definitely were present and accounted for with Maddie.

Those sparks now threatened to catch him on fire and destroy everything.

He turned left and made his way, slower this time, to his mom's driveway. A light shone in an upstairs bedroom.

At least they weren't asleep yet.

His mother deserved to hear the news from him and not through the gossip channels.

Especially since he determined to set things right with Livy in the morning.

He rang the doorbell and, a moment later, a bathrobe-clad Gary opened the door. "Reuben, everything okay?"

Like he cared. "Yeah, need to talk to Mom."

Gary opened the door wider. "Come on in. I can put a pot of coffee on."

"No need. Is Mom asleep?"

"No, she's actually not here."

Had his mother come to her senses and left him? Doubtful. "Where is she?"

"She and some girlfriends decided to be one with their youth and have an old-fashioned slumber party. Figured Fourth of July was a grand night for it. They left for Miss Agnes's house right after the city's fireworks. Giddy as a schoolgirl about it. Even borrowed a hair iron thing from Maddie that's supposed to make her hair all, uh, kinked or something like that?"

"Crimped you mean?" He only knew that because he had a sister who grew up in the early 90s.

"Something like that. So, anything I can help you with?"

"No. Just wanted to tell her some private news."

Gary padded in black slippers into the kitchen and yelled from the other room. "You mean the engagement?"

Reuben followed and leaned against the doorjamb between the kitchen and dining room and scowled. "How do you know about that?"

"Allie called." He handed Reuben a cup of coffee. "Said it surprised everyone."

Including the would-be groom. He shook his head at the coffee and turned to leave. "I'll come back in the morning."

Gary followed him and sat down on the bottom step of the front staircase. "Reuben, you never have told me why you're so angry with me. It'd be nice to know."

Reuben pivoted around to face the man who made his blood boil every time he saw him. "I can't believe you can even sit there and ask me that."

He held out his hands. "Give me a chance to explain."

Reuben pointed a finger at the man he had an extremely hard time not hating. "You took his life, then walked in and took over his home, his wife, and everything he loved. You don't deserve a chance."

He turned and slammed the door on his way out.

# 25

The hand came at him so fast he barely had time to flinch.

He winced at the stinging impact of Livy's palm on his cheek.

"I can't believe you did this to me. You kissed her, Reuben? While we were engaged?"

"Technically we were on a break, Liv. But still, it was wrong. You have every right to be mad."

Her cheeks blazed fire red as she paced his office, arms flailing. "Mad? You think I'm mad? Oh, buddy, I've gone so far past mad there are no words for it." She stopped and turned to him, her hands on her hips. "We just announced our engagement yesterday, Reuben."

A muscle in his jaw jerked, and Reuben dug into his gut and pulled out every ounce of reserve and patience he possessed. "You announced it and drug me along."

Her mouth dropped and she took a step closer to him, her finger poking his chest with each syllable. "No, no, no. You are the one who planned the Fourth of July engagement announcement, not me."

"That was before we took a break and you know it."

Anger fell from her face replaced by tears. "I can't believe you're doing this to me. Are you leaving me for her, Reuben? Is that what you're saying?"

Doubtful, given Maddie's silent treatment. "No. Maddie and I don't have a future. The kiss shouldn't have happened. She was as mad as you are about it."

Livy snorted her disbelief. "Yeah right. She's been making her move on you since day one, Reuben. I tried to warn you."

A moment of doubt seized him. But no, Maddie wasn't like that. "She only wants to get custody of her little brother and needs money and a stable job. That's it."

Livy crossed her arms across her black button up dress shirt. "And don't you think a stable boyfriend would be helpful too? One who has money?"

Given his shrinking bank account of late, Maddie was barking up the wrong tree if she thought that. "I'm not making excuses for what I did. It was wrong, but don't blame Maddie. She is just as much a victim as you."

Livy collapsed in the guest chair. "What does this mean for us, Reuben?"

Reuben leaned back against the edge of his desk. "I don't expect you to forgive me." He looked down at the woman who'd been a part of his life since he was sixteen years old. "I guess it means we're over."

The blonde-headed beauty looked up at him and stared for a full minute before responding, her voice quivering with emotion. "Fire her, Reuben. Fire her today, and we'll get through this. I'll forgive you, and we can move on."

He shook his head. For legal reasons alone, he couldn't do that. "I'm not going to do that, Livy."

She stood, her chin tilted high. She straightened her shirt and cleared her throat. "Then I guess we're through. If you'll excuse me, I need to get the dining room ready for lunch."

❦

"I have good news and bad news. Which one you want first?"

Maddie sucked in a breath at Corina's words as she turned the Tracker into The Emporium's parking lot. She was just getting there after her shift at the salon. "Let's get the bad over with."

She needed to end on a good note, because going in there to face the newly engaged moron-of-the-year was going to be difficult enough.

It was all she could do not to text him her resignation notice.

And would have, except she needed the job, and texts cost twenty cents she couldn't afford to waste on him.

"The Blakelys officially asked me for the petition paperwork. I anticipate having it back in the next week or two and scheduling their home study sometime in August."

No, no, no. This couldn't be happening. Maddie punched the steering wheel, and the horn blared, her bruised heart almost leaping from her chest.

"What was that?"

"Nothing." She dipped her head when eyes from inside the restaurant looked through the window in her direction. "How long do I have before I've blown my shot?"

"It'll probably go before a judge in September at the earliest."

Not a lot of time. She needed to get her house sooner than later. It'd take her a while to save up money to furnish it and show that she could handle another mouth to feed.

And September was less than two months away.

"What's the good news?"

"I've pulled a few strings and scheduled some time for Kyle to come visit you in Sandwich this summer."

Maddie's hands shook. "When?"

"If you can swing it, weekend after next. You do have a place big enough for him to stay, right?"

Even with getting paid this coming Friday, she would barely have the money for deposit and first month's rent, much less get any furnishings.

But they'd camp out on the floor if it came to that.

And Reuben had said the house was available immediately. "Yes, yes I do."

"You'll have to come get him and take him home."

The dollar signs added up with gas and meals. But she could pack PB&Js. "I'll make it work."

"What about your job? You don't work weekends, do you?"

Judy scheduled her an occasional Saturday, but she was sure she could swing that one off. "Not usually."

"I also think he can come again over Labor Day weekend before school starts. The Blakelys wanted to make sure you knew that they still planned to have you in his life, so this is their olive branch to you."

If the branch didn't include her brother visiting, she would have taken it and broken it into a billion pieces. "Labor Day would be perfect."

She discussed times then hung up the phone. A to-do list a mile long filtered through her brain, and her fingers itched for her steno pad at her desk.

The first thing on her list though: Make nice with her boss.

Because as mad as she was with him, she needed her job.

If she had to kiss a few frogs to get her brother-the-prince to safety, then this sister would pucker up and do just that.

# 26

The frog sat at his desk pounding hunt-and-peck style on his laptop keyboard. "You're late."

Maddie looked at her watch. Barely after four, a whole ten minutes late. Call in the firing squad now. Instead of defending herself, she opted for sarcasm. The one thing her boss understood. "You're cranky. I thought being engaged, you would be giddy and all floating in the clouds on the high of love."

"We're not."

"Not giddy?"

He didn't look up. "Not engaged. Now get to work."

That was fast. Not that she really cared. "Sorry about that."

His eyes met hers briefly before going back to the screen. "I told her we kissed. She wanted me to fire you, and I said no. Wedding bells flew out the window. Happy?"

Maddie swallowed and searched for words. Her shocked brain couldn't find many. "Sorry?"

"Don't be. Just get to work and don't make me regret not sending you packing."

She set her purse under her desk. His engagement, or lack thereof, shouldn't matter to her anyway. This was her place of employment. And that's all. "You have payroll hours checked for me to enter?"

He nodded to the basket she'd set on the edge of his desk. "Where you told me to put them."

Only a week ago he'd whined about implementing the basket and refused to use it.

Maybe being single agreed with him. "Thanks. I'll get right on it."

"I'm surprised you're talking to me again. I still expected the silent treatment."

She sat in her chair and booted up the computer. "First, let's remember. You kissed me. There is no 'we kissed' here."

"You kissed me back for a second."

Maddie spun around, her jaw slack. "I did not."

"Kid yourself all you like, but for a moment, you enjoyed it."

The egotistical pig. "I hated every gross second of it."

"What's your second?"

Maddie blinked. "What?"

"You said, 'first, blah blah blah.' That implies a second."

She swallowed the words she ached to call him. *Kissing frogs, kissing frogs.* "Kyle's coming for a visit. In less than two weeks."

His typing ceased. "Really? That's fantastic."

Maddie bit her lip. "Yeah, but I have a lot to do before then. Do you know if that house is still available?"

He nodded once. "We can move you in this weekend. I'll talk to Allie and we'll get it all arranged."

Resentment burned in her belly. While she welcomed help, she didn't need anyone controlling her. "I don't have anything really to move except my bags. I'll have to furnish a little at a time."

"You can't sleep on the floor."

She shrugged. "Air mattresses are cheap."

"What will you sit on?"

"The floor is carpeted. We'll survive."

"Utensils? Plates? Or do you plan to do take out everyday?"

She shook her head. "Paper and plastic. Don't worry, Reuben. I've got it handled. I just need your help contacting Tim so I can finalize the details. Actually, never mind. Gary or Betty can probably do that."

He sat back in his chair and studied her long enough that she squirmed and turned back to her computer. "You don't want to trust me, do you?"

She typed a few numbers into the payroll software. "Do I have reason to?"

"I kissed you, Maddie. And while I regret it, I think you'd hate me regardless."

Her fingers hovered before she let them drop to her lap. "I don't hate you."

"Really? News to me."

She shrugged. "I dislike men in general."

Reuben leaned his elbows on the desk. "Well, at least I'm in good company."

"If you call them good, then you're proving my point."

"Is it your dad or that old boyfriend you mentioned?"

Maddie pushed her chair away. "I'm going to get a drink."

"Running doesn't solve your problems."

She glanced back at him. "No, but it helps me shove them far away so I don't have to think about them for a very long time. And I'm okay with that."

"What was his name?"

Her hand gripped the doorknob. "None of your business."

"You're right. It's not."

She looked back at him, and something in his eyes, a genuine interest in caring for her, loosened her tongue. "Ryan. His name was Ryan."

"Give me his address and I'll make him wish he never set eyes on you."

She snorted. "He'd break you in two seconds flat."

"Probably. But I'd try."

As much as she wanted to hate Reuben right now, a small part of her thawed. He was joking, of course, but the thought was nice. "Thanks for that."

"What'd he do?"

She added a layer of mortar around the collapsing bricks that surrounded her heart. "None of your business."

He stood and walked over to her, hands safely in his pockets. "You can trust me."

She shook her head and opened the door. "No, no I can't." God was the only one who knew everything. The only one she could trust with the whole story.

And that was the way it would stay.

&

Why did he have to push? Why couldn't he have just left it alone as she'd asked?

Maddie lay on her bed, unwanted memories invading her peace.

It'd been four days, and she'd barely slept more than a couple hours total.

She'd come home from the Emporium early at Reuben's insistence. Said she'd been working too much and needed to rest.

But a nap had proved impossible.

She rubbed her bare arms as a shiver came across her body, despite the eighty degree heat outside. Memories of the men in her life overwhelmed her.

Mark had been her first. She'd only been fourteen and he was sixteen with a car, but by then her mom was dead, her dad was drunk every night, and she'd have given anything to get out of the house. So she started arranging for Kyle to sleep over at a friend's house and let Mark take her away for the evening. When she got home, her dad would be passed out on the sofa and, in the morning, didn't remember coming home to an empty house.

In her young mind, Mark was her savior. They'd go park someplace quiet, and he held her while she cried. Then he would kiss away her tears. Every time he'd go a little further with her, but when she asked him to stop, he did.

That went on for about two weeks until he got tired of being told no. He said that all the other couples did it, and if she really loved him, she'd let him.

And she did. The whole ordeal was awkward, painful, and humiliating. But Mark had said he loved her over and over. And she could deal with the pain as long as he loved her.

The next day at school, he ignored her completely. When she tried to talk to him, he winked at her and walked away.

Later, she heard some guys laughing and talking about it. Evidently someone had bet Mark to have sex with a stupid freshman, and Maddie had been the choice. The next week, she saw him walking down the hall with Tina, a tall, curvy blonde cheerleader, draped on his arm.

Her humiliation was complete.

But then again, Mark was only the first in a string of very bad men she would hook up with.

A knock filled the air of the small guesthouse, and Maddie breathed a thanks to God for the diversion from her thoughts.

She opened the door, and Reuben stood outside, looking as handsome as ever. She wanted to punch him.

"It's almost moving day."

Maddie forced a smile. "Yes, tomorrow."

Reuben's brow wrinkled, his eyes probing. "I thought you were going to nap. You look awful."

"Now that makes me feel so much better."

"What's going on, Maddie?"

"Nothing."

His expression told her that he didn't believe her a lick. Thankfully, he let the topic drop. "Allie, Stew, and the kids are going out for pizza, and I was going to join them. Thought you'd like to tag along?"

She almost said no, but getting out and away from her memories sounded like heaven.

"Sure, where and when?"

He smiled, a slight dimple appearing on his cheek that she hadn't noticed before. "Now, and we're going to Gene's."

"I'm not sure where that is. Will you give me directions?"

Reuben shook his head. "No, but I'll be glad to escort you there."

"I don't want to impose."

The man looked decidedly agitated as he put his fingers through his hair. "Look, think of it as my 'going green' initiative. I have to come back by here after we're through anyway. We'll save gas and the environment all at the same time."

"I didn't realize you were so altruistic."

The smile that came to his lips was a bit ornery. "There are many things about me you don't realize yet."

And that right there was the reason she wanted to drive separately.

# 27

*R*euben lied. Maddie forced a smile and clenched her fists so tight her nails cut into her palms.

"Surprise!" The gathered crowd shouted, but all Maddie wanted to do was run.

Reuben leaned over and whispered in her ear. "Don't blame me. It was my mom's idea."

Not what she wanted to hear. Reuben, she could take aside later, yell at, and punch in the arm. Betty, not so much.

Everyone started talking at once, the noise of it all overwhelming her. Reuben led her to a seat at the head of the table and took the chair next to her.

Most of the people around the table she knew, but a few faces were unfamiliar. There were a few waitresses from the restaurant who weren't on duty tonight, Miss Agnes, Cyndi and Judy from the salon, Betty and Gary, Allie and Stew and the kids, the pastor and his wife, and a few women from church she recognized as having been introduced a few times.

On a table off to the side sat a mound of wrapped gifts.

Betty stood and tapped her spoon on the corner of her glass. "Attention everyone." The room started to quiet down, and everyone's eyes turned to Betty, who in turn looked at Maddie.

"We wanted to get together to officially welcome you into our town and our hearts, and to give you a good start into your new home. Think of this as a housewarming shower."

Didn't they only have showers for weddings and babies? Neither of which she would be having anytime ever.

All eyes turned toward her and an uncomfortable silence followed. Realizing everyone expected her to say something, she scooted her chair out and stood. This was why she'd never become a politician. Being the center of attention wasn't her cup of tea, and lying through her teeth to a bunch of people didn't come naturally. "I appreciate everyone coming out tonight, for your kind thoughts and welcome. I'm—overwhelmed, I'm not sure what else to say."

A waitress approaching the table gave a much needed excuse for Maddie to sit down, and the chatter around the table started up again as the woman started passing out drinks. She gave a narrowed glance to Reuben. "You could have warned me, you know."

He looked affronted. "What? And ruin the surprise? More than that, I really don't care to risk the wrath of my mother."

"Your mom wouldn't hurt a fly."

Betty made her way to them. "Don't underestimate me, Maddie. Reuben learned long ago by a good hard whoopin' on his hind-end not to disobey his momma." She bent down and kissed him on the forehead.

Reuben put an arm around his mom's waist and squeezed. "That's right. I've been a perfect, obedient angel from then on."

She swatted his hand away. "Now, Reub, I also taught you not to lie, young man."

Maddie blinked away tears, memories of her own mom inching their way out of the box she'd hidden them in so long ago. As embarrassed as she was already tonight, no use topping it off with tears.

The waitress approached and put a Coke down at Maddie's spot. "They ordered this for you, but if you'd rather have something else, just let me know."

"It's fine, thank you."

The waitress left, and Betty made her way around the table to talk with the pastor.

Reuben put a hand to her shoulder. "You're not really mad, right?"

She shrugged, effectively removing his hand that was sending shivers down her back. "I'm not huge on being the center of attention, and I already feel like I'm mooching off you all too much, so presents just add insult to injury."

"I tried to tell her that, but Mom's persistent."

She smiled, a spot inside her pleased that he knew her well enough to plead her case. "I'm surprised you didn't have it at the Emporium though."

Reuben shifted in his seat and cleared his throat. "We were going to but changed the plans."

Maddie could guess the reason but wanted to hear it from the frog's lips. "Why?"

He took a swig of his drink. "I was in the mood for pizza."

A hand on her other shoulder startled her, and she looked up to see the pastor.

"I haven't had a chance to say hello on Sunday morning but wanted to formally welcome you to town and to our church."

The fault was her own, as she dodged out of church every Sunday for fear of someone grilling her. Given the sins of her past, Maddie preferred to stay in the background. She stood and accepted the hand held out. The man had kind eyes and a firm handshake and wore blue jeans and a polo shirt. Weren't pastors supposed to be in suits and ties?

His wife stood next to him, wearing shorts and a modest tank top, and a little girl behind her, age two at the most, stood sucking her thumb. "I'm sorry we haven't had a chance to meet yet. I'm Kathy, and this is our daughter, Rachel." The little girl scooted farther behind her mom's leg at the sound of her name.

Kathy just laughed. "Sorry, she's a little shy."

The little girl gave a grin, and raised her hand in a half-wave.

Maddie's heart constricted. Why did babies have to be so cute? It almost made her want one of her own. Almost. Maddie waved back and smiled. "Nice to meet you, Rachel." Then she looked and mustered up a smile. "It's nice to meet both of you. Pastor, I really enjoy your sermons."

He let out a pleasant laugh. "Glad to hear it. If you need anything at all, let us know, okay? And hopefully soon we can have you over for dinner."

She nodded. "I'd enjoy it."

The couple moved on, and Maddie sat back down to see Reuben staring at her. "What?"

He raised his eyebrows. "I didn't realize my feisty assistant suffered from social anxiety."

Had she been that apparent? "I don't. What are you talking about?"

"I'm not blind. You were about ready to pass out talking with them."

"Not true. I thought I did fine." She sipped her drink, irritated that he'd mentioned anything. "Was it that noticeable?"

"Only to me. You're always so chipper dealing with people, and you're different tonight. And you never hang around at church to talk to anyone either. How are you going to meet friends if you don't socialize?"

She straightened her spine. "I have friends."

"Like who?"

*You.* "Your mom, Allie."

"Besides them."

The guy needed to give it a rest. But still, she wracked her brain for someone else. Half the people at this table she barely knew, so they wouldn't count. Desperate, she played her wild card. "Livy."

In any other situation, the exaggerated incredulous look on Reuben's face would have been comical, but right now it just irritated her. "What? You don't think we're friends?"

"If you both are friends, I'd sure hate to be one of your enemies."

Maddie opened her mouth to rebut, but the waitress bringing out the pizza interrupted them once again, saving her from telling a big fat lie that had a snowball's chance in Mexico of flying.

⤞

"Don't worry about the gifts. I'll get them." Reuben plucked a box containing silverware from Maddie's hands.

The little spitfire put her hands on her hips. "What? Am I incapable of carrying a box now?"

"No, I just—"

She grabbed the box back. "I'm not disabled, pregnant, or a child. I'm perfectly able to carry stuff, Reuben."

Irritating female. He was just trying to help. "Fine. I'll go get some more."

Why did women insist on being so headstrong? A courteous gesture only got a man yelled at these days. God forbid he open a door for one. He stomped back into the restaurant, the force of the action helping to relieve the tension he felt. It'd been a wild day, and he just needed a hot shower and a good night's sleep.

He stacked up the last of the presents and picking up the large pile turned and started out of the restaurant. Maddie met him halfway to the car.

"Here, let me get a few of those."

He glared at her, then mimicked in a mockingly high voice. "I'm not disabled, pregnant, or a child. I'm perfectly able to carry boxes."

She rolled her eyes at his joke as he continued on. He was almost to the car when he tripped on the curb. Boxes shifted and started to fall, but after an awkward balancing act, everything stilled.

Maddie chuckled behind him. "Should have let me help."

Were all females so impossible? Safely depositing the presents in his trunk, he slammed the lid, then grimaced. No use taking out his anger on his poor, expensive, stupid car.

Maddie stood waiting for him, her arms crossed over her chest. "You ready?"

"Yes. I should have thought to get the keys from Tim so we could take this stuff right over there tonight to unload instead of having to load and unload it twice."

Maddie raised her eyebrows. "Why not just keep it all in your trunk overnight and we can unload it at the house tomorrow?"

First she insulted his manhood, now his intelligence. Why was he so attracted to her again? "You're right."

She smiled. "It's okay. I'm your assistant. It's my job to be right."

And she did it so well too. Reuben got in the car, and as soon as Maddie was seated in the passenger seat, sped off.

She eyed him. "Easy, Roadrunner."

He eased off the gas a little, but not enough to make her think she was getting her way. "Did you enjoy your evening?"

"Yes. Everyone was so sweet and thoughtful. I'm still in shock."

He did his best hillbilly impersonation. "We small-town folk stick together, ya know."

"Well, from where I come from, it's more of a take-care-of-yourself attitude unless you're in a gang, so this takes a little getting used to."

He realized just how little about her past he knew. "Were you ever in one?"

She shook her head, and he breathed a sigh of relief. "No. Almost once. Really close actually, but something stopped me. More like someone."

"Who?"

"One of my dad's girlfriends. I still don't know what she saw in him. Most of the girls he brought home were drunks or druggies just like him, but she was different. She was nice to us."

Reuben gradually slowed, hoping to make the trip home last as long as he could so she would keep talking. "How'd she keep you from joining?"

A far off look came over Maddie's face. "She loved me. Before she came, I was so lonely. I mean, I had Kyle, but I was like his momma almost, trying to keep Dad from hitting him, and keeping him from all the druggies that tried to get him to sell. He was only seven, and they still tried to get him to join their gangs.

"Anyway, some of the girls told me there'd be protection in a gang. That they looked after each other, had one another's back. It sounded nice to actually be around people who cared about you. But then Rachel came. She listened to me, hugged me, made me lunch, made sure I had breakfast in the morning.

She loved Kyle and took care of him too. She told me those girls wouldn't really have my back, that they were lying, and I believed her."

"She sounds like a great person."

Maddie was silent for a moment. "She was."

Reuben wished he had driven slower as he pulled up to his parents' driveway and parked. The woman was like this puzzle of pain and hardships that came together to make an awe-inspiring picture. Yet there were still giant pieces missing.

He turned to face Maddie, but she was already opening the door and getting out.

He followed her up to her door, and when she turned around, he noticed her eyes filled with unshed tears. The poor girl was probably used to holding them in for as long as she could.

"What happened to her, Maddie?"

She lowered her head and pressed her fists to her eyes as if summoning her inner superwoman. "I don't know."

The tears rolled in earnest then, and nothing could stop Reuben from taking her into his arms. Not a romantic hug. Just a man comforting a hurting little girl.

When her sobs subsided, he heard her sniffle against his shirt. "I'm sorry, Reuben."

"Don't be."

"No, I shouldn't be doing this to you. It's not your problem. I know I sound like I'm not answering your question, but I really don't know. I'm not sure why Rachel was ever there. She knew Jesus like Momma did, so why she lived with a guy like Dad, I'll never know. But one day, I came home from school and she was gone. Dad didn't say a word. He just sat in his recliner, and when I asked, he shrugged. Like he didn't care. An hour later, child services came and took Kyle and me away."

"Do you think she reported him?"

Maddie pushed away from him. "Yes."

"Where do you think she went?"

She took a breath. "To be honest, I think he found out and killed her."

Reuben sucked in a breath. "Why do you think that?"

"When I got home from school that day, there was blood on the kitchen floor."

# 28

*T*he moment the words slipped from her mouth, Maddie wanted to snatch them back. She'd told someone her secret. The one thing she vowed never to tell a soul.

Reuben's eyes were dark and serious as he looked down at her. "Did you report it?"

"No, and I shouldn't have told you. Promise me you won't tell anyone, Reub. Promise me."

"I'm not sure I can do that, Maddie."

"I have no proof of anything. I just know when I got home that day, there were splatters of blood on the floor, and I could tell someone had tried to wipe some of it up. I didn't talk about it to my dad, I was so afraid. But I didn't want Kyle to see it either, so I mopped it up as quick as I could. Right after he got home, the cops pulled up. Nobody asked about her, and I didn't say anything."

"You should have."

She shook her head. "I didn't know anything about her, not even her last name or who her family was. For all they knew, she never existed. Plus, I was only fifteen."

Reuben ran a finger down her cheek, and Maddie shivered. "You were very brave, Madison."

"I was a scaredy-cat. And I got mad. That's why Kyle and I weren't together. The first foster home we had was okay, but I was so angry all I wanted to do was hit someone, and usually that someone was Kyle or another little boy in the home. Eventually they sent me to a girls' home, because no one wanted a violent sixteen-year-old. Kyle went to the Blakelys."

"You're going to get custody of him, Maddie. I'll do whatever I can to help."

She hugged her sides. "Thanks. But it'll be a long shot. The Blakelys are filling out the official petition this week."

Reuben moved to hug her again, but she took a step toward the house, her back resting on the door. "Reuben, you have to stop hugging me. It's not right."

He stared at her. "I'm not engaged anymore."

She shook her head. "I don't care to be a rebound girl, or anyone's girl."

His lip curled into a daring smirk. "And if I hug you anyway?"

She raised an eyebrow. "I'd use some of the self-defense moves I learned on the streets of Chicago. You pretended to talk like a girl earlier as a joke. Well, you might just be talking that way permanently."

He inched back a hair. "All right then. I guess you have a good evening, and I'll see you in the morning."

"Not too early. Allie and I are going to check out a few garage sales. Can we meet here, say, ten-ish?"

He stepped forward a bit and touched a strand of her hair. "Have I ever told you that you're adorable?"

Her heart responded far too much to his compliment. Fiancée or no, he was still a no-no. The mushy night had just weakened her defenses.

Time to recharge them. Maddie reached behind her and opened the door. "Ten, Reuben."

Maddie yawned then took a sip of her coffee. "I can't believe you made me get up before seven a.m. on a Saturday."

Allie took a left down the residential street. "It'll be fun. The early birds get the best deals, you know."

"Yeah, but they also get very little sleep and are cranky the rest of the day."

"Oh, posh. A good deal drives the cranks away, didn't ya know?"

Maddie looked out the window as they drove by a perfectly good sale. "Why'd you pass by that one?"

Allie shrugged. "It didn't look interesting. Why? Did you want to stop at it?"

"I don't care, I just thought the purpose of this was to stop and shop."

"It is, but we don't want to waste time. That one had a measly two tables and most of that was full of clothes that probably have stains and are twenty years old. We'd have to stop the car, get out, look, get back in, start the car again, then go. We'd throw at least four good shopping minutes down the drain."

Good grief, the lady was a professional. Maddie had never been to a garage sale in her life. The idea of going up to someone's home and picking through their stuff that they laid out was just weird.

They stopped at several sales, but only found overpriced furniture with a nonhaggling owner or very few things that she needed. But then two hours into the expedition, Allie slowed the car at a large, two-story house with balloons hanging from its mailbox. The driveway was lined with at least six tables, and the lawn was scattered with various types of furniture.

Her friend turned to her. "Now, this, dear Maddie, is a mother lode of a garage sale. Let's go."

Taking one more sip of her coffee, Maddie opened the door and got out. She had to put a hand to the side of the minivan to steady her weary body. Early mornings weren't her thing. Especially after a week of no sleep.

Allie came around the van and rolled her eyes. "You're just being dramatic. Come on."

They headed for the furniture-covered lawn first. It sported a couch, a loveseat, and a decrepit-looking entertainment center that had seen better days, probably about twenty years ago.

The couch, on the other hand, looked promising. Allie plunked down on it and wiggled her tush, punched the cushions, tried to wiggle the arm rests. "It looks solid, Maddie. Come sit. What do you think?"

Maddie obeyed. The cushion was comfortable enough. And the light green khaki fabric wasn't too terrible. She actually liked it. "It seems like it would work." She looked at the loveseat. "That matches it too, but I really only need a couch."

Allie winked at her. "Let's see what kind of deal we can get."

The lady manning the sale approached them. "Good morning. You folks interested in the couch? I'm asking two-fifty for the pair."

And so it started. Maddie sat wide-eyed as Allie and the garage sale lady went at it. Allie offered her a $100 for both. The lady turned red and looked like she was ready to fight, but countered with $225.

Allie went up to $130, but the lady's voice raised an octave and said $200, final offer.

Maddie stood up to intervene, but her friend pushed her back down. Turning toward the lady, she took a step forward and got within a foot of her face, then said in a low, firm voice. "One hundred and fifty dollars, and that's our final offer. I'll throw in an extra five bucks to get the old entertainment center off your hands if you want."

The lady stared her down for a good twenty seconds, but finally relented. "Sold. I take cash only."

Allie finally looked at Maddie, who sat shell-shocked on the couch, then winked. "You have your money?"

Still unsure of what just happened, she doled out the cash to the lady, and Allie called Gary and arranged for him to come by with his truck and pick everything up later, then texted him the address.

Turning back to Maddie, she flashed her a grin. "And that, my friend, is how it's done."

"You really get into this stuff, don't you?"

Allie turned and started toward the main part of the sale, leaving Maddie no choice but to follow. "It's all about negotiation. Never ever pay full price at a garage sale." She stopped at a table filled with Christmas decorations. "Want to do some early Christmas shopping?"

The holiday was too far off for Maddie to even think about decorations, but the thought of having a place of her own at Christmas to put up a tree, hang a few lights in the bushes, with Kyle there on Christmas morning, made her want to cry right there in front of a bunch of obsessive garage salers. Instead, she walked to another table to get her mind off it. "No, Christmas is still too far off. I do like these light blue placemats though."

Allie joined behind her. "Ohhh, you're right! And they have cloth napkins to match!"

Maddie looked at the price. A quarter a piece? Really? Surely Allie wouldn't make her try to make the lady come down on the price this time. Talk about embarrassment.

"If you want them, hold on to them while we shop."

"Fine, but Allie, I'm not haggling with her over these, okay?"

Allie waived her off. "Of course not. I have a firm policy never to negotiate when someone's only asking a quarter. Otherwise it makes me look cheap."

Perish the thought. The woman should write a book about her garage sale rules.

"You look around here more. That table over there has kids clothes. Don't pay for *anything* until I get back, got it?"

Maddie put her hand to her forehead and saluted. "Yes, sergeant."

Allie rolled her eyes. "Ha, ha, funny. It's for your own wallet's good."

That part she appreciated. She only had three-hundred dollars for furniture and other things to set up home, money she could barely afford after putting a whole week's paycheck down on the house. But it helped that she was working obscene hours between full-time at the salon and nearly full-time at the restaurant.

She perused the tables in front of her, finding a few odds and ends that would be nice, then went over to check out how Allie was doing.

She found her friend knee-deep in children's clothes.

"Find anything?"

Allie's head popped up, and a grin spread across her face. "I told you this was the mother lode spot. They have like-new clothes in Sara's and Bethany's sizes, and she's only asking fifty cents a piece."

They spent the next twenty minutes sorting through piles of clothing and ended up with a whole box of clothes.

Besides the furniture, after minimal haggling, they left spending less than twenty dollars between them.

Maddie checked her watch and gasped. "I need to get back. I'm supposed to meet Reuben in a half hour."

"That's fine. I can only help until two this afternoon anyway, and we need to get you settled in. I'd say we did good today, wouldn't you?"

"Yeah, we did, although I guess I'll be sleeping on the couch for a while until I find a bed." She'd hoped at least to find something for Kyle to sleep on, to show Corina that she was capable of taking care of him.

Allie just nodded, making Maddie regret her words. Her friend didn't think her ungrateful, did she? Because that was the furthest from the truth. The Callahan family had been kinder to her than anyone had been in a very long time.

A little too kind.

As they drove home, Maddie tried to suppress a smile every time they drove by a sale. Allie would shift in her seat, drum her fingers on the steering wheel, and clear her throat each time. The woman was officially addicted.

"So, how are the kids doing lately? I haven't gotten a chance to see them." Maybe getting her attention on something other than sales would help Allie's withdrawal.

"Oh, they're doing fine. Cole's too big for his britches lately, and Bethany is just sweet little Beth. Sara misses you like crazy, keeps hounding me to let them come see you. She starts kindergarten next month, you know. She's entering the big times, that's what she said to me last weekend. Seriously, I have no idea where she gets her vocabulary."

Maddie could just hear five-year-old Sara saying it too. "Do you let her watch too much TV or something?"

"Hey, don't go blaming the mom, now. She has a dad too you know. They're probably glued in front of the TV as we speak watching Saturday morning cartoons."

"Mmm-hmm, now you're resorting to blame shifting."

Allie stopped the car in front of her parent's house. "Oh, shush. I am not."

Maddie barely heard her, because her focus was riveted to the gorgeous shirtless guy coming from behind the garage.

# 29

*T*o flex or not to flex? That was the question.

Or, the more proper question, should he go put his shirt back on? Not even ten and already the heat of the day beat down on him. Plus, he didn't mind the way Maddie stared at him.

*Liar.*

Fine, he really liked it. She probably didn't even know she was doing it, but as she got out of the minivan, her eyes stayed glued below his neck. When she shifted her gaze upward, the most beautiful blush he'd ever seen flared on her cheeks.

The day might prove to be highly interesting.

Allie walked around in front and grabbed Maddie by the elbow. "Come on. We have to finish your packing."

She shook her head, as if just coming around to her senses. "I'm pretty much done."

"Good, then we can load it all up and head on over while Gary and Reuben see to the big stuff."

Maddie frowned. "What big stuff?"

Reuben heard a grunt behind him, and turned to see Gary, his face cherry red from strain, carrying the solid-wood head-board on his shoulder.

"Let me help." He'd forgotten that he'd only come out front to make room in the back of the truck and was supposed to go back and help.

Gary let him take it, and Reuben walked past the wide-jawed Maddie and set the headboard against his step-dad's Ford, then hopped into the bed of the truck to rearrange things. "I got side-tracked, sorry."

"What are you doing?" The shocked female voice almost sounded mad. Shouldn't she be grateful?

He turned around to where Maddie stood, hands on her hips, fire shooting from her eyes. "Loading up your bed. What does it look like I'm doing?"

"Like you're stealing your parents' bed."

He forced himself not to grimace. The bed inside was Gary and his mom's bed, *not* his parents'. "Nope. Mom and Gary's bed is safely inside, where it belongs."

"You know exactly what I mean."

Gary walked up beside her and draped an arm around her shoulders. "It's a gift, Maddie, from Betty and me. We have another bed in storage that we'll be putting in the guesthouse. This one's yours now."

She shook her head like the stubborn woman she was. "No. I can't accept this. You've done too much already."

Reuben wiped a bead of sweat off his brow. "Now listen. We've already got the mattresses loaded, and I'll be dipped if you expect me to take these right back in there. If you don't want them, then feel free to start unloading it yourself." He knew he was being a grouch, but the confounded woman needed to learn how to accept help gratefully, if not gracefully.

Maddie narrowed her eyes then softened a bit. Ignoring him, she turned to Gary. "I don't know what to say, except thank you. You all have been way too generous."

"No such thing as being too generous when you're obeying God, Maddie." He stepped closer to Reuben and helped hoist the headboard onto the truck.

When they had it propped to the side with the mattresses, Reuben hopped out of the truck and wiped his sweaty palms on his jeans.

Allie tugged on Maddie. "Stop lollygagging around. I can't help long." She turned around and glanced back at the men. "Don't forget to go pick up Maddie's new couch, okay? You got the directions I texted you?"

Gary scratched his head. "Is that what the message thingy was on my phone?"

Reuben fought not to roll his eyes. "Yes, we got it, Allie. I'll get it from his phone, and we'll pick it up on the way to the house. And Maddie, don't forget all your stuff from the party last night is still in my trunk."

Allie stomped her foot in sisterlike fashion. "Shoot, I'd forgotten about that. I wanted to help get it all put up this morning." Her pout was *almost* comical if it hadn't been so annoying. "Oh, I have an idea. Maddie, you can just drive Reub's car to your house."

A female? Driving his car? Over his dead body. "No. I'll just follow the truck over there."

Maddie's forehead crinkled with confusion, and Allie's just steamed. "That's ridiculous, Reuben, we're going straight there, and you guys still need to pick up the rest of the furniture. If you don't want her driving it, then I will."

The laugh that escaped his lips was unintentional, but the thought of his flighty sister, who had been in three fender-benders just this year, driving his car was insanely funny. "You're joking, right?"

Her hands jammed onto her hips. "What? Don't trust me either?"

He'd never hear the end of this if he didn't let one of them drive. He fished a hand into his jeans pocket for his keys and tossed them to Maddie. She caught them midair. Impressive. "Don't wreck it, okay?"

Maddie looked at the keys and then up at him. "If you're so nervous about it getting a scratch, why'd you buy such an expensive car anyway?"

Allie rolled her eyes. "Take a wild guess."

Reuben clenched his jaw. He loved his sister, but she was stepping over the line. "Allie, put a sock in it, okay?"

"You know you never would have dreamed to spend that kind of money if Livy hadn't begged you to."

He didn't want to talk about Livy today. "I bought it for the business."

Allie pushed Maddie toward the back of the house and turned around as they walked. "You better watch out for lightning after that fib you just told."

Thankfully the sky was bright blue. "Just be careful, okay?"

Maddie sat at the red light, trying to figure out how to work the confounded windshield wipers on the fancy car. Who knew a storm could brew up so fast? Not an hour before, it'd been the perfect sunny day, and after they stopped to get some lunch, out of nowhere, dark clouds rolled in. She sure hoped the guys had gotten the furniture in before the bottom fell out of the sky.

The thing she tried made the headlights go off, not good in this weather.

Then the radio began blaring. Not it either.

A car honked behind her, and she glanced up to see the light had turned green. She'd have to try again at the next one. She pressed on the gas and drove slowly through the intersection, praying she could see anything important, like a car, pedestrian, or maybe, um, the road.

Water pounded the glass, making the street look like a giant kaleidoscope. Allie's van that was in front of her disappeared. She remembered the way, but she'd prefer to have stayed together in this weather.

If only Allie hadn't insisted on Maddie driving. Reuben hadn't been happy about the matter, in fact livid was too mild a term. She didn't know for sure what was up between him and his precious car, but the guy needed to chill a bit.

Maybe it reminded him of Livy. Now that they were officially broken-up, it made sense.

Inhaling, she took another whiff of the familiar scent that lingered. So totally Reuben. The designer cologne, or maybe aftershave, mixed with the smell of the hair gel she'd sold him. She smiled, thinking about his hair. Maybe it was the stylist in her, but it looked so cute when he tried so hard to make it perfect, but only just made it worse. And he thought himself so suave.

*Stop thinking about him!* It did her no good to dwell on her now-single boss. Nothing positive could come of it.

But all of that was fine anyway.

Because she was *not* getting involved with a man. Ever.

*Seriously, God. Never ever. I don't want one. You said you'd give me the desires of my heart. Well, that one ain't it, okay? Even though he is cute. And gorgeous. And a good dresser. And a good kisser.*

Ahhh!

She came to another stop light. She needed wipers on *now.* The effect of the swirling water against the windshield obviously was having a trancelike effect on her.

She pressed a few more buttons, and finally the wipers kicked into gear.

The light turned green, and she pressed the gas to go straight.

She was in the middle of the intersection when a flash from the left caught her attention.

Reuben took a hand towel and dried off as much of himself as he could. The rain had come out of nowhere, but thankfully they'd just finished putting all the furniture in the house when the buckets dumped from the sky. Unfortunately he'd been out shutting the back of the truck at the time, and now he resembled a drenched cat.

Gary sat on the couch, his eyes closed as he rested. It'd been a long morning. Reuben longed to join him, but he didn't want to soak through to Maddie's new couches. He looked out the window then turned around. "They left a half hour before us. They should have beat us here."

His step-dad opened one eye. "The rain probably slowed 'em down."

As if on queue, Reuben heard a vehicle pull in the drive. He saw Allie's minivan out the window.

Relief flooded him. Maddie should be right behind. With his car. Maybe she could park it in the garage so he could check it. . . .

Allie ran up the walk, and he held open the door for her.

She stomped her feet on the towel Reuben had laid down as a makeshift rug and shook her head, sending splatters of water all over him. "Phew, it's wet out there. I didn't think they were even calling for rain today."

"Me neither. What took you so long? Is Maddie behind you?"

"We stopped for lunch. I think I lost Maddie on the way out of town. I tried to slow down for her, but she didn't catch up. I'm sure she's just a minute behind me."

Five minutes later, there was still no sign of Maddie. Reuben paced the living room.

"Reub, she'll be here. Maybe she just got caught at some red lights."

He stopped and glared. "The whole two of them on your way here? I don't think so. Give me your keys. I'm going to go look for her." If the woman rear-ended someone, she was in a *deep* amount of trouble.

All he could think of was his poor, money-dripping car, its bumper crushed, dollar signs laying all over the pavement like shards of headlight plastic.

Allie tossed the keys to him. "Go for it. But don't blame me if you get wet for nothing."

Reuben ignored her. In the van, he stepped on the gas, retracing the route Allie said she'd taken. Close to downtown, the normally light Saturday afternoon traffic seemed to get busier, then finally came to a standstill. Blue lights flashed in the distance, punching him in the gut with each flicker.

He pulled over and parallel parked. He had to get up there and make sure everything was okay. Assess the damage. If she'd totaled it. . . .

He increased his pace to a jog, crossing an intersection, then fear clenched his stomach as the picture became clearer.

Three police cars. A fire truck. And an ambulance.

And one BMW with a Ford pickup smashed into the driver's side. His hands shook as the scene hit him with more force than the rain pelting his face.

Maddie.

# 30

*M*addie winced as the blood-pressure cuff squeezed her arm. Didn't they know accident victims were sore?

When the cruelty ended and the torture machine released its grip, the nurse unfastened it and scribbled on her paper. "You're a lucky lady, Maddie Buckner. I've seen much worse come through here from car accidents."

She didn't feel lucky at all. The Ford truck might as well have rolled over her twenty times for as good as she felt. "Thanks." No use sounding ungrateful.

"There's a few people who want to see you. Is it okay if I let them in?"

Maddie shrugged. There was one person she didn't want to see, but it would be inevitable. Might as well get it over with.

The nurse—what was her name?—Oh yeah, Molly, frowned at her, but turned and left the room.

*God, I know I need to be nicer. But this was supposed to be my good day. My fun day. The day when things started to go right for me. FYI—car accidents aren't fun! Wrecking my boss's car—not really a sign of things going right. Just so ya know.*

The whole thing was a reminder that good things weren't supposed to happen to her. She was Maddie—scarred, unlovable, unworthy Maddie. When she became a Christian, everything seemed to look brighter. There'd been hope.

But where was that hope today?

Oh yeah, it was sprinkled all over the asphalt at the corner of Route 34 and Main.

As the door opened, she closed her eyes and feigned sleep. Maybe she could put this conversation off a little longer.

Footsteps plodded along the floor until they stopped next to her bed.

She took in an extra long breath. Maybe she could catch a scent and figure out who it was.

The familiar spice gave Reuben away in an instant.

A chair scraped the floor, and a thud told her he'd sat down beside her.

Someone at the door cleared their throat. "How is she?"

Gary.

"Sleeping. The nurse said she had been awake but was pretty out of it and not really all there."

Maddie forced her lips not to move even though she wanted to yell. Not all there? She was in pain, not senile.

Gary's voice got closer. "I think they're planning on keeping her overnight for observation from what I overheard."

Over her dead body. This stupid hospital stay was already going to cost a fortune she didn't have. She and the doc had already had a little chat about that.

"Gary, you can go home. I'll sit with her until she wakes up."

Joy, oh joy. She'd rather Gary sit and Reuben leave.

"I don't mind staying."

No reply came. Maddie wished she could see his face.

Gary cleared his throat from somewhere near the end of the bed. "Reuben, this isn't your fault."

"You don't know what you're talking about."

"Yeah, I do. I struggled with it myself after your dad died."

The chair scraped against the floor, and Reuben's voice growled from somewhere up above her. "That's different."

"Is it?"

"You killed him then married his wife six months later." The words fired from Reuben's mouth like bullets emptying from a revolver.

"I didn't kill him. It was an accident."

The choked response told Maddie that Reuben's aim had been dead on.

"You were driving."

She sensed Gary's presence at the side of her bed, opposite Reuben. "Do you think I don't know that? That I don't have nightmares about it?"

Feet thudded across the floor toward the door. Reuben's voice was so low and deep she barely heard it. "I'll be out in the hall. Tell me when she's awake."

Maddie heard the door swish open then click shut.

Silence followed, then a creak of the chair sounded next to her again. "You heard it all, didn't you?"

She peeked open an eye to see Gary, one of the only men she had come to respect, sitting beside her. "How'd you know?"

"Your breathing. You held it for so long at one point I almost reminded you to let it out."

"I didn't realize his dad died in an accident."

Gary looked at the door, his eyes sad. "We don't talk about it much."

"What happened?" The moment the words escaped her mouth she wished she could snatch them right back. "I'm sorry. It's not my business."

"No, it's okay. I came to terms with it long ago. Matthew and I went into Chicago for a Christian men's conference. He'd asked Reuben to go along, but he'd said no, someone had to look after the restaurant. I insisted I drive because my small car got better gas mileage than his truck."

"That sounds logical."

"We were on our way home, almost ready to get off I-80, and were talking. It'd been an amazing conference. One I wish I'd have gone to years ago when Faith was still alive. I would've been a better husband if I had." Regret filled his words.

Maddie reached over and patted his hand. "I'm sure you were a fine husband."

He shook his head. "Matthew made me promise if anything ever happened to him, that I'd make sure Betty was taken care of, that I'd keep an eye on her." He smiled. "I'm sure he wasn't talking about marrying her, more like cutting the lawn and stuff like that. While we were talking, I guess I got distracted and the car drifted onto the left shoulder a little. I swerved back to correct it, but the car overcorrected and we spun. The car behind us hit the passenger-side head-on."

Maddie didn't need anymore explanation, especially since she'd experienced something similar that morning, but at city street speeds instead of Interstate ones. "I'm sorry, Gary."

"Betty was beside herself, but she never once blamed me. I did everything I could to help her, and in the process, fell in love with her. Believe it or not, she's the one who suggested we elope."

Maddie could see her doing just that. "So I guess Reuben was a different story."

"Reuben has hated me since the minute he got the news. He threw himself into the business even more than he had before."

It made sense. Not only did it honor his dad's legacy, but it kept Reuben so busy he didn't have time to have to think about it. Maddie understood her boss much better now.

But she still wanted to throttle his neck.

In front of her stood the most genuine, kind man she'd ever known. He was willing to step in and love Reuben, yet the stubborn man just threw it back in Gary's face.

Gary sat forward and put his elbows on his knees. "Wanna tell me why you were playing opossum?"

"I was avoiding the wrath of your stepson, something you probably know a little about."

"The wrath, yes. The avoiding, not so much. I'd much rather face him head on and get through it. He's the one skilled at avoidance."

She knew plenty about Reuben's anger. "I totaled his precious car. Believe me, the conversation he wants to have with me isn't going to be pretty."

"I think you'd be surprised."

He didn't have to work with the man everyday. "You think you could go find a doctor I could sweet talk into letting me out a little early?"

Gary smiled and stood. "Someone else is an expert at avoiding things too, I see. Why don't I just go check, and send Reuben in while I'm at it, hmm?"

He walked out the door before she could argue.

A minute later, Reuben entered. His face was pale white, and his hands balled into fists.

Yeah, her boss was steaming mad. And who could blame him? She'd totaled his car, his pride and joy.

And it probably gave him flashbacks of his dad.

"Reuben, I'm—"

He took a few steps closer. "If you tell me you're sorry, I might have to pinch you."

Maddie grimaced. "Fine, I won't tell you. The last thing I need now is another bruise." Plus, if he was going to be that much of a meany, he wasn't worth an apology.

His fists released as he neared her bed. To her surprise, he lifted his hand and caressed her cheek with the back of it. Even in her state of pain, the skin beneath his hand tingled.

"I hate to tell you, but you look like crap."

She let out a painful laugh. "Thanks a lot. I hate to tell *you*, but your car probably looks worse than me."

His hand stilled. Why hadn't she just shut her mouth and not mentioned anything?

"You do realize, Maddie, that I don't care a lick about the car, right?"

No, in fact, she did not. She wrinkled her forehead, but groaned at the effort. "I don't understand."

He pulled up a chair and sat beside her. "Back in the spring, I decided I needed new wheels. My old Chevy was falling apart around my ears, and since I was starting work on opening the two new sites, I figured I needed to start working on my image more, look more like the suave businessman I wanted to be. Livy insisted on going with me, saying that image was her thing. And she's right, it is. I wanted a nice truck, something manly and tough. You know, like me."

Maddie tried not to giggle, but it didn't work. Reuben was certainly manly and tough, but to hear him say it struck her as funny. "Sorry to tell you, but the BMW doesn't really shout 'tough guy'."

He grimaced. "You're right. But you have to admit, I looked pretty cool driving that thing."

She wouldn't admit it aloud, but yeah, he did. Instead she rolled her eyes and shook her head.

"Anyway, Livy talked me into it, even though the price tag almost sent me to the hospital."

"And now I wrecked it. I'm sorry, Reub. I really am."

He took hold of her hand gently and squeezed. "I know. And really, it's okay. I'll get an insurance settlement and go buy my big manly truck. So actually, you did me a favor."

The rock inside her gut dissolved to jelly. She waved her hand. "No prob. Anytime." No need to tell him that she could picture him climbing up into the cab of a big ol' truck and how cute an image that would make. Cute probably wasn't the look he was going for anyway.

The door opened again and Allie burst in, still in her jean shorts and tank top from this morning. "You're pathetic. You know that, right?"

Not exactly the welcome she'd expected. "Excuse me?"

"Going and getting in a car accident so we have to do all your unpacking for you. I know how it rolls."

The mischievous glint in her friend's eyes made Maddie smile. "You know me. Always trying to get out of something. Next time I'll pick a little less painful way, though."

"If you were anymore black and blue, I'd think you were a giant blueberry."

Did she really look that bad? She tried to move her casted left arm to touch her face, since her right was still in Reuben's hand, but the pain that seared through it stopped her.

Reuben squeezed her hand. "Careful. It's broken pretty bad. Other than that, you just have plenty of bruises. The doctor was outside a second ago and said he could release you today as long as someone stayed with you tonight. Gotta wake you up every few hours just to be sure."

Allie moved to her left side. "I've taken the honors of staying with you tonight, but really it's just so I can have a night out of the house without the kiddos. Devious, I know. I even had to fight Mom for it."

"You're too kind, but really, I'll be fine."

"Don't say another word. We're having a slumber party at your new house, and that's final."

Spoken like a mother of three. And given the massive headache that clawed at her brain, it was probably a good idea.

The nurse appeared a moment later and shooed the visitors out so they could get her ready to leave.

An hour later, Reuben wheeled her out of the hospital to Allie's minivan. "Your chariot awaits, ma'am."

She stood up on shaky legs, and Reuben's arm came around her back. The stance was almost like a hug, and despite her aching muscles, her heart beat faster at his touch. She could smell his spicy cologne with a hint of peppermint. Then she realized his face was bent close to hers, and he probably had a breath mint.

"You okay?" His voice filtered through the air in a low whisper.

It dawned on her that she'd gone limp, and his arm supported most all her weight. "I'm fine. Sorry."

His hand on her back reached around to her side and squeezed gently. "Nothing to be sorry about, Hon."

Hon? Did he really just call her that?

Okay, maybe she would faint right there.

*God, reminder. NO MEN. Still haven't changed my mind, still don't want one. Even though this one is awfully cute and makes my heart skip a billion beats.*

She allowed herself to be half-lifted into the van and settled back, glad for the solitude of the bench seat. Seconds later, Reuben slid in from the other side. The seat wasn't so solitude anymore with his hip brushing against hers and his arm scooting around the back, tugging her head toward him.

Unfortunately, her head rebelled against her and allowed itself to be cushioned against his shoulder. He felt too good. Too strong. Too nice to resist.

Maybe just this once. . . .

The ride back was quiet, stopping only at the pharmacy to fill her prescription for pain pills, and she thought she might have even dozed a few times.

They pulled up to the little house. She blinked. She'd expected to go back to Betty and Gary's little guesthouse and stay.

Then she remembered. She moved in today.

Reuben turned to her. "Can you walk, or do you need me to carry you?"

From the driver's seat, Allie snorted. "Yeah, he can carry you over the threshold, Maddie."

Over her cold, dead body. She'd crawl to the door if she had to. "No, I can make it."

The walk was a slow one, with Allie and Reuben on either side of her, supporting her down the path and up the steps. The door opened and Betty fluttered out. "Oh my dear. You come right in here so I can take care of you. I have chicken noodle soup and chocolate chip cookies waiting."

Maddie smiled. Not a usual combination, but oddly, it sounded good. Comfort food. Made by someone who loved her enough to take care of her.

Her frustrated prayer to God earlier in the hospital came to mind, and immediately she was ashamed. Crap happened. But God was providing for her through all the crazy stuff. She was alive, she had her house, she had this family who'd all but adopted her as their own.

And Kyle was still coming next weekend.

When she stepped through the front door, she sucked in a breath. Her house. Everything about the place fit her dreams to a tee. Stable, normal. Maybe a few more decorations eventually, but the couch was there, the old entertainment center, and someone had even brought over the small kitchen table from the guesthouse. She'd have to yell at Reuben later about it.

Gary replaced Allie's spot at her side. "Let's get her to the couch to sit down."

She hated feeling like a helpless invalid, but there wasn't a thing she could do about it.

Betty all but flew out of the kitchen with a bowl and tray in her hand. Setting the tray in her lap, she handed her a spoon. "Eat up. You need your strength back. I still can't believe they let you come home. They should have at least kept you overnight."

"Betty, I don't have insurance. Believe me, I'm glad they didn't keep me longer." The thought of the bills that would show up at her doorstep made her ill. No need to mention she'd begged the doctor to let her go.

Reuben sat on the arm of the couch and put a hand to her shoulder. "Don't you worry about bills. The accident was the guy's fault, and he even admitted it. His insurance will pay the hospital bills, and if I have anything to say about it, a good sum in pain and suffering too."

She shook her head. "No, I'm not going to be one of those people who run for a lawyer and try to live the rest of their lives off the insurance settlement."

"Some of those people deserve it, especially if they're confined to a wheelchair the rest of their lives because of someone's stupid mistake. That's why there's liability insurance."

She didn't want to argue about it right now. "Fine." At least she didn't have to worry about medical bills.

"And remind me when you get back to the office to give you medical insurance papers. I'll put you on the company's group plan for employees."

"I only work part-time, Reuben. You don't offer it to your part-time waitresses. Plus, it's still ridiculously expensive. I do your payroll, remember?"

He shrugged. "Let me worry about that, okay?"

Maddie tried not to fume. This was her life, her paycheck. She *needed* to worry about it. "Reuben—"

"No argument. Besides, you're eligible after a month if you work at least thirty hours a week, and even at part-time, you've been clocking in that. And insurance is just one more thing you can tell the caseworker you have available. It'll make you look more credible."

Allie brought her a glass of water. "Or, you could just find some hunky guy to marry. That would solve all your problems."

"Um, no. Not a chance." Even as she said it, she felt her cheeks heat up twenty degrees. "I'm not getting married. Ever."

She chanced a glance at Reuben, whose eyebrows were raised. Quickly averting her gaze so she didn't feel compelled to answer the questions she saw in those dark brown eyes, Maddie lifted a bite of soup into her mouth. Delicious, but hard to swallow knowing the stares she was receiving.

Betty spoke first. "Marriage isn't a bad thing, honey. But don't listen to Allie. You need to marry because you love the man, not just for your brother."

Marriage for them might be okay, but not this girl. Still, she'd keep her mouth shut from now on. No use arguing. "Thanks for the soup and cookies."

Gary put an arm around Betty. "We'll just be getting out of your hair. Give us a call if you need anything."

She nodded. "Will do. I doubt I'll feel up to church in the morning, so—"

Betty smiled. "We'll let Pastor know what happened. Beware though; you might get a visit tomorrow from him."

Oh, goody. "Thanks."

The couple left, and Allie said her good-byes shortly after, saying that she had to go home to get some clothes and get the kids to bed and would be back before bedtime.

Maddie hoped Reuben would leave with her, but no such luck. "Reuben, shouldn't you leave with Allie? You don't have a car here, and my Tracker's still back at your mom's house."

He took a seat beside her on the couch. "No biggy. I'll just wait until Allie gets back and borrow her minivan."

Just great. All she wanted to do was close her eyes and go to sleep, and now she'd have to entertain a guest. "That's fine." She hoped the smile she forced on her face didn't look as dishonest as it was.

"Don't mind me. Finish eating, then you can get some sleep. Or, do you want to watch some TV?"

"But I don't have a—" Just as she said it, the black box on her entertainment center caught her eye. She looked back at him. "We need to have a talk about all this. I am not taking your parents' furniture."

"You're not. Mom and Gary's house is still completely furnished. I thought we went through this earlier."

Oh, did she want to punch him. Hard. "You know what I mean. I can stand on my own two feet."

"Would it make you feel better if you paid them ten bucks for it?"

"No."

"It's all they would get for it if they sold it. Stores don't even sell tube televisions anymore. Mom wanted to put a nice little flat-screen out there anyway."

There was no use arguing, even though she wanted to with every cell in her body. Once a charity case, always a charity case. Would her life *ever* be her own? "Fine, but no more, okay? Can you bring me my purse?"

Then it hit her that all her stuff was probably still in the mangled BMW at some auto salvage place. Just great.

Reuben stood and walked to the kitchen, then returned with her knock-off Coach purse in his hand. "Here you go."

"But I thought—"

"Gary and Mom picked up everything from the car this afternoon."

She should have known. More hand-holding. She mumbled a thanks and took the bag from his hand. He looked out of place holding it anyway. Too . . . husbandly. Like those poor saps in the mall who were forced to be a bag holder for their shopaholic wives.

Fishing into the abyss that was her purse, she found her wallet and took out a twenty and handed it to him.

"What's this for?"

"Give it to your parents as payment for the TV. You know they won't take it from me."

He tried to hand it back to her, but she pushed his hand away.

"What makes you think they'll take it from me either?"

She shrugged. "Just leave it on the counter or something. They don't have to know I laid it there. Oh, oh oh! I know. Crinkle it up a little and put it in their laundry. That way they'll just think they washed it."

He crooked an eyebrow. "Are you insane? I think that knot on your head did more damage than the doctors realized."

She tossed the purse on the floor. "Shut up. Now, if you'll excuse me, I'd like to watch something on my new TV. Could you hand me the remote?"

He picked up the black device and sat down beside her, then flipped the power button.

Maddie held out her hand, but was promptly ignored. "Excuse me?"

Reuben looked at her. "Yes?"

She wiggled her fingers on her open hand. "The remote?"

He winked. "I've got it. What do you want to watch?"

Irritating male. How did she get stuck with a remote hog for a boss? "I'd like to make the choice while I flip through the channels on *my* TV."

He handed her the remote, but when she grabbed for it, he didn't let go. Their hands grazed each other, and Maddie released it as if it were a hot coal. "You're not being nice."

"You didn't say please."

At this rate, the guy was lucky if she didn't grab the remote and chuck it at him. "Pretty please with sugar on top. There."

He moved to hand her the remote again, but when he let go, his hand went in front of her and settled on her bruised cheek, and his face inched closer to hers. He was going to kiss her again. She didn't want him to. But she did.

No she didn't. She really, really didn't.

But why then was her face moving closer to his?

His lips connected with hers, and a rush of warmth poured through her veins.

As quick as it started, Reuben ended the kiss. He sat back and winked at her. "Just needed my sugar on top. So, what do you wanna watch? I think there's a game on."

*God, why are you doing this to me?*

Maddie settled in her seat and flipped the channel until she found *Wheel of Fortune.* She ignored Reuben's groan beside her. Served the man right.

# 31

What did he ever do before Maddie?

Reuben scratched his head as his gaze scanned the mounds of paperwork that needed to be dealt with. There were bills, payroll, supply orders to be sent in, and a billion other things that needed handled today.

Then again, distance was probably a good thing.

She was proving dangerous.

Every time he was with her, an overwhelming urge to protect her came over him. Maybe it was a brotherly kind of thing.

But the kiss he stupidly snuck the night before said otherwise.

At least she hadn't slapped him.

If he could only figure her out. But from what he knew about women, that was no easy task. Every time he came close to her, she blushed brighter than ketchup on white bread. But she insisted on holding him at arm's length.

He should never have kissed her. Especially the first time, but even Saturday night had been a mistake. She wasn't ready for that, and if he were honest with himself, he wasn't either.

Maddie deserved to be more than a rebound.

He'd given her strict instructions that she wasn't to come to work this week. She'd called Judy to let her know she couldn't work for the next few weeks until her arm healed enough to trust it with people's hair. The owner hadn't been happy, but was astute enough to know that a one-armed stylist wouldn't be good for business.

But the little firecracker had tried to convince him that paperwork one-handed wouldn't be hard. As much as he'd love her company, it wasn't happening.

He picked up a piece of paper from the top of the pile and groaned.

"You desperate yet?"

Reuben's head jerked up at the sweet sound of his pistol of an assistant. "I thought I told you to stay home." She looked pitiful with her arm in the sling, a knot on her forehead, and dark purple bruises on her cheek and chin. He just wanted to pick her up, take her home, and put her back to bed.

"And I thought I told you I'd be here if I felt up to it. And I do. Besides, I was going stir crazy in the house by myself."

"I'd have come over tonight to keep you company."

She glowered at him. "Thanks, but no thanks."

As much as he wanted to send her packing, he'd known the woman long enough to realize that she wasn't going anywhere without a fight.

"I'll let you stay, but promise you won't overdo it. I have a meeting in a bit, so you'll be on your own this morning."

"Maddie is tough girl." Her voice lowered as she imitated Tarzan. Then she smiled and returned to her normal sassy self. "I mainly want to get payroll done and some invoices paid. See, just call me selfish. I only came in so I'd get paid on Friday."

"I'm here to see Mr. Sanders." Reuben fiddled with the change in his pocket. He'd been waiting for this day for a long time. The final go ahead on his dad's dream. He glanced at his watch. Two minutes early, which was a miracle given the time it took to drive there. As much as he hated Maddie coming into work today, it'd been a godsend.

"And your name, sir?"

"Reuben Callahan. I have a ten o'clock with him."

The receptionist picked up the phone and punched in a few numbers. "A Mr. Callahan is here to see Mr. Sanders." An exaggerated pause and frown from the young woman behind the desk made him tighten his fist. He had gotten the time right, he was sure of it. "I see. I'll let him know."

She hung up the phone. "I'm sorry, sir, but Mr. Sanders left early for a lunch appointment. It seems we received a call this morning canceling your appointment."

That made no sense. Who would do that? "Do you have a record of who called?"

"His secretary said a woman phoned in, I believe your assistant. Said you had changed your mind about the project."

What kind of game was Maddie playing? Was she that mad about the kiss the night before? Reuben gripped his briefcase and tried not to act too mad. No use being fodder for office gossip. "I'm sorry you were given misinformation, but I'm still very much interested in using Mr. Sanders's services. Can I reschedule?"

"Sure." Her fingers tapped on the keyboard. "He has a two o'clock three weeks from Thursday open."

A three-week setback was not what he needed at this point. He needed the plans to get a cost estimate from the builder, which he needed to get to the bank so they would approve his loan, the loan that stood on very shaky ground. "There's nothing sooner?"

"I'm sorry, sir. He's going on vacation for two weeks starting next week, so his schedule's pretty full right now. He's getting married, you know. It's his honeymoon."

What he would give for a very large punching bag right now. "Fine, that will have to do."

He turned and stalked out of the office trying to figure out what just went on.

Surely Maddie wasn't that mad about Saturday night. It just didn't make any sense. He slid into the driver's seat of his rental car, a Toyota Camry. A nice car by most people's standards, but a step down from his BMW, no thanks to Maddie.

He pounded the steering wheel with his fist and blew out his breath. No, the accident wasn't her fault. He didn't blame her. She was a victim, just like his dad had been.

But today. Today was unacceptable.

Pulling his cell phone from his suit coat pocket, Reuben hit the speed-dial for the restaurant.

"The Sandwich Emporium, how can I help you today?" He recognized Livy's voice, in her sugary-sweet customer tone. It's what made her good at her job.

"Liv, I need to talk to Maddie."

"Oh, I think she's busy—"

"*Now!*" He didn't mean to yell, but his nerves were wound tighter than string on a fishing pole.

"Is everything okay, Reub?"

"Fine, Fine. Just put her on." Livy would only rub it in his face if he vented to her. Their working relationship was odd at the moment anyway. He'd expected her to quit when they broke up, but she'd stayed.

He heard the standard hold music, light jazz that his dad had always favored, and a minute later Maddie answered. "Reuben? How'd the meeting go? That was awfully fast."

The woman had some nerve. "No thanks to you."

"Excuse me? What's that supposed to mean?"

He gripped the phone tighter, wanting to throw it at something. "You canceled my meeting, Maddie. What do you think I mean? Now I can't get in to see him for another three weeks, so I'll have to postpone the meeting with the builder and this might even affect me getting the loan."

"So let me get this straight. Your meeting got canceled somehow, and you think I had something to do with it? Why in the world would I do that?"

"Good question. Why would you?"

A huff sounded over the line. "I wouldn't, because I didn't. I've barely been here an hour and am still knee-high in paperwork. You've been nothing but kind to me. Plus, I like working for you. Why would I do something to jeopardize that?"

Her words were like a pin jabbing into his bubble of anger, blowing the air right out of him. "I thought you might be mad because of Saturday night."

"What? The whole remote thing?"

Despite himself, he grinned. That had been cruel of him. "No, I meant the whole kiss thing." Even as he said it, he realized how stupid it sounded. Besides blatantly ignoring him for the rest of the evening, she'd never acted mad. More like embarrassed because she'd liked it.

"I wasn't mad that you kissed me, Reuben. But really, you do need to stop. You're my boss, and . . . I'm not kissable material."

He begged to differ, but given his confusion over the appointment cancelation, he wouldn't voice his opinion now. "I just don't understand who would cancel it then."

"Who all knew about it?"

Closing his eyes, he thought for a moment. "My mom, you, Gary, Livy, Allie, Stew. . . . That's about it."

"Well, do this. Come back here, and in the meantime, I'll call and see what I can do about getting your reschedule moved up."

"Good luck with that." But even as he said it, the stress eased from his muscles. "And—I'm sorry. For accusing you. I was just stressed out and—"

"No need to explain. It's behind us, okay?"

Maddie sat back in her chair and covered her face with her hands. What had just happened? Did her boss really think she was out to get him or something?

He'd bent over backwards, against her wishes, to help her out. Never in a million years would she hurt him. Not on purpose anyway.

She moved to Reuben's desk and shuffled through papers, trying to find the architect's phone number. He kept it on speed dial in his cell phone and handled all matters related to the new restaurants, so she'd never even called them before. Finally, she found an invoice with letterhead containing a phone number.

As she picked up the phone on Reuben's desk, the office door opened.

"What are you doing, Maddie?"

She replaced the receiver. "Somehow an appointment of Reuben's got canceled this morning. I was just trying to call and reschedule."

Livy leaned against the doorjamb and crossed her arms. Her blonde curls were swept back into a low ponytail. She looked the height of professional with her perfectly pressed black dress pants, tapered white blouse, and short black vest.

"Reuben's time is valuable. You need to be careful and not make mistakes like that. I'm sure he's not happy."

Maddie's jaw dropped but she recovered quickly, standing up straight even though all she wanted to do was sit and slouch. Her entire body was still aching, and being so tense with this woman in the room wasn't helping. "I didn't make a mistake. I don't know how it got canceled."

She shrugged. "Well, maybe they canceled the wrong one, who knows. Reuben just sounded mad on the phone, and I wanted to make sure everything was okay." She turned to leave, but glanced back before she shut the door. "Oh, and if I were you, I wouldn't rummage around Reuben's desk too much. Invasion of his privacy won't get you very far either."

The door slammed, and Maddie bit her lip to prevent herself from screaming. What had Reuben ever seen in such a frustrating woman? Sure, she was all chic and dressed to the nines. But if she was what he found attractive, both in personality and looks, then Maddie must only be a temporary diversion.

And she didn't want to be temporary or permanent in Reuben's love life.

But even while she thought it, the memory of his brief kiss Saturday night flooded her. Gentle, sweet, and quick, but left her heart mushier than wet bread.

Despite what she tried to convince herself, Reuben wasn't like the other guys. He didn't take pleasure in hitting her. He didn't force her into his bed. He didn't broadcast to the whole school that she was lame in the sack.

Not that he had a school to broadcast anything to or experience in bed with her to know.

Maddie sat down in his chair and closed her eyes, willing the memories to stay away. But the ache of her body in its bruised state transported her back not too many years ago.

It'd started with Mark. Even though almost every guy snickered at her behind her back, she realized that not many girls would put out, and even though she didn't want to, something about being with a guy made her feel powerful. Like she was in control of what she was doing.

Thinking back, maybe it had nothing to do with the control thing at all. Because really, they were mean jerks, the whole lot of them, and they held more control over her than she wanted to admit.

She just didn't want to be alone.

Until that last time. Maddie cradled her cast-covered arm as she remembered his fists.

As her memories turned toward that fateful day, Maddie pounded her fist on Reuben's desk. No, no, no.

She wouldn't go there.

The architect. She still needed to call him and reschedule before Reuben got back. It'd get her mind off old nightmares better left buried.

And maybe she could figure out what happened to cause the whole scheduling mess.

She punched in the phone number and a high-pitched receptionist answered. "Good Morning. Sanders office, how may I assist you today?" The woman had obviously had a nice dose of sugar this morning.

"Yes, can I speak with Mr. Sanders's secretary please?"

"You sure may. Hold one moment please and I'll transfer you through. Have a most wonderful day!"

Gag. She hoped Reuben didn't expect her to talk like that. If so, she might as well go back to cutting hair.

She spent the next several minutes talking with a much older, and saner, secretary, who claimed she'd taken the cancelation call earlier.

"I'm sure the caller wasn't you though, dear. The woman who called had a lower voice. Almost raspy, like she had a cold."

Strange. "And she said her name was Maddie?"

"Oh, no. She just said she was Reuben's assistant. Let me see here what I can do about his schedule though. You know, I think I can squeeze him in right before lunch tomorrow. About eleven-thirty? He doesn't have lunch plans but he does have a one o'clock."

Maddie drummed her fingers on the desk. She'd have to make a decision, and hope it worked out for Reuben. *Please, God, let this be okay!*

"He'll take the eleven-thirty and, if it'd be okay, they can probably finish their discussion over lunch."

"That would work just fine. If there's a problem, I'll call and let you know. Otherwise, just plan on that."

Maddie hung up the phone, proud of herself for making the decision and fixing the problem, but hoping Reuben wouldn't be irritated. If anyone had control issues, her boss fit the bill.

She stood from his chair as the subject of her worries walked through the door. The poor guy looked depressed, his face drawn, almost defeated.

"Hey, Maddie."

Why did she have this overwhelming urge to run and give him a huge bear hug? The only thing that held her back was the thought of the pain it would cause, in body and heart.

"You don't look so hot."

He eyed her as he set the briefcase down beside his desk. "Thanks. Appreciate the compliment."

"I didn't mean it like that." She moved to allow him room to sit in his chair, but he just leaned against the desk and ran his fingers through his hair, messing it up.

She smiled. It looked cute messed up.

"I don't suppose you were able to get the time moved up."

"Oh ye of little faith."

His head jerked up. "You did?"

"Tomorrow at eleven-thirty. You meet him, then have lunch. Hope that's okay, but it was your last chance."

She found herself swept into his arms and squeezed tighter than an almost empty tube of toothpaste, crushing all the air from her lungs. Thankfully she'd moved her arm out of the way, but it still hurt like the dickens. "Reuben—"

He let go, but moved his hands to her shoulders. "I'm sorry for blaming you, Maddie. I should have asked first and not accused."

She shrugged. "I don't blame you. I just hope you can trust me though."

He nodded and squeezed her shoulders. She tried to hide her wince. "Of course." One of his hands moved toward her cheek, and she backed away, pretending not to notice the move.

She walked back to her own desk and flipped back on the monitor. "I do wonder who made the call though. The secretary said the person just said she was your 'assistant' and that her voice was raspy, like she had a cold."

"That's odd, but to be honest, I just want to put the whole thing behind me. Maybe someone else called to cancel and the secretary misunderstood."

Maddie shrugged her shoulders and got back to entering the payroll. She wasn't sure she liked the idea of just letting it go. If someone had made the call, they were doing it to be malicious. There'd be no other reason.

# 32

*I* can go by myself." Maddie crossed her good arm over her chest and dug her heels into the gravel driveway.

Reuben held open the door to his rental Camry and pointed inside. "I'm driving you, and that's final."

"I've been driving myself to and from work for the last three days and you didn't have a problem with it."

The obstinate man didn't budge. "A five-minute drive is a little different than an hour."

She didn't relish driving with her arm out of commission, but showing up with Reuben on her elbow might not look that great. Especially with her history. "I don't want Mrs. Blakely getting the wrong idea about us and telling Corina."

"I don't see what your love life has to do with Kyle visiting you, or even your request for custody."

Maddie flung her arm in the air. "Oh, yeah. Showing up on my kid brother's foster parents' doorstep with my drop-dead gorgeous boss isn't going to wave any flags. Two seconds after we leave she'd be on the phone with child services telling them about how I'm shacking up with my boss to keep my job."

He didn't move or back down an inch. "That's ridiculous and you know it. Just because I offer a ride to my invalid employee to help her out doesn't mean we're involved in any-way." A smile crept onto his face. "But I'm flattered you think I'm drop-dead gorgeous."

Ugh, that wasn't what she meant at all. Sorta. "Fine, but you stay in the car when we get there, okay? Maybe I can just say you're a guy from church and the brother of my friend."

Maddie climbed into the passenger seat and wiggled around trying to buckle her seat belt one-handed. Stupid broken arm.

Reuben got in the driver's side and took the buckle from her hand and fastened it.

Great. Next he'd be brushing her teeth for her.

After they were on the road, Reuben popped in a CD. "Matthew West. That okay?"

She nodded, having never heard the group before. Usually she had the rock station on in her car, but in the last month she'd taken to just turning it off. She still liked the songs, but wasn't sure that God wouldn't zap her dead for listening to something unchristian.

Better safe than sorry.

The music filled the car, and a peace settled over her as she listened. Christian music was an anomaly to her outside of sit-ting in the pew at church and singing. Maddie closed her eyes as a song started about being strong.

Something she could totally relate to. She needed to be strong enough to get through the next few months. To fight for Kyle.

As the song played, Maddie squirmed in her seat. *Not* strong enough? Completely different from what she thought it was going to say.

Who could sit there and admit to being weak? To talk about failing?

Her mind raced to Kyle. Admitting failure and weakness was giving up.

*God, who do you think you are to try and tell me I'm weak? I think I've proved that I'm tough. Geez.*

Blah.

Blah, blah, blah.

Reuben flicked the volume button down a hair. "You look madder than snot."

Maddie squirmed in her seat. "It's nothing."

"Bull. Spill it."

Baring her heart to her boss, letting him know her doubts and irritation with God, didn't sit well with the health of her job. "I was just thinking about the song. Interesting message."

"How so?"

Couldn't he just leave it alone? "You're such a nag."

"We have a good forty-five minutes left of this trip. We have to talk about something, and the reason for your scowl sounds like a good place to start."

She looked out the window and watched the corn fields fly by. "I think the singer is an idiot."

Reuben laughed. "I'm sure Matthew would appreciate that a lot."

"What man would admit to being weak and sing about it to the world? Talk about losing your man-card. There's no way I'm going to sit here and sing, 'I'm weak and broken, not strong at all, look at my flabby muscles, ladedadeda.' And I'm a girl, the supposedly weaker gender. Blows that stereotype out of the water."

The man beside her laughed so hard she was pretty sure she saw tears. "I don't remember the line about flabby muscles in the song."

Maddie just stared out the window. "Don't laugh at me. I'm serious."

He blew out a breath. "Sorry."

"We might as well change the CD now. I can't respect a word this guy sings."

Reuben pressed a few buttons and another song on the same CD started to play. "Listen to this one."

Maddie shut her mouth while she listened. Now this she could deal with. Survivors. That's what she wanted to be. Unstoppable until God calls her home.

When the song ended, she glanced at Reuben. "Matthew needs to make up his mind. First he's a weakling, now he's a survivor."

"The point he's making is that as humans, we're weak, but we get our true, lasting strength through God. When we lay ourselves at God's feet and admit that we can't do everything, that's when God can really work. We're survivors because of God's strength in us. It's in the Bible."

"Yeah? Where at?"

Reuben frowned. "I don't remember. But there are a lot of places it talks about God's strength being made perfect in our weakness. If we were all strong, we wouldn't need God."

It made sense. She could admit she needed God. What she could not admit was that she needed Reuben. Or anybody else. "This is getting too deep for a car trip. Wanna hear a knock-knock joke? Or play the alphabet game?"

∼∙∙∽

Reuben reached for Maddie's hand and squeezed it. "You know you're the queen of avoiding a topic, right?"

She pointed to an exit sign. "I see an A."

He smiled. "I'll say one last thing, then let it drop, okay? I learn more every day just how much of a failure I am when I try to do it all myself. When I try to be strong and drive my life, I crash. You've seen that first hand. When I admit I can't drive worth anything and let God have at it, I may go down some roads that confuse me, I may be lost, but God knows where I am, and He won't let that car veer off the path, no matter what happens. He loves you, Maddie."

She finally turned toward him, her lip curling in a half-smile. "God's love is why I came to Him in the first place." She wiped her hands over her eyes, erasing tears that threatened to fall. "Anyway, fine. I'm a weak failure and God is big and strong. Happy? Oh, and there's a B on the Burger King sign."

A weak failure described him exactly. "Tell me about Kyle."

She snorted. "He's a cute little dorky eleven-year-old who has the attitude of a sixteen-year-old and the smarts of a fifty-year-old."

"An odd combination."

"Just wait until you see him. He gets straight As and is in advanced classes, which is not normal in the city, yet will smart off to you quicker than you can blink. The very typical troubled foster-care kid in that department."

He spent the next twenty minutes having all the letters of the alphabet pointed out to him in signs and hearing all the past escapades of the boy who, while Reuben would never in a million years tell his assistant this, reminded him very much of Maddie. By the time he took the exit off I-80, he looked forward to meeting the mini male version of Maddie even more.

Following Maddie's turn-by-turn directions, they pulled up to a small but presentable house in a so-so part of town. Not the slums, but definitely not the suburbs either.

Before he got told to stay put, he stepped from the car and walked around, opening Maddie's door for her.

"I thought I told you to stay in the car."

"We'll explain it. Don't worry."

But the frown on her face told him she would do it anyway. They walked up to the house, and as they approached the porch with chipped white paint, the front door swung open.

"Maddie!" A boy with shaggy brown hair, looking a little older than Reuben had pictured, threw himself into Maddie's good arm.

Maddie wrapped her arm around him. "Kyle, you've grown a foot and it's only been two months. What's up with that? I specifically told you not to grow until I saw you next."

He pushed back and stood up straight, a smirk on his face. "Shut up. I'll grow when I want to." The response was gruff but typical eleven-year-old words. Kyle glanced at Reuben and immediately stiffened. "Who's this?"

Maddie nodded toward Reuben. "A friend from Sandwich. I busted up my arm last weekend so he offered to drive me."

Kyle turned toward him and tried to get in his face, except given his height, he only reached his chest. "You hurt my sister? There'll be hell to pay if you did."

Maddie stepped in between them, a dash of red painting her cheeks. "Be nice. Reuben's the brother of my friend, and my boss. He's been nothing but kind. I was driving his car and wrecked it, and he didn't even yell. The fact that I'm still employed should tell you he's a pretty great guy."

Kyle still studied him through squinted eyes, then looked back at his sister. "How'd you break your arm then?"

"Car accident. Reuben wasn't even there. I swear."

Reuben nodded at the boy. His level of respect for the little man sky-rocketed. "I'd never hurt your sister, man. I promise. I just wanted to help her out. She'd planned on driving here by herself, and no way was I going to let her drive with one arm out of commission."

Kyle nodded. "Yeah, she can be a stubborn brat sometimes."

Reuben decided wisely not to respond.

An older woman, probably in her early forties with dark hair streaked with a few strands of gray, stood in the doorway. "I see you've already found a man. Didn't take you long."

Maddie flashed him an *I-told-you-so* glare. "It isn't like that. He's my boss, and my best friend's brother. Just helping me out is all."

The roll of her eyes told how much she believed her. "Kyle needs to finish eatin' before he can head out."

Reuben took a step forward and opened his mouth to defend his assistant, but the scorned woman put a hand to his arm and looked up at him with pleading eyes.

Fine, he'd be quiet this time. But Mrs. Blakely was just plain rude.

At the same time, Reuben couldn't help wondering the details of his assistant's past. She'd mentioned more than once that it wasn't good but hadn't offered any details. Not a boss-asking-his-assistant kind of question though.

Despite not officially being invited, they followed Kyle into the house, which was neat, clean, and slightly outdated, but other than that, shouted of normality. A blue flowered couch in the living room, family pictures covering the fireplace mantel, and a collection of bells from a variety of states in a corner china cabinet. For some reason, the term "foster parent" had equated itself with "poor losers who get kids for money." A totally unfair stereotype, he knew.

And maybe Mrs. Blakely was just concerned about Kyle. Maddie herself had said she was quite wild not too long ago.

The older woman motioned to a spot at the table. "Have a seat. Want something to eat or drink?"

"No thanks." He sat down at the plain, solid oak wood table on the other side of Maddie.

The woman sat across the table and sipped an iced tea. "So you're Maddie's boss?"

"Yes, ma'am. I own a couple restaurants. Maddie has been a godsend to me. I'm in the middle of another expansion project to open two more restaurants, so she's been helping keep some of the day-to-day administrative work taken care of so I can focus on the building project."

Mrs. Blakely eyed Maddie. "What happened to the hair thing?"

"I still work there actually. I am working both jobs."

"Must take up all your time then."

Maddie sat up straighter. "I work hard, yes, and am saving up money while I have the time. Eventually, I'll quit one of them so I can be home more often."

Reuben's heart thudded in his chest. She'd said "one of them." Surely she wouldn't quit on him.

"You might not want to say that with your boss sitting right here, girl."

"Reuben knows where we stand. I'm not worried about it."

He did? She wasn't? A private talk would be needed, as Reuben didn't have a clue what was going on under that adorable brown hair of hers.

Kyle pushed his chair back. "Ready to go. My stuff's already by the door."

Mrs. Blakely pointed at his plate. "You know the rules."

He rolled his eyes. "Whatever." But he still threw the paper plate in the trash.

Reuben stood and held a hand out to Mrs. Blakely. "Nice to meet you, ma'am."

She grasped his hand and held tight. "You better not hurt either of them, you hear?"

"Wouldn't think of it. I'll protect them with my life." And he meant it too. A fierce sense of obligation overtook him when he saw Maddie trying to help Kyle with his things, and the boy refusing assistance. The two were special, and God and Mrs. Blakely held him responsible for their well-being. He determined not to let either of them down.

# 33

*M*addie unlocked the front door and stood aside as Kyle and Reuben brought the luggage in. She could barely keep still. Her little brother was here. How cool was that!

Kyle tossed a duffle bag onto the floor. "So, where do I sleep? And what's for dinner? Cool, at least you have a TV. Any video games?"

Typical boy. "I only have the one bed, but you can take it while you're here, I'll sleep on the couch. I'm ordering a pizza for dinner and no video games. Sorry." She'd tell Allie to help her keep an eye out for some at garage sales.

"Pineapple and ham?"

She laughed. "Is there any other?" They'd survived on ham and pineapple pizza after Mom died. The Pizza Hut guy in their old neighborhood knew them by name.

Kyle shouldered the duffle and took his other bag and pillow from Reuben and headed down the hall. Her boss stood in the middle of the room looking ultra-hot in his jeans and button-up plaid shirt.

Maddie set her purse down and fished out her wallet from the chaos. She really needed to learn to throw away old receipts and church bulletins. "Thanks for driving me. How much do I owe you for gas?"

He tucked his thumbs into his jean pockets. "Not a dime, and you know it. I enjoyed it."

"Driving for me and listening to me whine the whole time? If that's enjoyable, you seriously need to rethink your brand of entertainment. I insist on paying you something."

"How about we use the barter system?"

Maddie turned from him and headed for the kitchen, trying to create distance between them. "I'm not paying you with a kiss, so you can just forget about it."

He'd followed her and took a seat at the table. "That wasn't what I had in mind, but now that you mention it—"

"I'm not a rebound girl, Reub. In fact, I'm not going to be any man's girl. Ever."

"So I've heard. Why not?"

"Because men are pigs."

He turned in his seat. "Well, thanks a lot."

She picked up the phone book she'd found in a drawer and flipped through the yellow pages. "It's not your fault. You can't help that you were born into the male species. But as nice as you are sometimes, you do have some jerkish qualities."

He drummed his fingers against the table. "Like?"

The list was quite long. Where to start? "For one, you think you can tell me what to do."

He shrugged. "I've just been trying to help."

"And there's another one. You butt your nose into my business even when I don't ask for it. You kiss me like you have this God-given right to claim whichever woman's lips you'd like. And really, you just make me crazy sometimes."

He stood and scooted his chair back. "All horrible things, I must admit. See you later then." He walked toward the front door as Kyle was returning.

"Where you going, man? Thought you'd stay for pizza."

"Your sister isn't too keen on jerkish men, so I'm letting myself out."

The preteen shrugged. "Maddie can be weird sometimes. Sorry."

"Not your fault." He slapped him on the back. "See you around."

She wanted him to leave, but curiosity and guilt won out. "Wait."

He opened the door, but turned to face her. "Yes?"

"The barter. If it wasn't, uh, the other thing, then what did you have in mind?"

"Pizza. Thought I'd stay over and eat with you guys, but not sure I want to stay where I'm not welcome."

Kyle flopped onto the couch. "Mad, be nice and let the dude stay. He seems cool."

She did owe him for the gas. "Reuben, we'd be delighted if you stayed and ate pizza with us."

The door closed. "Even if I'm a jerk?"

She shrugged. "Kyle's here anyway. Might as well make it two." A cushion from the couch flew through the air and hit her in the leg. "I was going to get some cheesy bread, but if you keep that up, you can forget it."

"Sorry, sis. Won't happen again. But you did just call me a jerk."

"Call 'em like I see 'em." She laughed as she ducked into the kitchen to side-step another cushion.

That settled, she called in the order as the guys settled on the couch and turned on the TV. Typical men/boys. But there wasn't much else to do. For the first time, it hit her that Kyle would be there for two days and she had no clue how to keep him entertained.

What if he went back to Chicago and begged Mrs. Blakely to not make him come back? What if he hated it here? She needed to find some video games, pronto.

"Hey sis."

She peeked out of the kitchen. "Yes?"

"What we doin' tomorrow?"

And it started. "I'm not sure yet. Why?"

"Reuben was saying maybe we could go hiking or something. He knows some trails. . . . "

Not her first choice of activities, especially if her boss was along, but anything was better than sitting here all day and counting the flecks of gold in the carpet. "Sure, that sounds fun." About as exciting as a root canal.

"You don't have to go if you don't want to. I know you aren't, like, a hiking kinda girl."

What was that supposed to mean? Did he think her a stuffy diva who spent her days getting her nails and hair done? Sure, that *sounded* really nice right now, but . . . "I wouldn't mind going. Reub, what time you thinking?"

"Earlier the better, before the heat of the day."

Scratch any ideas of shopping garage sales with Allie for video games. "Okay, like eight?"

"Uh, thinking more like six."

Maybe she needed to take a few Q-tips to her ears. "In the morning?"

"Too early for you?"

"You do realize you're asking me to go hiking with a broken arm, right?" She turned, not wanting to see the pity in his eyes. Her broken arm was a convenient, and true, excuse to get out of hours of walking, getting dirty, and spending two insanely early Saturdays in a row.

"Sorry. I forgot about your arm. If you want, I can take Kyle. But if you have plans—"

She shook her head. "No, if Kyle wants to go, that's fine. Allie and I might go garage saling anyway." Maddie would put her foot down though. She wasn't getting out of bed a minute before eight.

Kyle beamed at her. "Thanks, sis."

"Do you all want something to drink? I have pop."

They both replied in the affirmative, and Maddie reentered the kitchen to fix their drinks. As she took them into the living room, the doorbell and her cell phone rang simultaneously.

Reuben stood and took the drinks from her. "You answer your phone, I'll get the door."

Who would be calling her? Maybe Allie about the morning. She picked her phone out of her purse and stilled when she saw the number on caller ID. She'd screen the call if Reuben wouldn't become suspicious.

She answered, despite her desire to throw the phone through the window and be done with it.

"Maddie, it's Livy." No, really? She never would have guessed. "I just want to let you know that I know what you did."

Maddie glanced at the guys in the living room, starting to dig into the pizza. It irked her to no end that Reuben had probably paid for it. So much for the barter system. "I'm sorry, what did you say?"

"Don't play innocent with me. If you don't tell him, I will."

What was the woman talking about? Had she officially gone bonkers? "I—"

"I don't want to hear your excuses. Tell him by Monday, or I will."

A click signaled the end of the call.

Fear clutched its talons into her heart. She had no clue what was going on. How could she confess something she didn't do, or didn't know that she did? What did Livy know? Surely it wasn't—

The room began to spin, and she leaned on the table for support.

"Maddie?" Reuben's concerned voice made it to her ears, but she couldn't respond, her throat like rough sandpaper.

A moment later arms closed around her and she was pressed against his chest. "Who was it? What's wrong?"

She shook her head. No way could she explain Livy's phone call without raising his suspicions. No, she had to figure it out first. "Nothing. I, just, I got dizzy all the sudden."

"Let's get you to bed. I think we've overexerted you for the day."

She shook her head. Tonight was Kyle's first night here. She wouldn't bail. "I'll be fine if I can just sit down for a bit."

Before she could protest, Reuben swung her up in his arms, his arm supporting her knees like a little baby. How humiliating.

But thankfully he set her down on the couch beside Kyle, then took the place on the other side of her. "There's a movie on TV. We can all watch that while we pig out on pizza. Okay?"

Maddie nodded, trying not to think of Livy or of how good it felt to be snuggled between her two favorite men.

Even though she'd never let one of them know that. Just like she couldn't let him know about her past. But if Livy had found out, there might not be any other choice.

And if that happened, she might just lose everything.

⁓

Reuben pressed a sleeping Maddie closer to his chest. She fit perfectly against him, and he would be just fine to keep her there for a long time to come.

On the other side of her, Kyle stood and stretched. "Well, I better get to bed."

"Hey, man. Do you mind taking the couch? Maddie's still in pain from last weekend, and I think she'd sleep better on the bed."

"Yeah, I planned to make her sleep there anyway. I put my stuff in the empty room."

The boy had a lot more respect than Reuben expected for a foster kid. He obviously thought the world of his big sister. He nodded his head in approval, not wanting to make a big deal out of it.

"Can you go turn down her bed? I'll carry her in there."

The boy paused. "You two aren't sleeping together, are you?"

Hearing the words from an eleven-year-old tore at his heart. That he even had to ask was sad. "No, we aren't. I'd be lying if I told you I didn't like your sister. But I believe in respecting women and not sleeping with a woman unless she's my wife."

"Do you, like, wanna marry her?"

This conversation wasn't taking the greatest of directions. He shook his head. "I've only known her a couple of months, and just recently broke up with my fiancée. Plus, your sister has some issues with guys. Seems to think she's destined to be single."

The boy laughed. "That'd be a switch. Maddie hasn't been without a guy in her bed in I don't know how long."

That he talked about it with no embarrassment worried Reuben even more. "Well, she's been alone since she moved here and is doing pretty good."

"Yeah, she said she got Jesus or something like that and wasn't gonna sleep around anymore. I didn't believe her though."

"Why do you think she was like that? I mean, with so many guys."

Kyle shrugged. "I dunno. Dad was such a jerk, I figured she'd hate guys forever. Anyway, I never realized what she was doing, making me sleep over at friend's houses all the time. But then we went into our first foster home, and she got caught sneaking out at night. I heard them yelling about it all the time. Then I went to the Blakelys and Maddie went to some other place. I heard Sarge tell Sid she was gonna get pregnant or sick if she didn't stop."

Reuben had no clue who Sarge and Sid were, but his stomach churned at the thought of Maddie as a teen. "How old is your sister?" He already knew the answer, but right now, he just wanted to get the subject off of sex.

"I dunno. Her birthday is in September, that's all I know. That's why Corina is gonna let me come back over Labor Day. Her birthday is on Monday."

"We'll have to throw her a party, won't we?"

"Okay, but just a small one. She isn't big into parties."

She had been a bit out of place last week at her housewarming party. "Why not?"

"Dad used to throw some with his drinking buddies. They'd drink all night and get real mean. Pretty scary. We both decided that parties weren't all that great."

He wanted to find the guy and clobber him. "It'll just be small, with my family and you. Okay?"

"Whatever." He nods toward the hallway. "You can bring her? I'll go get the bed ready."

Reuben lifted her and smiled when her arms went around his neck, her cast rubbing against his skin. She was a hundred-ten pounds, if that, and looked too cute asleep against him.

He could get used to this way too easily.

The covers were turned down when he got into the room, and he laid her on the bed and took her sandals off her feet.

Her toenails, a pink metallic color, sparkled against the white sheet before he tucked the bedding around her.

Kyle stood beside him, hovering as if to protect her if he tried anything.

Reuben motioned him out of the room and switched off the light as he closed the door. No need to tell the boy this wasn't the first time he'd carried his sister to bed. That first night at his mom's house still stirred his senses. She'd clung to him just like tonight, and he'd taken off her shoes and socks, something oh-so-personal for a guy to his new assistant.

If he were honest, in that moment he'd started to question his relationship with Livy.

Now he was single.

But Maddie still held a lot of hurt and a lot of questions. She was young. Almost seven years his junior. She'd been through more in her life than he could even imagine. Would he be able to help her heal? Could he deal with the issues she was bound to have pent up inside of her?

He just wasn't sure.

Kyle plopped back on the couch and used a cushion as a pillow. "I'm beat."

"You get some sleep, I'll just clean up here and let myself out. See you bright and early at six, okay?"

"Sure. If I'm asleep, wake me up."

Reuben was glad he had a spare key. "Will do."

He picked up the empty pizza box from the floor and tossed it in the kitchen trash. He put the cups in the sink, rinsed them, and added them to the dirty dishes in the dishwasher. Maddie could start it in the morning.

Turning to leave, he noticed her cell phone sitting on the kitchen table.

Whoever had called had disturbed Maddie more than she let on.

A glance at Kyle told him the boy was already asleep, the sound of his snores drifting into the kitchen.

It'd be an invasion of privacy to look. But fierce protection smoldered inside of him. It was for her good.

He picked it up, then set it back down. It was wrong. He wiped his sweaty palm against his pants. If she wanted to tell him, she could.

# 34

"I'm bored." Kyle lay on the couch, one arm under his head and the other flung across his body.

If Maddie heard those words one more time, she might give up and scream. Older boys were so much harder. Had it only been a few years ago when he would entertain himself with Tonka trucks and playing cowboys and Indians?

The video game system she and Allie had scrounged up that morning worked for about an hour and a half after Reuben dropped him back off this afternoon. But now she was out of ideas. If he were here permanently, she'd put him to work around the house, and there'd be school for him soon, friends he'd make.

But a visit was harder than she'd imagined.

"You wanna watch a movie?" She'd also splurged and bought a DVD player at Walmart. Using the TV to entertain probably wasn't the wisest parenting decision she could make, but desperate times called for whatever would keep Kyle happy.

"I guess. We gonna go rent one?"

"Yeah, and we can stop by the grocery store too. Maybe bring back chicken for dinner?"

He shrugged. "Fine."

They headed to her Tracker and were on the road when Maddie finally worked up the nerve to ask the question she'd being dying to know the answer to. "So, what do you think of Sandwich?"

The shrug of his shoulders made her stomach tighten. "It's cool, I guess. Hiking was fun this morning."

*He likes it here! Thank you, Jesus!* She'd have to tell Reuben.

She turned into the parking lot of Art's Supermarket. Making sure her short list was in hand, they walked into the store. Buying with an eleven-year-old boy in mind was much different than for just herself.

Halfway through the shopping trip, it became clear that grocery shopping with Kyle was a monumental error in judgment. Her cart was full of junk food. Somewhere buried down there was a bunch of bananas, but other than that, not a healthy item in the bunch.

"Hey sis, these are awesome." He held up a box of snacks that shouted 100-calorie packs on the front. At least they were better than the three packs of little cake snacks he'd thrown in a few minutes before.

"Kyle, we need to cool it with the junk food. I haven't even gotten half the things on my list."

"A boy's gotta eat when a boy's gotta eat, Sis." His eyes lit up. "Oh! Oreos! Buy one get one free. Sold."

Maddie groaned. "Let's just get this finished, okay? And no more junk food."

They made it to the checkout with only a few arguments over purchases. The cashier rang everything up and told her the total.

Maddie gulped. "How much again?"

She repeated the three-digit number.

The balance in her bank account ran through her brain. It'd be cutting it close, like within pennies.

She glanced at the bagger packing the bags, and Kyle standing behind her. Usually she'd just put a few things back, but it'd be too humiliating with everyone staring.

"Is there a problem, ma'am?"

"No, sorry." She bit her lip and swiped her card. *Please, Jesus, don't let it reject. I have no clue how these things work, but please make it go through.* The machine prompted for her PIN, which she entered.

The cheerful cashier handed her a slip of paper. "Here's your receipt, ma'am. You have a wonderful day."

*God, thank you.*

Kyle helped her load the groceries into the Tracker, but instead of heading to get a movie, she ran by the bank instead. "Just need to check something."

If her balance was in the negative, she could transfer some from the tiny amount she had hoarded in a savings account. Oh, why hadn't she done the overdraft protection like the bank lady had recommended when she opened the local account?

She pulled through to the ATM and slipped her card into the reader to request a balance inquiry. The machine spit out a receipt.

Maddie looked at the number printed, then blinked and reread it. Was there some kind of banking error?

"What's wrong, sis?"

"I think there's something wrong with my account. Hold on a minute. I'm gonna check the transactions on my phone."

Since she didn't have online access to her account at home due to no computer, she had the toll-free number on speed dial to get transactions voiced to her.

The prerecorded information droned in her ear, and after entering her information, she finally was able to press one for the five most recent deposits.

After hearing the first one, she almost dropped the phone.

The deposit on Friday for her paycheck was a good two-thousand dollars more than it should have been.

# 35

"What's wrong?"

Maddie clicked the end button on the phone with her shaking thumb. "Nothing. I, uh, just calculated wrong. There's plenty of money, no worries." *Liar.* She didn't want to explain to Kyle yet. Not until she'd decided what to do about it.

What was Reuben doing? She didn't need his handouts. She wanted to strangle him. Couldn't he just leave well enough alone?

"Cool. Let's go get a movie. I'm starving, and the chicken's gettin' cold."

No longer worried about her meager bank account balance, she drove to the Walgreen's Redbox. After picking up a chick flick for herself and some strange teen dragon movie she'd never heard of, she drove home, drooling as she did every time she entered the Lake Holiday subdivision. What she wouldn't give to have one of the lakeside homes that cost an arm and a leg.

Kyle pointed out a particularly cool one that sported a For Sale sign in the yard. "You should buy that one, sis."

"You have about six-hundred grand to loan me?"

"Wow, are they really that much?"

She nodded but didn't divulge that the only reason she knew was because she'd sneaked onto their lawn last week when driving home late and took one of the "Take one" flyers by the sign. She'd almost fainted upon seeing the over half-million-dollar price.

"You should see Reuben's house. His isn't quite as big, but it's still quite nice."

"See, you should just hook up with him, sis, and you'd have it made."

She gripped the steering wheel. She'd have done just that not even a year earlier. "I'm not 'hooking up' with Reuben, by way of marriage or any other method. Besides, I'm done with men."

"Oh, yeah, Reuben told me about that. Why? I thought you always had to have a man at your side?"

"I found Jesus, remember? He's the only man I need now." She loved how "good" she sounded when she said that.

Immediately she chided herself. Surely such a thought was prideful or some other sinful attribute that would cancel out any benefit of her no-man-but-Jesus attitude.

"So Jesus says you can't have sex anymore?"

*God, please please stop this conversation. I do not want to talk to my little brother about sex. I know, I want him to live with me, the subject will come up. Can't I, like, take him to a pastor or something? Seriously? Please?*

Reuben flashed through her mind, but oh no. Asking her boss to sit down and have a birds-and-the-bees talk with her little brother was beyond humiliating.

She'd have to brave it by her lonesome.

"The Bible says that the physical side of a relationship should wait until you're married. I'm not, so I will stay in my own bed." There. That sounded . . . motherly.

"That's new. Last I heard you were warming the bed of every guy in high school."

Maddie slammed on her brakes, screeching to a stop in the middle of the street. "Excuse me? Where did you hear that?"

He shrugged. "Sarge."

Air refused to fill her lungs. "She told you that?"

"No, I heard her telling Sid."

Cold-blooded fury coursed through her veins as she tried to control her breathing. How dare that . . . that . . . that *female-dog* woman. She hadn't wanted to swear so bad since moving to Sandwich, a habit she'd determined to leave behind in the projects of Chicago.

A horn honked behind her, so she pressed the gas again, gently because if she let her emotions take over, they'd be going ninety in the twenty-mile-an-hour zone. She remained silent until pulling into the driveway, then turned to face Kyle, who was picking at his fingernails. Obviously this was an issue that didn't sit well with him either.

"I didn't sleep with every guy in high school." Although it was closer than she wanted to admit. She took a deep breath. "And what I did do is behind me now. Jesus takes all of the crud in our life, throws it out the window, and lets us start over fresh. I'm not saying I'm perfect now, but I'm trying, Kyle. So when it comes to guys, they're off-limits. I know my weaknesses."

"Yeah, that you're easy?"

She clenched her fist on the steering wheel. *Lord, help me.* "No. That big, strong guys can steer me wrong oh so easily. Girls are different than guys, Kyle. There's some weird, rooted desire in us to have someone protect us. Dad was never there for me, you and I both know that. So I let guys do that for me."

"So, now what, you don't need protection anymore?"

"I didn't say that. I'm just letting God do the protection and relying on him."

"Whatever. I still don't understand why you can't get married. That's dumb."

There was no way to explain it to him. He wouldn't understand.

☙

A knock sounded on Reuben's office door, and he glanced up from the papers that littered his desk. "Come in."

Livy peeked her head in. "You busy?"

"A little, but I can make time. What's up?"

She closed the door behind her and took a seat in the office chair across from his desk, the picture of professionalism. "I've been meaning to talk to you."

"About?"

"Maddie."

He didn't want to discuss Maddie with Livy. Maddie was on her way to Chicago with Allie driving, returning Kyle to the Blakelys. "What about her?"

"I see that she's not in today. Everything okay?"

He shrugged. "I gave her the day off."

She rolled her eyes, her face smug. "Must be nice."

He didn't have to explain it to her, but she'd pry until she found out anyway. "Her little brother was in town for the weekend, and she's taking him home. She worked all last week despite being in a lot of pain. She deserves the day off."

Livy held up her hands in mock surrender. "I wasn't saying you shouldn't have given it to her. I'm kind of glad she's not here anyway so we have a chance to talk." She leaned over and dropped a manila folder onto the desk. "Take a look."

He eyed the folder. The file tab had "Madison Buckner" typed in bold all-capped letters. "What's this?"

"Something sat wrong about her with me. So I took the liberty of getting the normal check done that we do on all employees. As you know, you hired her, not me, so nothing was ever run."

"And what gave you the right to do it now, behind my back?"

"Just open it."

He didn't want to. After talking to Kyle, part of him was scared of what he'd find.

The other half of him was dying to get a peak. No need to let Livy know that though and validate her devious handling of the matter. "Thanks for the information, but next time, ask my permission before you spend company funds on something like this, okay? Is there anything else?"

Her cheeks burned red and her eyes squinted. "That's it. Let me know if you need anything else."

She stomped out of the office in typical, Livy-like fashion.

The moment the door closed Reuben opened the folder, then clutched it closed again. No. He wouldn't do this now. He had a billion other things on his plate today, and even if there was something to see, he couldn't do a thing about it now.

*Chicken. You just don't want to think about it. You're afraid of what you'll find.* He brushed the thought aside. Her past was just that. Her past. Before she came to know Jesus.

Didn't everyone do things they came to regret later?

It was none of his business.

He shoved the file in his desk drawer, then settled into his chair and wiggled his mouse.

The envelope icon at the bottom of the screen alerted him of new e-mail.

He clicked on his e-mail software and saw three unread messages. The first was a joke forward from Allie.

Delete.

The second he flagged with a reminder to look at later.

The last one he actually opened. It was an e-mail from the company that processed his payroll, which was odd, because they usually dealt 100 percent with Maddie now.

*Mr. Callahan, attached is a copy of the special payroll journal as requested. We apologize that this was missed last week. If there's anything else I can do for you, please let me know and I'll be happy to assist.*

*Sincerely,*

*K. Barnes*

*Payroll Specialist*

*PayPeople America Inc.*

Reuben frowned. He hadn't requested a copy of the journal, and every other week, it always went to Maddie. Before her, he'd just moved the e-mail to a folder without reviewing them. Someone would let him know if there was a problem.

What concerned him most was the "special payroll" note. Since when did they process those? Maybe there'd been a mistake.

He clicked on the PDF file.

Blinking, he leaned closer. Was that Maddie's name? Yes, and. . . .

His heart froze. A bonus . . . for how much?

A mistake. It had to be.

He picked up his phone and dialed the phone number at the bottom of Ms. Barnes's e-mail signature.

"Good afternoon, PayPeople America, this is Karla speaking, how may I assist you today?"

"This is Reuben at The Sandwich Emporium. I got your e-mail about the pay register?"

There was a pause, then she cleared her throat. "Yes, I, uh, was there a problem, sir?"

"Yes. I have no idea what it's for. I never requested a special payroll."

"I, um, can you hold on one moment, sir?"

He wanted to shout no, to tell him what was going on right now, but instead he muttered yes. Maybe she had to look something up. It had to be a mistake.

The woman came back on the line. "Sir, I'm going to transfer you to my manager. Hold one moment."

The music and advertisements broadcasting their other services came on the line again, grating on his nerves even more. He didn't care about Section 125 plans or 401k services.

A moment later the irritating tirade stopped. "Mr. Callahan, this is Melanie Bristol. How are you doing this morning?"

"I'd be doing better if I knew why a special payroll was being cut without my permission."

"Actually, sir, you gave permission for your assistant, Madison Buckner, to submit all your payroll information with no restrictions."

"You're telling me Maddie called in a bonus to herself?"

"Yes, one of our other specialists took the call last week. There was a note that she'd requested no register be sent, that you'd given her a raise and a bonus but that she didn't need the paperwork."

He blinked. "Her rate of pay increased too?"

"Not on this last check, but she changed it going forward. Quite a generous increase too." The figure she quoted was almost double the rate Maddie currently made.

"If she requested no register be sent, why did Karla send me one today?"

The woman cleared her throat. "Karla is your normal specialist and speaks to Maddie quite often, and when the other specialist mentioned taking the call for her last week, she got suspicious. Maddie is usually very insistent on getting all her paperwork timely, so it just seemed out of place, especially with the bonus being for herself. We felt it prudent to send you a copy just to be on the safe side."

Nothing about this made sense. "Are you sure it was Maddie?"

"We asked her to confirm her social security number to verify her identity, sir."

Hurt pinched his heart. "Thanks for sending the register to me. Can you please put a note that all raises or additional pays out of the norm should be cleared by me?"

"Certainly, sir. Is there anything else we can do to assist?"

"Not right now."

He slammed down the phone, not sure what he should do.

What could she need the money for? He would have given it to her if she'd asked. There had to be some mistake.

He tapped his foot for a moment, then pulled out the file he'd shoved in the drawer.

Scanning the report, his mouth dropped open.

Anger slammed through his veins.

He slammed the folder shut and looked at his watch. She should be home or close to it by now.

Maddie had some explaining to do.

# 36

$M$addie rested her head on the arm of the couch and settled in for a quiet evening of watching TV and eating popcorn for dinner. She'd survived her first Kyle visit, and while a little bumpy, it had gone well.

She couldn't wait until Labor Day weekend. She planned to have the house much more ready by then, and Kyle's room decked out with stuff to make him feel comfortable, as much as her budget would allow. No more sleeping on the couch.

One thing was sure, though. She would be returning every penny of the bonus Reuben had given her the moment she arrived at the restaurant in the morning. She'd even gone to the bank after they'd gotten back in town and withdrew every penny in cash.

She'd provide for her brother, and as sweet as it was, she didn't need Reuben's help.

A knock on the door startled her.

Dragging her weary body off the couch, she padded to the front door and opened it to find Reuben standing there, the old familiar frown on his face, except this time, she almost saw steam coming out of his ears.

What had she done now?

"I wasn't expecting you."

He walked around her and into the room, but didn't say a word.

"Reub, is something wrong?"

He thrust a piece of paper into her free hand. "Explain this." The words shot right through her heart like a bullet shattering it.

She looked at the sheet. It was a payroll journal.

With her bonus on it.

Her hand shook as she handed it back. "I was going to ask you the same thing."

He paced the floor. "Don't act innocent, Maddie. I'm a lot of things, but I'm not stupid." He stopped in front of her, his eyes boring into her like a drill. "If you needed money, why didn't you just ask? Why did you have to go behind my back?"

Maddie blinked. "Excuse me? You think this was me?"

"No one else is going to call in a bonus for you."

If she had two good arms, she'd punch him right now. Her voice rose a decibel. "And how stupid would I have to be to call in one for myself?"

"You know, I don't pay attention to payroll that much. You had the perfect gig, giving yourself a raise too."

His words were like someone kicking her in the gut. She wasn't even mad anymore. Her heart just plain hurt. "I can't believe you'd think I would do that."

"I got your background check back. There's a lot of things in there I didn't believe you'd do."

Maddie put her hand to her chest. Her heart lay limp inside, bloody from the massacre his words created. She choked out her words through tears. "How dare you."

He stepped toward her, his eyes hard and black. "You know, I think it's better that Kyle stays with the Blakelys. He needs a good influence on him."

She slapped him on the cheek as hard as she could. The pain of the impact on her hand shot up her arm, but she ignored it. He deserved it and a thousand more.

Reuben stood silent, a red mark streaked across his cheek.

Maddie walked over to her purse and took out the bank envelope with the bonus money in it and walked back to him, slamming it into his hand. "There. Every penny of the bonus. I thought you were just being typical Reuben, trying to take care of me, and had determined to give it back to you in the morning. Instead, you're a bigger jerk than I expected."

His jaw clenched, and he opened his mouth to speak but she stopped him. "You know? You have this innate ability to judge everybody. Reuben the prosecutor, judge, and jury, and no one ever stands a chance. Since I've known you, you've blamed me for ruining your hair, your car, your restaurant, and now stealing money from you. And of course, I'm going to pollute Kyle too."

She took a step forward and got as much in his face as her height would allow. "I made mistakes. I'll be the first one to tell you that. I don't know what your little report told you, but here are just a few."

"Maddie, I didn't—"

"No, no. If you're going to accuse me of things, I want you to know exactly what I have done, not some made-up crap. At my last count, I'd slept with about fifteen guys, give or take. That waitress job I told you I had for a day? Not only was I bad at it, I also lifted a watch, a wallet, and purses from various customers before I was caught.

"And at a particularly low point after high school, I walked the streets and contemplated prostituting myself for money so I could eat. Almost did it too. Lucky for me, the guy who offered was a cop. Instead of going through with it, I got put in jail."

His face blanched white and he put his hand on her arm.

Maddie shoved them off. "Don't you dare touch me. Get out of my house."

"Maddie—"

She pointed. "Now."

He turned to leave, but at the doorway, stopped. "I—"

"One last thing." She held the door in her hand and took a deep breath. "You have the most amazing stepfather I've ever met and all you can do is act like a total jerk to him. You accuse him of some pretty crappy stuff, and while I get that your dad died, it doesn't give you the right to make Gary and your mom miserable just because you can't get over it. It's called showing grace, Reuben. Look it up."

She slammed the door in his face, then opened it back up to see his shocked face. "Oh, and I quit."

She shut the door a little tamer the second time.

# 37

$\mathcal{A}$ hand shook her shoulder. Maddie stretched in bed and turned to see Kyle peering at her. "What time is it?" Her voice grumbled even to her own ears.

"Eight. I let ya sleep in."

She sat up in bed and stretched. Labor Day. And her twenty-first birthday.

The only birthday present she wanted was the eleven-year-old who stood beside her bed holding a cookie sheet with breakfast on top. A bowl of cereal, toast—she thought anyway—and milk.

She couldn't hold back her cheesy grin. "You're so sweet. Thank you."

"Allie told me I had to. And the toast is black."

It indeed resembled a chalkboard. "It's perfect."

Sitting up in bed, she took the tray from him and settled it in her lap. She took a bite of the Frosted Flakes and paused.

Kyle was staring at her, so she smiled and forced herself to swallow the lukewarm, soggy flakes. "Mmmm. Yum. How long ago did you get breakfast ready?"

He shrugged. "About an hour ago. I wanted it to be ready for you whenever you woke up. I didn't want it to go bad, so I finally woke you up."

The poor guy was about forty-five minutes late for that, but no one could drag the truth out of her. "Well, it's fabulous. Thanks."

He smiled and turned to leave. "I'm gonna go get dressed. We're going to the fair today still, right?"

"Of course."

They'd decided no party, just a fun day at the Sandwich Fair and a sickening amount of cotton candy.

When Kyle was out of site, she set the makeshift tray on the bed, grabbed the bowl, and dumped its contents into the trashcan beside her bed, then emptied the tissue box from the dresser into the can to hide her crime.

*Note to Maddie: Take out the trash ASAP.*

She bit into a piece of the toast, but it caught on a tooth.

Glancing at the door, she reached down and tucked the rock-hard black bread under some of the tissues.

She was about to do the same with the glass of milk when Kyle walked by her room and poked his head in. "You done already?"

She shrugged. "It was good, what can I say." To prove her point, she lifted the glass of tepid milk and chugged it.

Her stomach almost revolted, but thankfully it obeyed and kept its churning to itself.

"Hey, can Reuben come to the fair with us today?"

Just hearing his name made her want to throw the glass across the room. She hadn't seen him in a month and a half, and she'd love to keep up the record. "No, I'm sure he's working or something."

She would have no idea what the man was up to. When Allie tried to fill her in, she refused to listen.

The only thing she knew was that Livy wasn't working for him anymore, and that he'd hired a new assistant. She knew that only because a customer at the salon had droned on and on about it. Maddie would have told her to shut up if not for the fact that she was an amazing tipper.

"Did he fire you or something?"

She rolled her eyes. "No, now drop it or we'll sit here and watch soap operas all afternoon."

"Fine. Hurry up and get ready so we can go."

"We're meeting Allie and the kids at eleven, remember? We have almost three hours."

She needed to pick up the house a little anyway. Corina was coming tomorrow to get Kyle and was doing her home study at the same time. Maddie had finally saved enough money to make the house look presentable and have a slim but fighting chance at getting Kyle, so she had filled out the formal petition two weeks earlier.

They were waiting for a final court date to see what the judge would decide.

"I'm going to play video games then. Let me know when you can go."

"You could help me pick up ya know."

"Or I could not. It's my last day of freedom. You gonna make me spend it cleaning?"

So much for birthday pampering. "Fine, go."

"We could always go out to breakfast."

Maddie frowned. "But you already gave me breakfast in bed."

He rolled his eyes. "Which you then threw in the trash. I'm not stupid, sis."

"Let me get dressed. Where you wanna go?"

A speed clean and a McDonald's stop later, they arrived an hour early at the fair.

Kyle shoved his hands in his shorts pocket. "Let's ride the rocket launcher."

The ride that threw its occupants around in circles for an ungodly amount of time was a no-go for her. "Or not. That thing looks like it could kill someone. I was thinking more like bumper cars."

"Wimp."

Maddie nodded. "Yep. I'm fine with that title."

They walked through the crowds, and Maddie bought cotton candy to help keep the scary ride suggestions at bay.

She pinched a puff from the fluffy pink mound and stuffed it in her mouth. Yum, Yum! Pure sugary goodness. She offered it to Kyle, but a throat cleared behind them.

Her breath caught in her chest and a piece of pinky fuzz threatened to choke her.

Kyle smiled for the first time since they arrived at the fair. Traitor. "Hey Reuben. Maddie said you were working today."

Reuben raised an eyebrow in Maddie's direction then looked back at Kyle. "Nope. Took the day off to hang out with Allie and the kids. I heard you were in town, though. Having fun?"

He rolled his eyes. "Maddie only wants to ride the sissy rides."

Maddie rested her hands on her hips and kept her eyes trained on Kyle. She didn't even want to look at the man. "Safe rides, not sissy rides."

Kyle kicked a rock on the ground. "Whatever, same thing."

Reuben's baritone voice thudded against her ears. "Do you think she would mind if I rode a few with you?"

She sat up straight. How dare he talk about her like she wasn't even here? "That won't be necessary. I can ride with him."

Kyle shoved another piece of cotton candy into his mouth. "Even the Blue Thunder?"

Maddie swallowed. The ride moved every which way, in circles, and upside down at ridiculous speeds that no human should be allowed to travel outside of an airplane. Especially one who'd just gotten a cast off two weeks prior. "Of course, even that one. Now, let's go. I think Reuben has things to do."

Reuben's mouth tipped up into a mischievous smile. "Actually, the Blue Thunder sits three in a seat. We can all go."

Kyle whooped and hollered and pulled Maddie toward the ride.

When they got to the short line, she stepped back. It was probably short because no one else was stupid enough to get on it. "You two go. It's okay. I'll just wait."

Reuben leaned down and whispered in her ear. "Chicken?"

She narrowed her eyes. The man had some nerve. "Fine. Let's go."

Marching in front of them, she held her head up high. She could do this. How scary could a ride at a country fair be?

⟳

Maddie heaved into a trashcan beside the Blue Thunder.

Reuben was in so much trouble. She'd done just fine without him. Why couldn't the man just leave her be?

She walked back toward them, wiping her mouth, and praying her stomach would stop revolting. "I guess that McDonald's this morning didn't agree with me or something." She glanced at her watch. "Kyle, let's go. It's about time to meet up with Allie."

And get rid of Reuben.

Her ex-boss smiled. "I was going to meet her too. She said she'd be over by the food tents. I'll walk with you."

Maddie looked at Kyle who grinned from ear to ear. She smelled a setup. "Well, let's go then."

Her nose twitched the closer they got to the "food" section of the fair. Normally the smells would be delightful. Now the greasy corn dog mixed with sweet funnel cake aroma made her eye the midway for another trashcan.

Allie and her crew waved to them from where they stood in line at a hot dog and funnel cake stand. "Yoo-hoo, Maddie, Reuben, over here!"

Maddie weaved in and out of the crowd, dragging Kyle along behind her, until they reached the crew. "Hey there. We got here a little early so were checking out the rides."

"Good! The girls just wanted something to drink real quick. We had a late breakfast so we aren't hungry yet."

Phew. Because she'd leave if she had to watch anyone stuff their face right now.

Cole looked from his Mom to Kyle, then back to his mom. "Hey, can Kyle come with me and the other guys to ride rides?"

Allie shrugged. "As long as it's okay with Maddie." She turned to her. "The boys from the youth group at church are all meeting up in a few minutes to do the rides together. Kyle's welcome to join them if you'd like."

Kyle used his best begging stance, tugging on her arm and looking at her with puppy-dog eyes. "Please, Maddie? I'll be fine. Come on. You want me to like it here, right?"

Corina had finally agreed to mention Maddie's request for custody to Kyle. He now used it as leverage.

The boy was good. Too good. "Yes, but I just don't know if it's safe. "

Reuben cleared his throat. "Maddie, I think it'll be all right."

She glared at him. "I don't remember asking you."

He shrugged. "I know the guys. They're good, and there's a few older ones in the bunch. It's normal for the teens to hang out together at the fair. You're not in Chicago anymore, Dorothy."

Maybe she was being a spoiled sport. But letting her little brother roam around the fair without her, even if he was with the youth group from church, just didn't sit well. She wanted him to get to know other kids here though. "Fine. Go. But take my cell phone. Allie is the number three speed-dial. We'll call you when we're ready to leave, or vice versa." She tossed her phone to him.

He flipped it open and nodded. "Who's number one and two?"

*Do not blush!* "Voicemail's number one."

Reuben's phone blared out a saxophone ringtone.

Kyle smirked. "Guess Reuben's number two then, huh?"

Maddie wanted to throttle him. "Just go and have fun, okay?"

"Cool. Thanks, sis!" He took off with Cole.

Allie paid for her drink and handed it to Sara. "I need to take the girls to the kiddy ride section. I'm sure that will be boring for you guys. How 'bout I meet up with you in a few hours at the exhibits?"

Maddie looked from a smiling Allie to a wide-eyed Reuben. A set-up if she ever saw it. "Wait. I thought the point was to walk around together."

The fiend smiled. "It is. And we will . . . in a few hours. Have fun." She pushed the stroller and pulled Sara along before anyone could argue.

"So, I'm your most important speed-dial, hmm?"

She cast Reuben a barely-tolerant glance. "No, that would be voicemail, remember? Besides, you're only number two because you were my boss and are highly demanding. I just forgot to change it, so don't get a big head."

"Too late. I'm already flattered. Can't take it back now."

"You just don't know about the dartboard with your picture on it hanging in my bedroom."

A mischievous glint sparkled in his eye. "You hang my picture in your room?"

The man was utterly impossible and egotistical. "Listen. Neither of us wants to walk around the fair together. I'll just go look at some chickens or something, okay?"

"After Allie went to so much trouble? I think not."

This was not how she wanted to spend her birthday. At all. And her stomach had tentatively regained it's land legs. "Fine, you can buy me cotton candy then." He deserved to buy her a billion cotton candies.

He shook his head. "I think we can do better than sugar on a stick."

Five minutes later, they walked away from a vendor stand with the biggest elephant ear Maddie had ever seen drenched in powdered sugar. She tore off a piece of the dough and lifted it to her mouth.

Heavenly. She could feel her arteries clogging.

Reuben tugged at her arm and when she jerked it back, he brushed his thumb against the side of her mouth. "Just a little wayward sugar."

A tremble ran from her cheek all the way to her toes at the feather-light touch. She gulped. "Thanks."

"Wanna go on the Ferris wheel?"

Being suspended in air with the man she wanted to use as a punching bag? "Not really."

"Humor me."

They stood in line, and Reuben helped her into the seat when their turn came but she shook his hand away. "I can do it myself."

She tripped and landed in the basket with a thud.

He slid in beside her and lowered the bar to hold them in. "Should have let me help."

The ride lurched and moments later they were airborne.

Then they stopped. She looked around. Had they broken down? "What's going on?"

Reuben settled his hands on the bar in front of them. "Just loading more passengers. It'll be a few more stops until we get going."

Duh. She knew that. Why had she just remembered that little fact? Maybe because they were suspended in the air and with each spurt of movement, the metal machine transported them higher.

Reuben butted her shoulder with his. "You scared?"

She looked down at her white-knuckled grip on the bar. "Um, no. Not at all. Nothing is as bad as the Blue Thunder at least."

"Liar. You need to stop that, you know."

"I know. But then you'll know all my weaknesses, and that just wouldn't do."

The ride heaved forward again, but this time didn't stop. Maddie caught her breath as they circled around.

"I'm sorry, Maddie."

She tore her eyes from the view of the fair to the man beside her. "You should be."

"I fired Livy."

Now that was news. She'd heard that Livy had gotten tired of Reuben's tyrannical rule and left. It was the first time she'd cheered for the woman. None of it mattered though. Reuben, Livy, and the Emporium were none of her concern anymore. "It doesn't really matter now, does it? That's between you and her."

He continued as if he hadn't heard a word she said. "I went back to the restaurant that day and got to looking at things.

Nothing had added up for a while. So I dug into the back-up documents and found where she'd doctored invoices and pocketed the difference and changed receipts to show more tips and less sales. She never admitted to it, but I'm pretty sure she was behind the whole payroll thing too."

Maddie had guessed that a long time ago.

He breathed a hard sigh. "When I fired her, she begged me not to. Seems she'd racked up a lot of debt I didn't know about and was barely paying minimum payments. Livy liked to live nicely. I just . . . I guess I just never realized how much she was spending. The payroll thing, I think she was just jealous. It's the only thing I can figure."

Despite her best intensions, he'd roped in her curiosity. "Jealous of who? You?"

"No, of you, Maddie."

Maddie shook her head. The idea of "Miss Supermodel" being jealous of Maddie Buckner was hilarious and not possible. "I'm nothing compared to her."

He took her chin and tilted it toward him. "You're right."

She pulled away and looked out at the crowds below. "Thanks a lot."

"You're so much more, Maddie." His voice was low and husky.

She snorted. "Yeah, when cows fly."

"You're smart, funny, and you tell things like they are, even when a certain boss is being a complete idiot."

"At least you got one thing right."

"I'm serious. I love your honesty. You don't sugar coat things and you aren't fake. I know exactly what I'm getting when I'm with you."

Tears stung her eyes. "What you'd be getting is a used woman with a big mouth and a bad temper."

He shook his head and used his thumb to wipe her tears. "No, you're refurbished. The Bible says we all are, and thank God for that." He took her hand in his. She let him, but refused to squeeze it like he did hers. "I messed up royally, Maddie. But you were able to open my eyes where so many others had tried and failed. Gary and I had a long talk, and you're right. I was withholding grace and trying to act like God. I think I just wanted someone to blame, and he was convenient."

She permitted one side of her mouth to curl into a partial smile. "I'm glad you figured it out."

He leaned closer, his gaze roaming her face as if he were studying her, his lips but an inch away. His hot breath against her face made her shiver. "I want to kiss you again, Maddie. For real this time."

It'd only take a small shift of her body to show him her heart. Her body, her soul, her heart longed to just throw the past out the window and give in to this beautiful present Reuben offered. Her stomach churned, her pulse raced. But her head screamed stop.

What if he hurt her again? He'd crushed her before not with his fists, but with his words. She wasn't sure she could handle it again. She looked out again over the fairway. "Aren't the lights beautiful from up here?"

"Can I ask a question?"

No. "Okay."

"Why are you afraid to kiss me?"

She lifted her chin and swallowed the pain of her lie. "I'm not afraid. I just don't want to."

"That's not why, and we both know it."

Her heart slammed against her rib cage. If she were on land, she would run. But being up here, her feelings were harder to stuff away, no matter how much she wanted to.

He leaned closer, his mouth dangerously close again. "Maybe a better question is, do you like kissing me?"

She blinked away the tears that threatened to drop. "It has nothing to do with like or not like."

He withdrew. His voice went from husky to low and serious. "What is it, Maddie? I want to help."

She turned to gaze out again, and found herself snuggled closer to Reuben. "The last time a guy kissed me, before you, it wasn't pleasant."

"What happened?"

She'd never talked to anyone about that night. For some reason, her heart ached to unload. Maybe a by-product of the altitude. "Let's just say Ryan wasn't very gentle."

"You mentioned him before."

She closed her eyes, the picture of him imprinted in her brain. "He was into some bad stuff, but his muscles were big, his talk was tough, and I thought he hung the moon. He made me his girl, and let everyone know it. My social status went through the roof. Like everyone respected me overnight because I dated him." The memories tugged at her. The euphoric feeling as she walked down the hall, people standing straighter as she passed, smiles directed at her instead of sneers of disdain. Every girl's high school dream.

It didn't take long for the dream to be smashed as sure as a pumpkin after Halloween. "Ryan didn't do things halfway. The first times we . . ." She blushed at what she'd been about to say. "I mean, he wasn't mean at first. I was so proud, because with everyone else, he acted like a gruff, tough guy, but with me, he was gentle and sweet. I told myself I brought out the good in him. But right about the time I started thinking the L word, he started to get rough. I didn't like it, but he got mad when I told him so.

"Then one day, in school, he pulled me aside and started kissing me, right there in front of everyone. At first I didn't care, but then people started laughing, so I pushed him away. Big mistake. Right there, with everyone watching, he started in on me. He slammed me into the locker and kissed me, then slapped me and started punching. It took a few minutes for a teacher to come out and stop him."

Reuben tightened his arm around her, his hand rubbing gently. "I'm sorry, Maddie. That guy was a big jerk."

"My own fault. I should have known. The good thing was, after that I decided men weren't worth the trouble. If I was going to make a life, I'd do it by myself."

"Even God?"

"Except for God. He's the man I'd been looking for. He's all I need." Just saying the words reminded her of her mission. God, Maddie, and Kyle. They could do it, without the help of anyone else.

Reuben's thumb rubbed a circle on her arm. "What if God wants to use a guy to help you?"

"What if He doesn't?"

"But what if He does, Maddie? God uses all sorts of people. His will is perfect, so if His will is to give you a helpmate in life, don't tell him no. You'll regret it."

The air had gotten too thick up here. She elbowed him to lighten the load. "You're just saying that so you can get a kiss."

His chest shook with laughter. "I won't lie. I want a kiss. But I'm saying that because I care for you, and I know that telling God no isn't a great idea. Believe me. I learned that the hard way."

"You have firsthand experience in that?"

"A topic for another time." He turned her face back toward him, his eyes probing hers. "I'm still waiting for my kiss."

Before she could question her motives or talk herself out of it, Maddie unclenched her hand from the bar and covered his cheek, then leaned closer. "Okay."

He leaned down until his lips grazed hers.

She sucked in a breath, and he leaned back and studied her eyes. "You okay?"

More than okay. She nodded and put her hand behind his neck to draw his lips to hers again, this time savoring every moment. The fear of their first kiss was gone.

Their lips mingled while she ran her fingers through his hair, his hand pressing against her back, inching her closer.

The wheel slowed and then jerked to a stop, the movement causing Maddie to break away.

The reality of what happened drifted into her clouded brain. She'd kissed him. "Reuben—"

He put a finger to her lips. "Shhh. Don't ruin it. We've talked enough, we'll save more for another day. This weekend. Friday night, just the two of us. Our first official date. Okay?"

As their bucket reached land and the attendant opened their bar, Maddie's senses floated back to earth as well. She couldn't do this. It would only end badly.

"Reuben, I—"

The dangerous kisser shushed her as his phone rang. He answered it as they walked down the plank. "Reuben speaking."

Maddie glanced at him and instantly her stomach tightened.

His face wore that old familiar Reuben scowl.

"We'll be right there."

"What happened?"

He pulled her to him and put an arm around her shoulder. "It's Kyle."

# 38

"He spray painted what?" Maddie clenched her fingernails into her palms.

"A cow, ma'am. Seems they thought it would be funny to write the words Blue Thunder on the prize winning cow over at the Ag exhibit. The owner's none too happy."

She bit the side of her cheek to keep from yelling. Loudly. "Oh, the sister's none too happy either. Where is he?"

He motioned for Reuben and Maddie to follow them. Sitting inside the barn was Kyle. No accomplice had come forward, but there was no way he'd done this on his own. He didn't even have any spray paint.

"Kyle, what on earth were you thinking?"

He stared at the floor and shrugged.

Maddie pressed her fingers to her temples. She looked at the security officer. "Can I take him home, or are charges being pressed?"

"No. The owner said as long as he'd get disciplined at home, he wouldn't file a formal complaint."

Well, glory be for that. "Thank you." She turned to Kyle. "Let's go. Now."

He stood and followed her out of the barn, his feet dragging the whole way, Reuben on his heels.

Maddie turned. "Whatever possessed you to do such a thing?"

He only shrugged.

Reuben walked around and put a hand on Kyle's shoulder. "How about I walk you to your car?"

Maddie shook her head. Getting her head mixed up with Reuben got her into this mess. She should have never let Kyle out of her sight. "No, we've got it. I'll, uh, see you around sometime."

"That's it?"

She glanced back to see him standing, his arms spread apart. "Kyle's my priority. I forgot that up there for a minute."

"Maddie, it doesn't have to be this way. I want to help."

"Good-bye, Reuben."

✑

*God, please. Please, please please, let Kyle come here to stay. I need my family, and he's the only person I have left. Even though he does spray paint cows. . . .*

Kyle walked into the living room and tossed his bag beside the couch. "I'm packed. This stinks. I don't want to go back."

"Your cow painting didn't help things, you know."

"I told you I didn't do it. That other kid told me he wanted to show me something cool. I went with him and watched him do it. When someone started yelling, he threw down the can and ran."

While the intelligent sister in her said he was full of bologna, a part of her actually believed him. Kyle may have an attitude, but Sarge ran a tight ship. He didn't get out of line too often.

"It doesn't matter who did it. You weren't supposed to leave the group, but you did and look where it got you."

As if on time, the doorbell chimed. "Can you get that?"

She turned back to the kitchen to finish wiping the counters and heard Reuben's voice float through the house.

Her heart skipped a beat. What was he doing here? He probably decided to come support her while Kyle left. She wished he would just leave. It made it even harder.

She laid the rag on the sink and walked out to the living room. "What are you doing here?"

Without taking his gaze from hers, he cocked his head toward the back sliding door. "Kyle, can you give us a few minutes? Alone?"

The boy shrugged and headed outside.

Maddie lifted her eyebrows. "Corina will be here any minute."

"I know. I came to lend moral support."

She wiped her sweaty palms against her shorts. "I'm doing just fine as it is."

"You know what I think?"

"That sandwiches should be America's national food?"

He smiled. "Besides that."

"Please, do share. Only because I don't think you'll leave until I let you."

"I think you're a rotten receiver."

Maddie rolled her eyes. "I don't see how football has anything to do with me. I probably would be a lousy receiver."

He took a step toward her. "I can't figure out if it's your pride that keeps you from accepting help or the fear of being let down. So which one is it, Maddie?"

She turned to look for something to clean to get out of this conversation. But everything was finished. "Listen, I don't have time for this. Corina's going to be here any time."

Reuben took two steps until he stood directly in front of her. "You told me once that I needed to extend grace. Well, you, my dear, were right. But you also need to accept grace and help from others. Be a graceful receiver. No one can go through life alone."

"I have God. He's all I need."

"News flash, Maddie Buckner. God is in the business of using his people to do his work. So when you reject help from, say, my mom or Gary, or Allie, or me, when we're just trying to do what God asks us to, then you're rejecting God too."

She backed up a step. "But—"

The ding of the doorbell saved her from having to formulate a reply.

Kyle walked in from the backyard and glanced at the pair. "You done yet? Geez, kiss and make up and be done with it already."

"We're not—" Reuben said the words in time with Maddie, and they both looked at each other as Kyle opened the door.

Corina stood with a smile on her face and a clipboard in her arms. "Good morning. Sorry I'm a few minutes late. Rush-hour traffic out of Chicago is a bear. Kyle, how was your weekend?"

"Awesome. I don't want to go back."

"You know the drill. We have a few hurdles to get through yet."

Kyle looked back at Maddie, a glint in his eye that scared her. What was he thinking?

Maddie tore herself away from Reuben, who looked proud as a papa to be staying. "Corina, come sit. Do you want a drink?"

"No, and we don't have long. I just wanted to talk with you, tour the place, take a few notes. And who's this?" She nodded toward Reuben.

"This is my, uh, former boss, Reuben. I told you about him.
. . ."

"Yes you did." She held out a hand to him. "It's so nice
to meet you. I have a few questions for you too, if you don't
mind."

He nodded. "I'd be glad to."

Kyle stepped in between the two. "Yeah, Reuben and
Maddie have some great news."

Maddie frowned. They did? "Kyle—"

He crossed his arms over his chest, a smile exploding on his
face. The boy looked downright proud of himself. "Yep, they're
getting married. See? Now they'll be together, I can come live
with them, and everything will be cool. Right?"

# 39

Reuben couldn't move. Married? What was the boy talking about?

He liked Maddie and all. Wanted to date her. But married? Maybe eventually. . . .

The social worker raised her eyebrows. "Well, this is a new development. I guess congratulations are in order?"

He stood speechless as she held her hand out again. Dumbly, he shook it, not sure his voice would work yet.

Maddie stood a foot from him in a similar state of shock, staring in horror at her little brother. "Kyle, we aren't—"

The boy patted her arm. "I know, you weren't going to say anything just yet." He turned and gave Reuben a private, pleading stare. "But don't you see? This fixes everything. If you wait too long, the court might let the Blakelys adopt me."

The social worker smiled, but the action didn't reach quite to her eyes. "So when did you pop the question?"

Kyle spoke for them. "He asked her on the Ferris wheel last night at the fair."

He did? They'd done a lot of things on the Ferris wheel, including some cold-shower-invoking kisses, but a proposal? He would've remembered that.

Maddie put a hand on his elbow. "Corina, can you give us a minute?"

She nodded. "Sure. I'll just go check out your yard. This really is a nice neighborhood, Maddie."

Kyle waved to them. "I'll go show Corina around, okay?"

The moment the door slid shut, Maddie turned to face him. "Reuben, honest, I have no idea what he's talking about."

No doubt about it, given the expression on her face when Kyle made his announcement. "The boy is desperate to be with his sister and saw an obvious solution. I gotta be honest, it was brilliant on his part."

She pressed her fingertips to her eyes, something she did when trying not to cry. A classic, tough Maddie move. "I don't know what to do. I can't lie to her."

He took her hand. "Then don't."

The door interrupted them again. Kyle and Corina stomped the grass off their feet on the door mat. "The backyard is gorgeous, Maddie, you did a . . . " Her voice trailed off as she caught sight of Maddie's tears. She sent Reuben a protective *you-better-not-have-hurt-her* glance. "Is everything okay?"

Maddie turned and brushed her eyes with her fist. "Yes, but we need to tell you that—"

Reuben put a hand on the small of her back. "That we'd love it if you came to the wedding. We don't have a date planned yet, but you're more than welcome."

Corina smiled and nodded. "I'd be delighted. Now, don't think this makes you a shoo-in for custody, but it does help the odds quite a bit. Reuben, I'll need to do some background checks on you, and there will be paperwork to fill out eventually, especially if you want joint custody."

He nodded. "We do."

Maddie looked up at him, her eyes wide in confusion. "We do?"

"Yes, of course we do." He gave the social worker a wink. "She's so deliriously in love, she keeps forgetting her own name even." For emphasis, he pulled Maddie to him and placed a chaste kiss on her lips. "Right, love?"

Her good hand fluttered in the air and landed on his stomach. He was quite sure she didn't even realize it. "Um, right. Yeah, in love."

Corina laughed. "Okay, I get it. Save the mushy stuff for after we leave, please. Can I get a tour of the inside?"

Kyle grabbed her arm and took the lead. "I'll show her, Maddie."

As soon as they disappeared down the hall, Reuben put his arms around her and pulled her close. "I'm sorry. I had to wing it a little. But I was serious."

"You were?" Her voice croaked hoarser than a frog.

"I think I've loved you since I saw your back plastered against my window."

She snorted. "Liar."

"Okay, maybe a little later than that."

"I can't lie to Corina. She's more than just mine and Kyle's social worker. She's become a friend."

He put a hand to her cheek. "Is being saddled with me for the rest of your life all that bad of a thought?"

"No, but—"

He covered her lips with his to silence her. "Then good. We'll talk about it later. It's not like we'll get married right now. But if our engagement helps you get custody of Kyle, then I'd be happy to push up the formal announcement, as long as you're okay with it."

She looked up at him, her eyes searching his. "Are you saying you *want* to marry me?"

For a guy who'd dragged his feet for ten years over marrying a girl, Reuben thought it almost comical that he did, indeed, want to marry Madison Buckner, whom he'd known for all of three months. "We have a lot to learn about each other, but yes, I believe I'd love to marry to you."

She blinked away tears. "But—"

"I need to get back to the office. But once they leave, come over there okay?"

"What about your new assistant?"

"She only lasted a week."

"Why?"

He kissed her nose. "She wasn't you."

# 40

*E*ngaged. A word Maddie still couldn't wrap her head around. Was she really engaged to Reuben? How crazy was it that she had no clue. On one hand, Reuben seemed ultraserious. On the other, it'd been Kyle's fault, and was he maybe just playing along to help her out?

The whole thing was all fuzzy.

*God, this day is so not turning out how I thought it would.*

But, nothing in her life could be classified as normal. Maybe she was destined for a weird, complicated existence. Like poor Moses.

Fine, maybe comparing herself to the guy God used to free a whole nation of people was a tad bit self-indulgent. But the dude went through some wacky stuff.

Almost killed when he was a baby, saved by Pharaoh's daughter in a river, raised as a son of Pharaoh himself. Then he committed murder, hid out for a while, then was commanded to go back and free the Israelites. Burning bushes . . . plagues . . . Ten Commandments . . . dealing with the impossibly stubborn and rebellious Israelites.

She wasn't sure the guy ever had a break. Then to die just short of the Promised Land he'd worked so hard to reach? That had to bite big time.

She pulled into a parking spot at the side of the building beside a black Ford truck and made her way to the familiar front office.

Maddie gulped as she knocked on the door.

"Come in."

She slipped in the door and shut it behind her.

Nothing was changed. Except for additional stacks of paperwork everywhere. Reuben still sat in his big office chair.

"Did Kyle get off okay?"

"Yeah. I told him I might try to go see him at Thanksgiving."

He stood and walked around the desk. "That'd be nice."

She picked up a stack of invoices and fanned through them. "You need to hire another assistant."

Reuben moved toward her, his eyes and gait determined. She set down the papers and backed up as he came closer, not sure what he intended, but after a few steps her legs hit his desk, and she almost sat on it.

"You offering?" He stood directly in front of her, offering her no room for escape.

Hope sprouted in her heart. "Reuben—"

He caught her lips as she tried to argue, kissing away any words until her brain couldn't remember what she'd been trying to say. His hands found hers, and they stood, touching only at the lips and hands, until Maddie came to her senses. She broke apart and looked at him. "I thought the Bible said it was better to give than to receive."

He put his forehead to hers and smiled. "If someone gives something, then someone else is receiving. It's as true as the law of gravity."

"But it's greedy."

An impish smile came over his face. "You can be greedy with my kisses every day of the week, Maddie."

She punched him playfully in the stomach. "I'm serious. You agreed to this engagement thing to help me. Your mom and Gary have given me more than I could even add up. All I ever do is take, take, take and I just . . . I just want to feel like I can stand on my own two feet."

Reuben pushed a strand of hair behind her ear. "We all want to feel that way. But we just can't do it. The Bible is full of times where people needed help. Good grief, Jesus's first miracle was because a party ran out of wine. God created us to need Him, to need one another."

She looked up into his eyes. "But you don't need anything. I mean, besides an assistant of course. But on a personal level."

"What I need is someone who will yell at me when I jump to stupid conclusions. Someone who will forgive me when my temper flares and will tell me when I'm overly obsessed with work. I need someone to take me, faults and all, and love me."

She snickered. "That's a good answer. I figured you'd just say you needed another kiss."

He winked at her. "Is it bad that I want to kiss my future wife?"

Then he was serious . . . no doubt about it. At least, she was pretty sure. . . . "No, I guess not."

He wiggled his eyebrows. "It's just the two of us. Alone."

Very much aware of the situation, Maddie gave him a gentle shove. "You're right. Thanks for the reminder."

"Hey, hey. I didn't mean for you to do that." He grabbed for her hands and tried to pull her back, but she resisted.

"I know, but . . . I just feel better with a little distance between us."

His eyes twinkled. "Am I too tempting for you?"

Hardly. Well, maybe a little. "You flatter yourself. But I've been down that road, Reub, and don't want to revisit it."

He took a step forward. "I wasn't going to clear off the desk and make love to you right here. I promise. I'm a 'wait for marriage' kinda guy."

"Are you a—" She couldn't even bring herself to say it. Since when did saying the word *virgin* make her blush?

He nodded. "I am."

Maddie gripped her hands together and studied them. "You already know I'm not."

Reuben put a finger under her chin and raised her head until their eyes met. "But that was before you came to know Jesus, and it's all in the past. He's forgiven you, and your sin is gone."

Her teacher had told her the same thing, but knowing it didn't take away the shame, the feeling of inadequacy and remorse.

Suddenly, she needed to know. For sure. "Do you really want to marry me, Reuben? Are you really, truly serious?"

He stepped closer and lowered his forehead to touch hers. Their noses grazed as he smiled. "Really, truly. I love you, Madison Buckner."

She wrapped her arms around his neck and brought him close, burying her head in his shoulder. "I love you, Reuben Callahan."

*Thank you, God. I prayed long and hard that you'd keep Reuben away from me. Thank you so very, very much for telling me no.*

# Epilogue

*M*addie twirled in front of the mirror for the billionth time. White had never been her favorite color, but today was a major exception.

"Sis, come on. You'll get a complex if you keep staring at yourself." Kyle stood behind her, a big frown on his face. Tuxes weren't cool, or so he said, and he'd argued with her about it right until she sent him to the other room to put it on.

But he sure did look handsome. At twelve, he was just starting to hit a growth spurt, but his weight hadn't quite caught up with his gangly height, not for lack of eating.

"I'm almost done. I just like seeing my dress twirl." So it gave away her youth a little, but she'd be twenty-two in a few months, and Reuben didn't seem to mind, even when she teased him about being *so* old at age twenty-eight. She'd even plucked a gray hair for him the other day. He hadn't been pleased.

The door to the small office opened and Corina entered, a white veil in hand. "Okay, the groom is now in the building, so no more coming out of this room, you hear?"

"Yes, drill sergeant."

"Don't sass me, young lady. Here, let's pin this in your hair."

The tulle draped over her face finalized the picture-perfect image. Never in her life had Maddie imagined getting married, much less to a handsome, sweet, lovable guy like Reuben. The last year had been full of ups and downs as they "dated."

Reuben had decided opening one restaurant at a time was his limit, so most of his time had been spent working on those plans and keeping everything moving, not to mention the court date for Kyle, which was canceled at the last minute. A week before scheduled, Sid had an episode and was diagnosed with a blockage in his heart. The bypass went fine, but Sarge, er, Mrs. Blakely finally admitted that Kyle was better off with Madison and Reuben. Maddie had even invited them to come visit, so she'd know that everything was going well.

A new court date was now set, one for after they were married.

She smiled, knowing that the couple who only wanted the best for Kyle sat outside the door, waiting to wish them well.

Betty fluttered into the room, looking all fancy in her sequined mauve gown. "It's time, dear. Are you ready? Oh, my goodness, you look beautiful. Just lovely." She rested her hands on her arms and squeezed her from behind. Looking at her in the mirror, she smiled. "Your momma would be so proud of you, darling."

Maddie smiled. She and Betty had some long, heart-to-hearts over the last year, so the older woman probably knew her better than any shrink child services had sent her to back in the day. "I miss her."

"I know, sweetie. But today is a time for rejoicing and new beginnings. Just remember that."

Corina cleared her throat. "It's time, ladies."

Betty went to fluttering again. "Oh, yes, yes, it is! Corina, you have your flowers?"

She waved them in front of her. "Check."

"Good good. Now, I'll go get my seat. Allie and Gary are right outside with Sara, ready for your cue."

Butterflies did the jive in her stomach as Corina walked in front of her and Gary met her at the door. "You ready?"

She nodded. "As I'll ever be."

The dining room of the new restaurant had been parted down the middle, the guests taking seats at tables and booths on either side of the dining room. In front of the waitress stand stood the pastor, and beside him, Reuben.

Maddie caught her breath. He looked so handsome she thought she would melt on the spot. That would put a whole new spin on the sandwich "Reuben melt."

Gary urged her down the aisle, and she was only semiconscious of her hand being placed in Reuben's.

His strong grip reassured her. This was the man she loved, and in just a few moments, they'd be one.

The pastor went through the motions of the ceremony, and Maddie managed to say all the right things at the right times with only minor prodding. Her eyes were for Reuben alone.

That is, until the closing line. "I now pronounce you man and wife. May you go with God, and may He be the peanut butter that holds you two lovebirds together. Reuben, you may kiss your bride."

The crowd snickered, and Reuben smiled, but the humor of the moment didn't keep him from his mission. He lifted her veil over her head and claimed her lips to his.

❧

Getting married in a restaurant had its perks, the biggest being no need for a change in venue for the reception. And in keeping with the menu and theme of the day, they'd be serving sandwiches. Maddie walked from table to table on her husband's arm, greeting the guests and thanking them for coming.

When she approached the last table, she almost stumbled. Reuben gripped her arm and steadied her. "You all right?"

Maddie couldn't answer. Instead, she stared at the guest whom she hadn't seen in over five years. "Rachel?"

The woman who looked not much older than Maddie, stood, her hand fluttering to her chest. "Maddie, oh, Maddie."

Tears flowed as Maddie moved to hug her. "But . . . how? I thought—"

"I saw your announcement in the newspaper. I told myself to stay away, but I just couldn't. I needed to make sure for myself that you were all right."

A million questions ran through Maddie's mind. "But what happened to you? I . . . you left, and there was blood, and—"

Rachel nodded. "Your dad was . . . not a nice man, as you already know. I finally had enough that day, and told him I was leaving and taking you two with me. He . . . well, let's just say it didn't please him. It killed me to leave you two there, but after he left, I called child services, and . . . I called my mom."

"Your mom?"

Rachel smiled. "In case you didn't guess, I wasn't much older than you are now when I met your Dad. He was older, and I was in the mood to rebel. After I moved in with you all, I saw his colors real fast. But by then, I couldn't leave. Not with you and Kyle there, all alone with that brute of a man. My mother, bless her heart, prayed for me every day I was gone, so when I called asking to come home with my tail between my legs, she rescued me. I just hated not knowing what happened to you and Kyle, if you were okay."

Maddie hugged her again. "It's okay. We're fine. Kyle lives with me now, and as you can see," she looked over her shoulder and winked at Reuben, "I'm doing very well for myself."

Two hours later, Reuben and Maddie stood beside their big ol' black truck, a Ford F150 Reuben finally decided on, that was decked out with cans, streamers, and balloons. Maddie had tried to convince him they should drive the Tracker as their get-away car, but he'd put his foot down.

They waved good-bye to the crowd of well-wishers, and Reuben helped Maddie into the truck to escape the barrage of rice being thrown at them. He hopped in the other side and revved the engine.

"You ready to ride, little lady?"

She slid over closer to him and put a hand in his. "Ready if you are."

Later, as they parked at the hotel outside of Chicago where they would stay the night before catching a flight to Hawaii the next day, Maddie pulled a cooler out of the back. "Did your mom pack this?"

Reuben shrugged. "She likes to send food."

Maddie lifted the lid and found two sandwiches, with a note from Betty. "*Maddie and Reuben, just in case you get hungry, I packed some sandwiches for you. Love you!*"

"That was sweet of her." She sniffed and grinned. "I think it's PB&J."

Reuben took the container from her and brought her lips to his. His kiss ignited a passion inside that Maddie had tried desperately to keep under wraps. "Reuben, I—" Why couldn't she seem to get a breath?

"I gotta be honest with you, Maddie."

She smiled at his husky voice. "Hmm?"

"A PB&J sandwich is not what I had in mind tonight."

She giggled. "Oh really? Maybe a tuna sandwich?"

He kissed her again, deeper this time. When he came up for air, he shook his head. "No, more like a Reuben and Maddie sandwich."

# Discussion Questions

1. Maddie had some interesting experiences with her bosses. Have you ever had a difficult boss? How did you handle it?

2. The Callahans were "givers." They took Maddie in and helped her without questioning her past because it was what God called them to do. How would you have reacted if you had been in their shoes?

3. Maddie was clearly a little rough around the edges. Imagine her coming to your church before she was saved. How would she be welcomed? What about after, when she was a new Christian but had no clue the "rules" that many view for Christians? Would she be welcomed in *your* church then?

4. What do you think it means to be a graceful receiver?

5. How does one balance being a graceful receiver with not wanting to take advantage, or, in the extreme, not being greedy?

6. Reuben struggled with being in a relationship with Livy while not knowing if he was still in love with her. How do you know the difference between affection and true, lasting love?

7. Related to the above question, many couples divorce these days because they "fall out of love." Is there such a thing? Or is love a choice? If it's a choice, should Reuben have stayed engaged to Livy and chosen to love her regardless?

8. Reuben had a habit of making harsh judgments before getting all the facts. Is this something you struggle with? How do you overcome it?

9. Maddie was irritated with God for not answering her prayers in the way she would have preferred them to

be answered. What are some times God has answered your prayers in a way that wasn't what you expected? How did you deal with it?

10. What's your favorite type of Sandwich? (Me? I like a good ol' PB&J!)

Want to learn more about author
Krista Phillips and check out other great
fiction from Abingdon Press?

Sign up for our fiction newsletter at
www.AbingdonPress.com/fiction
to read interviews with your favorite authors, find tips
for starting a reading group, and stay posted on what
new titles are on the horizon. It's a place to connect
with other fiction readers or post a
comment about this book.

Be sure to visit Krista online!

*http://reflectionsbykrista.blogspot.com*